AFTER THE FALL

The Engineer and the Apocalypse

yodacat
books

For Ursula

For putting up with it

Content warning

Real life isn't nice, and this book is set after the apocalypse where life is less nice. It deals with themes of violence and includes scenes of murder and sexual assault.

Prologue

August 3, 2019

Armageddon. Nuclear war. The end of life as we knew it.

***

No one expected Armageddon to be so shit. Such a damn damp squib. We expected hell — fire and brimstone. We expected the nukes, a flash of light, and then nothing ever again. Inter Fucking Continental Ballistic Missiles all crossing paths as everyone fired them, all at once, wiping out every major city in the world, sending clouds of shit into the atmosphere to kill anything that was left in a nuclear winter.

We expected that the earth would get over it, and the cockroaches would rule, creating a benevolent cockroach society, an insect utopia of art and music with no people to scream and hit them with a shoe.

We thought that God would reach his hand down, taking the righteous in a glorious rapture, leaving us sinners to repent under darkened skies. Maybe that's what happened. Maybe God did take the righteous. The truth was that none of us really knew.

We knew that there were bombs. The missiles crossed paths in the upper atmosphere and crashed to Earth, but only a few worked, and most of those missed. All those huge nuclear arsenals? It turned out that they were about as reliable as my '89 Fiesta.

Seattle was hit dead on. Destroyed. I was there to watch it happen. A six-week trip to the USA, and I was there for day one of Armageddon. Just my luck. The nuke destined for Los Angeles missed completely and landed a hundred miles out in the desert; acres of sand were turned to glass in an instant.

Vancouver was a direct hit, but the bomb didn't explode. All over the world, from what little we know, most of them didn't go off. Still, clouds of dust went up into the skies, filling them with shit, darkening them, settling months later into not so much a nuclear winter but more of a nuclear Irish summer. Cloudy and grey and raining. A miserable, damp old Armageddon. Albeit it a wet existence punctuated by end of the world storms.

It was everything else that went wrong afterwards. That's what killed billions, wiping most of the population from the face of the Earth. We think. The TVs stopped working right off, the radios not long after. In the years that followed, we pieced together the rumours and stories. They were hard to believe, but then so were our own tales of the disaster. Nuclear plants melted down and left the whole east coast a nightmare of glowing rocks and radiation. Stories of horrific cancers, mutant babies with thankfully short lives, a disease-ridden, rotting heap of corpses.

Then the tsunamis hit. Fun fact: if you detonate a nuclear bomb big enough in the middle of the ocean, it can cause a big wave. That was our best guess as to what happened anyway. How could we know? We just saw the aftermath. I heard that half of Los Angeles got washed away just as everyone was congratulating themselves on escaping a nuke. All that was left were a few ultra-rich in the hills who hadn't evacuated yet. They were outnumbered by their gardeners and maids.

A bloodbath of epic proportions followed. I heard descriptions of a movie exec who was shredded with a lawnmower. The story may even be true. I've seen worse.

The storms came next. Another fun fact: even a half-assed nuclear war can contribute more to climate change than four hundred years of burning coal. We got droughts, we got heat, we got rain, and when the storms came, no one was ready. Winds stronger than anyone had ever seen. Gales that destroyed everything in their path. That's a problem in America—they build so much out of wood. Nothing's built to last. Though I think they expected it to last longer than this.

Lastly, there were the plagues. The cities were destroyed, and suddenly, all these people who had never done anything in their lives were fleeing, and they couldn't find food, clean water, or shelter. I say this like an expert, but back then I couldn't do much either. I just ran. No food, no water, no shelter. Bodies were everywhere. Disease spread quickly. The stores were looted in the first few hours, leaving only empty aisles. Most were destroyed, though, by the fires, the waves, or the bombs. Gunfights over bottled water, kids dying for want of an aspirin.

With all the cities destroyed, refugees spilled into the countryside, looting and fighting over the little that was left.

There was no God, not now, if this was Revelations, then we were left behind, and I was on my own.

Chapter 1

Four years later

I stopped the bike as it reached the top of the hill. Shaking, I took a moment to catch my breath. I climbed off and almost fell, knees weak beneath me. I looked back. Nothing. I'd left the dim lights of New Seattle far behind, and there was no one following. I strained to listen. Was I safe? Wind in the trees, the ticking of a cooling bike, and the thudding of my heart were the only sounds.

I was still trembling. Jimmy was dead, and I'd run. Maybe running was a mistake, but I didn't think so.

I got back on the bike and kicked the starter. Nothing. I tried again. Nothing. I swore, calling on every swear word from Marley's impressive vocabulary. Fear pumped through me. I checked the tank, still mostly full, so I kicked the starter and again, nothing. I kicked again and again, jumping up and driving my whole body down, but the motor didn't catch.

Terror took over. In my mind, I could hear the engines following as Zeke and some of the Patron's boys came for me. My imagination running wild showed me the lights of chasing trucks. In a panic, I jumped off the bike, ready to run. Just leave it all behind and escape into the woods. Better to die in the cold wastes of the mountain than to be caught.

I stumbled and fell into the light snow. The cold shocked some sense back into me, running blindly into the trees was futile; I needed to be rational. I took huge gulping breaths as I tried to stand. I forced myself to calm, hands on my knees, trying for slow big deep breaths before I looked back. The road was clear, but terror still drove me as I grabbed the bike and pushed it the last few yards to the crest of the hill. Jumping on, I shoved off and let it go.

When it sped up enough – ten, fifteen miles an hour – I dropped it into first and eased off the clutch. The back wheel skidded in the snow. I feathered the clutch in and out, the wheel catching and spinning, and then locking and skidding for what seemed forever. I almost cried as I looked ahead at the rising mountains that I would hit all too soon. Almost halfway to the bottom, the wheel caught on something, some rough part of the road, a patch free of snow, or some gravel, I don't know what, but the engine turned over, cracked and spat, and came to life.

Relief like you'd never know swept over me, and I drove on another minute before I could think clearly enough to drop back to neutral, motor idling to save fuel. I had a long way to go, six thousand miles or so, and only enough gas for a few hundred of them.

There I go again. Gas, like I'm an American or something. Dollars and apple pies, beer that's weak piss, cars that are too big, and guns for kids who are too small. No, I was going back home. I had petrol or ethanol or whatever gunk the bike was running on. I was going home to Ireland, to Marley, to a place where this madness would end.

I was freezing. The temperature was below zero. I'm not sure what that is in American, I'd never got the hang of Fahrenheit. Miles and pounds were fine, but it could be eighty degrees or ten and I wouldn't know. I knew that I couldn't feel my hands anymore, the gloves only blocked some of the cold.

I'd come to another peak and down ahead I could see a small pinprick of light, four, maybe five miles away. Without thinking it through, I killed the engine again and got off, then took off my gloves and held my hands over the exhaust like I was sitting in front of a fire. It cooled all too quickly and now my hands stung, needles stabbing everywhere as blood rushed to frozen fingers.

I studied the lights ahead. Brehem, a new town that had sprung up as refugees fled the coast. The town had two wind turbines in an area that some freak aspect of mountain topography left always windy, but that never saw the gales. Since the Fall, the climate had changed, bringing droughts in spring, months at a time without a drop of rain, when before it had rained buckets every day, and snow and heat and rain all on the same July day. Snow three feet deep in mid summer, to be gone the next day in a blistering heatwave. The storms had gotten worse, winds, two hundred, three hundred miles an hour, or more, flattening whole towns, but Brehem was protected in some way from it. We had little to record the weather, no meteorologists had survived that we knew of, but the cold, the heat, the rain and the wind, we knew shattered all records.

In Brehem maybe four hundred people were packed into a small collection of low sturdy buildings. Workers for the Patron, mining in the hills or cutting wood to be hauled by horse and cart to New Seattle. These were the ones who didn't get to live in New Seattle. Not as useful in society, prisoners mostly. Not in a jail with a ball and chain, just the kind of prison where there's nowhere to run. If you were caught you could be shot. Or worse.

I was in for the worse if I was caught.

There were still some lights on even now, at close to four in the morning. I tried to place them, to remember the town layout from when I was last here to fix a turbine. The lights were spaced well apart. The guard huts at either end, I guessed.

I pulled out my battered Michelin Road Atlas, one of my most treasured possessions. I'd traced the lines with my finger so many times. In my head, a long shining line merged, page after battered page, to show me the way east to the Atlantic coast. The nearest it would show me to home.

Now, in the light from the bike, it showed me what I remembered. There was no way around Brehem. There was one road through, and that was guarded. Day and night. Even here, a town under the Patron's long arm, there was still a threat from wild animals, from people trying to run, and from the gangs who would pass through and leave nothing alive.

I checked the tank. Almost empty. I filled it from one of the three cans tied to the bike. I breathed deep, sucking in courage from the cold air, and got back on. Out of habit I checked behind me. Was that a flash way off there? Way, way back? Miles and miles, but it could be a headlight behind the trees.

I kicked the bike, it started this time, and pushed off downhill, not conserving fuel and going way too fast for snow covered rough ground.

Chapter 2

As I came closer, the narrowing walls of the valley confirmed that there was no other way around. Thick forest and steep slopes rose on each side. Even in good light it would take forever if it was even possible at all. I'd have to talk my way through.

"Cold out," said the man at the heavy gate, nodding at me.

I didn't recognize him, some big guy with a long beard streaked with white. Tall, with muscle run to fat, like an out of shape wrestler. The kind of heavy the Patron liked to keep around.

"Yeah, freezing."

"Bit late to be out riding," he said, cradling his rifle. Not pointing it, but making sure I saw it. So sure, so confident. I was an ant he was watching, ready to stamp.

I shrugged. "I just go where I'm told. Someone broke down out near Vantage and the Patron wanted it fixed. Like yesterday. Zeke gave me the bike and said to go."

"The doc? I thought that looked his bike."

His gun lowered slightly.

"Yeah, someone has something the Patron wants I guess, so he wanted the job done. Like I said, a truck out at Vantage somewhere. Probably just outta gas. You've no idea how often that happens."

"I don't know you. And I didn't hear of anyone breaking down," he said, flatly. He wasn't accusing, just dropping the facts, laying them out on the ground in a neat line for everyone to see.

"Radioed in. I'm Haley, the mechanic. Ask Joel or Ted. I was out with them on the turbine last month. They'll know me."

He looked at me. I knew they'd not pick up any radio signals here, not in this valley. Radio didn't work well any more anyway with all the shit in the air.

"And you got any gas?" I asked, pushing my luck. "Running a little low. The bike can't take that much."

He paused to consider. Joel and Ted ran this town. I had met them. Assholes who had whistled at my ass as I'd climbed up the turbine. But they also ran the town. If he was new, this guy wouldn't want to piss them off.

"Yeah," he said finally. "Go on up to Ron on the way out. He's got the truck there, should have gas."

I didn't thank him, just kicked off and headed through the town. Ron knew me. Well, he recognized me. It wasn't a town that had a large population of women. He was suspicious, but he knew who I was and he knew the bike. Everyone knew the bike. Everyone knew Zeke.

"Didn't hear about a truck breaking down," he said as I filled the tank and my jerry can. I could see he was unsure. He knew I was the mechanic, but this was well out of the ordinary. If he delayed me when there was something urgent ahead, he'd be in a lot of trouble. If he let me through and there wasn't, it could be much worse.

"I'll probably need this," I said as I took one of his full jerry cans and tied it to the bike. "Yeah, all the way out at Vantage. Fucking freezing weather, too. Couldn't have run out in the morning when there's at least a bit of sun. Patron wanted it fixed in a real hurry. Just as well

Zeke was there, and I could take his bike. Would have liked to take the jeep, but it's busted again."

I realized I was talking too much, so I stopped.

He nodded. I think it was Zeke's bike that pushed him over. Everyone knew Zeke, the smiling, helpful doctor. Most knew he had a hard side too, but they didn't know him like I did. And they all knew the Patron. If he decided at four in the morning that he needed something, he got something by four fifteen.

Ron let me go. There was no reason not to. He was tired and at the end of a long night. There'd been no alarm, no cry. I knew Zeke couldn't radio ahead, not until he was much closer, and I hoped he wasn't. There was a radio in that shed beside Ron, I knew that, and I willed it to stay silent.

Next year the Patron said there'd be a phone line again. It wasn't here yet.

I tried not to be obvious in glancing back. I was wasting time here, but I saw no lights coming. Twisty roads and heavy trees, but they could still be back there. Gaining on me. Getting closer and closer every minute I threw away here. But I needed the gas.

I finished, filled everything, said my thanks, and headed off. I think my heart only beat again when I was a mile away, and then it came with a huge thud that shook my whole body. I'd made it.

I was ninety, a hundred miles away from New Seattle and I'd topped up my gas. Othello, or what was left of it, was another hundred or so miles away, a border town on the Patron's ever-expanding territory. A thousand or so people were living in the ruins. I gunned the engine and rode off through the lessening snow, out on to the plains. Nothing out here but the occasional cluster of houses behind high walls and fences. There were roads marked on my map that I could use to avoid those.

When I got out far enough, the snow cleared. Down out of the hills, it changed to frost. In the east the sun was rising, hidden behind thick clouds but it would warm up a few degrees and clear the road of the patches of ice. I hoped.

Still, it was slow going. I fell once, skidding on a bend and sliding off the side of the road where I had to push myself out of the scrub I'd landed in. I was exhausted. I'd been fleeing all night in freezing weather after a long day of hard and heavy work, but I couldn't stop. I had to keep going. They could be just behind me in trucks, swapping drivers, all-wheel drive, with lots of gas to waste. Along with guns and bullets.

Zeke would be there; I hadn't hit him hard enough to stop him. The Patron's men. Tough, hard and brutal. Zeke would have told them I was a killer. I could expect no mercy.

I passed the crossroads. South lay Yakima, but the area was wild and empty, only a few Wanderers and the gangs of the Kings there. An area riddled with dumps of radioactive waste. Nowhere to run. The road was mud, and behind me the tracks from the bike were clear to see. Zeke would see where I turned. He might follow or just leave me to my fate.

Chapter 3

I came to what was left of Vantage, once a nothing main street on the Columbia River. Now there was nothing left. Shells of what were once houses. Concrete walls, broken and crumbling. Some patches of tar between the piles of mud and debris.

I'd heard what had happened. In a huge storm, the river had risen to wash everything away. The hills turned to mud and collapsed, covering what was left of the town. The bridge, the only way across the river for miles, was gone. A broken spar remained on each side, rusted fingers pointing at each other. Almost a mile from one side to the other.

No one lived here anymore. The river was a polluted mess, though we didn't know what from. Chemical spill, a radioactive leak or some ancient curse. Anything it touched died. Nothing grew around here. You couldn't drink the water, or you'd get sick.

A long, thick and rusted cable joined the broken spans of the bridge. A ring around the cable was bolted to an old flat steel barge that served as a ferry. It was a hard job to pull it across, or so anyone who had ever done it had told me. A length of rope ran to the ferry and to a wheel on each side to haul it over if it was on the other side.

Of course, the ferry was on the other side.

I drove the bike down and hauled for all I was worth on the big wheel to wind in the heavy rope and slowly pull the ferry across.

Usually, two men turned the wheel and even then, it was slow business. I was alone, exhausted, frozen, and bruised from my falls. It was all I could do to turn it a few inches at a time. Dragging the heavy barge across that distance of slow-moving river was almost beyond me.

Across the river the sun was up. I was settling into a panic. Zeke could be here any moment. I paused often to look around, behind me, to listen for the sound of an engine.

I dragged at the wheel and tried to decide if I could do it, just jump in the river if he came. A awful end in the deathly stew of the Columbia, but better than being caught.

The barge moved. It was maybe halfway across, but the river was wide; there were still seven, maybe eight hundred yards left. The current was slow now, making it easier for me. If the river had been in flood, I don't think I could have moved the barge at all.

I pulled, grabbing high and dropping my body down to turn the wheel, my hands ripping on the flaking rust, now getting slippery with my blood. I hauled, I pulled. I thought about abandoning the bike and climbing on the cable, but I knew I couldn't make it. I wished I could harness the bike engine to turn this wheel but there was no time. The closer it got, the more tired I became, but as all the rope came out of the water, the weight dropped, and it became a little easier.

When the barge made it to the small dock I whooped with relief and pushed the bike on, letting it roll down the short ramp and fall on its side. Was that an engine in the far distance? Panic swept over me again, and I checked again behind me.

Now I pulled on the cable, gripping tight and trying to walk towards the back of the barge to pull it across the river. One length. Two. Hands screaming in pain. Another length, and another. I paused. It was an engine, I was sure. Still far away but coming at speed over the empty land.

I pulled and pulled and moved the ferry out. I was halfway across and I could hear the motor clearly, coming into town, out of sight, the noise echoing down to the river.

Another length. Another and then I could see it. An old Chevy truck that I immediately recognized; I'd cleaned the carburettor on it just last week. One of the Patron's. Just one so far, but I was sure that there would be others.

It stopped. Two guys got out. One was the tall, slim figure of Zeke, the other I vaguely recognized. Dave, I thought, one of the hunters who came through town occasionally. I could see Zeke's grin from here.

They grabbed the slowly spinning wheel behind me and held it. I wasn't even half ways across. Immediately the barge stopped moving and then as they put their weight on the wheel, the barge reversed. I tried to stop it, but there was no way; there were two of them and they had all the leverage.

I was ready to jump, ready to end it all in the mire of the Columbia. Better than going back. But I had other options first. A knife, a quicker end if needed.

I grabbed the knife from my bag on the bike and jumped to the rope. The barge was tied to a thick steel cable, a large loop to keep it from sliding off down the river, but for moving it across there was just a long and old rope tied to each side. I sawed at the rope they were pulling. My knife was sharp and before I'd gone back more than a yard, it was cut.

"Where to now, Haley?" shouted Zeke. I could see the damage I'd done. His eyes were black, his nose crusted with blood. His arm obviously hurt, judging by the way he held it, but he was grinning.

Separated by a four or five hundred yards of water, I could see that grin. He was going to get revenge.

I grabbed at the cable and started hauling again. I checked ahead. Sooner or later someone would come on the other side. He could radio them, probably. Coming down out of the mountains, he might have gotten through already. They could already be on their way, bringing another boat to come out after me. I heaved as hard as I could.

A shot rang out, and I dropped to the deck.

I looked up wildly. Zeke had a rifle. Another shot, this one hitting something with a clang. The barge I hoped and not the bike. I peeked over; he was taking aim. I dropped again but the shot came nowhere close. Zeke was wasting precious bullets. He was never a good shot.

I couldn't stand up to pull the ferry over. I'd lose the waiting game.

I wasn't going to give in.

I grabbed the wrench from where I'd left it tangled in the brake and clutch cables of the bike. A big heavy wrench, the ends still splotched with blood. I moved quickly, and I could see the grin fall from his face.

He gave the rifle to Dave. I jerked at the bolts, the ones holding the braided cable to the loop around the long steel run across the river. I pushed, shoving forward with my feet, and the bolt came loose with a scream of tortured metal and rust. As I fell forward another clang rang out, right where I had been.

Dave was a better shot.

I stayed as low as I could, working frantically at the bolt. It came loose, and the second one was easier. But the next one was stuck. Rusted tight.

I heard the clang of the bullet right beside me just before I heard the shot. I could see the spark it caused. I dropped the wrench with a yelp, diving for cover, but knew I had no time. I picked it up, hunkered as low as I could, and gave everything I had to the bolt. It came loose.

The last one I pushed at it, all my weight against a rusted thick bolt, and with a creak it moved. And then stopped. I gave it everything, another creak and then a shot. The bolt was almost free, caught now as it bent, the current pulling the barge south and the cable holding it fast until the last thread gave up and the current won.

I dropped to the deck as another bullet hit nearby. I saw it strike the frame of the bike. I jumped and dragged the bike away, pushing myself behind it, hoping the low sides of the boat were enough.

The rope from the east side spooled out as I went slowly south, staying too low for a shot. Then the rope reached its end and the barge jerked on a slow arc to the shore.

I risked a glance. I'd moved slowly, but I'd moved enough. I was in the middle of the river where I'd already drifted fifty yards downstream and toward the far shore.

Dave was aiming, taking his time, carefully sighting down the barrel. I ducked but he never took the shot. When I looked again, they were in the truck. I stood, watching as they took off, parallel to the river and following me. When the barge hit the shore, I was lucky, the slope was gentle and the river wider.

A quick prayer to any god that might be watching and I started the bike, lying with it in the bottom of the barge, and then hauled it up and over the side. A shot hit the barge, but I had the engine gunned, the front wheel lifting from the ground as I sped up the bank, behind the first building, and out of sight.

Chapter 4

I hoped I was free. The radio in that truck barely worked. I knew that because I'd installed it. If I could get a half hour more of a start, I might make it. I could get lost in the mess of roads ahead.

They'd need to go back. They could wait for someone to come out, but it would take time to fix the barge. More to piss off the Patron, but hey, in for a penny, in for a slow and painful death.

I rode on, pausing when I felt I was well away, a half mile or more, atop a slight rise. Looking ahead the road was clear, my fear of someone coming the other direction gone. Behind me, I could make out the truck, a figure, Zeke was standing by it, looking at me. I crested the rise and moved on.

The road, the one that was mostly clear, went on east. Another old road, a broken and damaged trail of concrete and tar, moved south. The ground was clear enough that I left no trail so I headed south. There were smaller roads leading off to the east and west back towards the river. Mostly clear land, lots of empty space, a mix of sand and scrub. Not much to hide in. At the third or fourth junction I headed east, careful to make sure that the ground was too rocky to be leaving a trail.

The roads were a mass of cracks and holes and dirt and gravel. Abandoned cars and burned out trucks dotted the way. I wanted to stop, to curl up beside one out of the wind and sleep, but I couldn't. I was still too close. I could still be found. But I was exhausted.

I stopped to check my maps. The river would curve east soon, forcing me back towards Othello. I was sure by now that the message would have gone ahead. Even Zeke could have found a radio signal on top of a hill. Girl on a stolen bike. Murder, death. Hold her.

The map showed a road going south over the river, but the bridge was long gone. Only the ferry at Vantage remained. That was gone now. Zeke would need a boat, someone to meet him on this side with a truck, or else go halfway to Canada to find a way across. I had a tenuous head start. I needed to make use of it.

I was exhausted. But I kept going.

The progress was slow but finally up ahead I saw shelter. I needed sleep. I had to risk it.

A log cabin, half fallen, but built of logs heavy enough to withstand most of what the world had thrown at it. I needed just an hour maybe. Shut my eyes for a second, out of the wind and cold.

A heavy log sign lay on the side of the road. I was almost past it before it registered. Before it woke me with a slap across the brain and fear shook my body almost throwing me from the bike.

Hanford Reach National Monument.

I knew this place. I'd not just heard of it but visited, part of a tour when I 'd first come to the US. A national park, beautiful and wild with neatly well-kept roads to drive through. Postcard log cabins with rangers and pic-a-nic baskets.

I'd met one of the rangers later, in New Seattle. Six, seven months after the Fall. He'd died a week after he'd arrived, his skin peeling and blistering, his teeth and hair falling out. He had sores popping and bleeding, gushing a vile smelling shit all over. He was twenty-three.

Hanford Reach National Monument was beside the Hanford Nuclear Facility. The one that had fallen apart when systems shut down and power failed, when bombs shook the earth and storms threw us around. Portland, on the Columbia river, was a mess. Everywhere south along the river was a place of death. The sludge I'd crossed in Vantage was nothing compared to the disaster here. Nuclear waste everywhere. Some even swore the river glowed at night.

How long did I have before the decaying uranium pelted my cells with enough radiation to cripple my DNA and leave me to a messy death? I jumped to start the bike again and went full speed back the way I'd come, upriver and away from the spill as fast as I could. Already in my mind I could feel the plutonium attacking me.

I was fleeing, running from the image of that ranger dying in agony, faster and faster. I had to get back, go north past Vantage before anyone on this side of the river came looking for me. Up where I could lose myself, Canada maybe. Anywhere far enough away from Zeke, from the Patron.

Pushing ever faster, I rode like crazy over what was left of the road. And then the front wheel hit a rut and the bike bounced and flew and I was losing control and the old army truck loomed up ahead, burned and rusted and pulled across the lane. I yanked at the bars and the bike leaned. I tried not to fall, but went smack into the ditch at the side of the road, bounced out of the saddle and into a heap with the bike.

Down in the mud, I struggled to get my face out of the inch or so of water, as I pushed at the bike to free myself and sit up. Everything hurt, I'd hit hard, but when I checked, nothing seemed to be broken. Except the bike. The bars were twisted slightly, but worse, much worse, the kick start had caught on something and snapped off. I stood the bike up and went to retrieve my pack and the jerry cans that had all come off.

I tied them back on, put the bike in neutral, and tried to push it back to the road. It was hopeless; the slope was too steep. I pushed and shoved but got nowhere and just as I fell back again, I heard it. An engine. Somewhere in the distance, the sound of motor.

I dropped to the ground with the bike and listened. It was back on the road, a long way off, but in the silence the rumble of a broken muffler carried. Was I far enough down from the road to be hidden? I was small and covered in mud, I could hide. The bike though was a bright blue. Even now, thirty years out of the factory, the paint was still bright. I grabbed my old blanket from my pack and covered the worst of it. The blanket was a muted brown. I hoped it would do.

I grabbed the wrench in one hand and my knife in another and crawled slowly to the edge of the road to watch. I hid in the ditch, peering underneath the old truck. In the distance, I could hear it coming, the rattle of a piece of shit car going slowly. It came to the top of the rise, maybe half a mile off. It slowed, and then stopped.

Two guys got out and looked around. They both had rifles. One took something from the back. *Binoculars*, I thought. They looked around quickly, then got back in, turned around, and drove off. Faster than they'd came. Relief came, but so did the fear. They wouldn't come any closer to Hanford than that. And they had run off quickly.

I stood up and looked around. South was the river. West further on was the river. East, the river curved slightly north, a whole area of nightmares. North was the road where people were already looking for me. To cross to the road north of me there was an emptiness, what had once been farmland. Once high desert carved to circular fields with irrigation, now it was a mess of scrub and brush.

I picked up the bike and walked that way, staying as far east as I dared. Looking for a place to hide. A place to sleep. It felt like forever but was probably only an hour before I found it.

A large old farmhouse was now a mess of rubble, destroyed in a storm, a house of straw when the wolf came blowing. I crawled under what had been part of a wall, sheltered enough from the wind to not feel its bite, wrapped myself in my blanket, and slept.

I woke up cold. I looked around, but it was pitch dark. I strained to listen, but the night was silent. I shivered. I wanted a fire but out here it would be seen for miles. Instead I worked by feel, going through my pack, eating a little food, finishing my water, and then building up the walls around me to make a smaller, closed in space. Then I wrapped myself back up. My exhaustion beat the cold outside and I slept.

I got up again at dawn. My little shelter was still cold but warmer than the frigid air outside. I needed to plan. I started with the bike. It was an old Yamaha DT200, built for rough trails and cross country. The kick starter was snapped off; without it, on this rough level ground there was little chance of starting the bike. There were side and top boxes mounted on the bike. The side boxes were old aluminium cases someone had found, and in better times, Jimmy and I had mounted them there.

The boxes had only what I had put in them. A small amount of food, a knife, basic tools, a now empty water bottle, my blanket, and the other t-shirt I owned. All my other clothes, I wore.

The top box was a heavier steel box, locked with a padlock as it had been when I'd taken the bike. I took the wrench as a hammer and a screwdriver as a lever, and it snapped on the third blow. Cheap. Once I opened it and saw what was inside, I knew I was in a whole world more trouble than I'd thought.

Chapter 5

Two days earlier

New Seattle is in the mountains. High enough up that the snow comes early. High enough and far enough away from the coast to avoid another tsunami.

I was useful there.

Useful was what kept me alive. All those years growing up on a farm had given me skills I never wanted at the time but were life and death now. I hated growing up in the arse end of the middle of nowhere, but learning to grow food, to fix things, kept me alive now.

All that time studying mechatronics at university, not so much. Not at first. I thought my trip to Amazon to study their robots would turn into a great career, making the next robots to fly into your house and stock up the fridge. A robotic arm was no good anymore. A knack for old engines like Dad's Massey from the seventies was much needed. Knowing about crops, that helped.

Later, knowing how to generate electricity from the rubble of civilization came in handy. Actuators, cogs and pulleys, magnets, induction and currents. This was all later, after food and shelter. When we stopped running and talked of rebuilding.

You had to be useful here. The Patron didn't accept anyone who couldn't contribute. Those who couldn't help ended up in the forests and the mines or out in the wilds where no one lasted long. I fixed the cars with Jimmy and we got the solar and hydro power going. When help was needed in the fields I went, but mainly I worked in the shed.

Jimmy was about seventy, small and thin and bent over. He'd spent forty-eight years as a mechanic, he told me. Forty-eight. He was retired six months and the world went and ended on him. He should be fishing in Florida he told me. If there was still a Florida. Not fixing cars. All the same, he knew his stuff.

Nothing worked anymore. The cars we had to work on were old, they had to be, none of the modern cars would start. Computers just failed. An EMP some said. A curse from God the preachers told us. A virus from North Korea, some guy who swore he had worked on NASA's mars lander had told me.

We ran out of gas in the first few weeks, so later me and Jimmy brewed our own. A mix of ethanol and whatever we could make, from whatever we could spare. A rough still made from all the copper we could scavenge. You could try to drink it, probably kill you, and I'm sure that some tried, but it worked. It would run the '84 Datsun Jimmy owned, the older jeeps the Patron liked, and the bikes that we needed for the terrain.

New Seattle had once been nowhere, a few cabins for the summer and ski seasons, a few houses and a road. People fleeing the coast had streamed through, half destroying it, and the original residents fled or took up their guns to protect themselves. Alfred talked them into letting us join; we'd be useful, he convinced them. We could keep them safe. Now it was a growing town, ten thousand people or more, walled and secure.

We ended up there at the tail end of the exodus from the coast, huddled in the few houses over winter and building small shelters. We worked with the people to make a town, to build up their barricades, to build more shelters. When the winter storms hit, many died frozen in the cold. Two houses fell, the new ones we'd built to shelter the growing population. The rest held up, more from the cram of bodies inside than anything else.

We learned we needed concrete buildings, solid stone and heavy thick planks of wood. Not the cheap shingle and siding that came apart at the first gust of a hundred mile an hour wind. Houses built for the longest winters, the worst storms, the deepest snow. Town walls to keep out the bandits.

Four years later and I was cleaning the carb on a battered Ford Ranger. Ethanol burns off quickly and leaves a thick deposit on the carburettor. Myself and Jimmy, we shared a shed, a small shed that once would have parked one car. Miraculously it survived the first huge storm and we prepared it for the next ones, piling up dirt against the walls. People helped us. Even back then, before he was the Patron, Alfred was leading us, and he saw how we were useful and needed a place to work. He needed us to work for him. To get cars running, to make the power. He could use us.

So, I was cleaning the carburettor that evening, and drinking tea. Not good tea, probably not even tea but something Jimmy boiled in a pot. It was late. We'd spent the day pulling out the generator from the river and replacing coils. Slow, cold work. It was September, I think, I'm not sure of the days anymore, but I knew it could snow any time.

The door slammed open, no knock, just shoved open, and the beaten blue end of a Yamaha pushed in. Zeke followed it, already half drunk.

"Piece of shit died a half mile back," he yelled, pulling a flask from his coat pocket.

"I'll take a look," said Jimmy calmly.

"I don't care what it fucking is, just fix it," he almost screamed, his face turning redder.

He was looming. That's the word for it, looming. I thought he might hit Jimmy. He'd had to push the bike in himself, and he was never one for hard work.

"Hey Zeke, why don't you go over to Bob's?" I said. "We'll fix this up and I'll come get you. Someone brought in a deer last night and he's been cooking it all day. Get yourself some before it's all gone. We'll get on this and have it for you by the time you're done eating."

I could see the change in his eyes. Hot food, good food, fresh meat, was a rarity these last few months. Even for Golden Boy Zeke there'd been less this year than any other. Anytime someone brought in a deer, it was worth showing up. And Bob would have some booze. He'd rattled the flask in his hand, it was empty. He was still angry though.

"Just hurry it fucking up you, two. The Patron needs me tonight,"

"Sure thing Doc," said Jimmy, already reaching for tools to work on it. "Get right on it."

We'd had another doctor in town, but he died during a storm when he got caught in a shelter too far from town and the wind and hail destroyed it. Zeke took over. Not that he was qualified, but he was all we had. He'd almost finished medical school. He was clever, I'd give him that, but he was also a cunt.

He left, and Jimmy started disassembling the carburettor. It was gummed up, so he got to cleaning it with a small pick and a rag. I continued with the truck

Jimmy took off the tank and drained it before rinsing it out. There was gunk in there, too. I ran the gas through an old coffee filter and put it back in. Topped it off.

Jimmy put the rest back together.

"Should I go get him?" I asked.

"Let him have another beer and calm down a bit more," he said.

We took up our cold tea and sipped while a kettle boiled on our stove.

I didn't want to go outside. It was cold and my coat was old, taken from a body four years ago. Some old man with an old coat. The shed was warm. The wooden walls were old and cracked, but the outside was piled high with dirt, so we were half buried from the wind. Jimmy had built a small stove from an old exhaust pipe. He'd cut a grill and a hole in the muffler and we lit tiny fires that we had to feed constantly, but the whole thing heated the shed and kept water hot enough for tea.

"Fuck it, I'll go get him while that boils," I said, and shrugged into my coat.

The air was biting, it would snow tonight. Bob's wasn't far. Maybe four or five hundred yards. Another old shed, bigger than ours, but banked against the storms in the same way. More of a hobbit hole than a house, it was beside the Patron's place. His was the grandest house, a proper log cabin built for the ski season a long time ago from trunks heavy enough to have survived this long.

Bob's was the bar, the community centre, the town meeting place, and where we all came together. It had been a storage shed for some snow equipment and was big enough. The Patron had seen the advantage in giving us an outlet like this. Control the beer and the drugs, and you control the people. Guns backed him up.

Bob had run a bar in Seattle, and he'd known the Patron back then when he was a small-time dealer in Belltown. Now he served bathtub gin and a piss he called beer. It was also the town store, where food came in and got doled out. Where we met and prayed, fought, or played.

Zeke was at a table near the back. Drunker than before, laughing raucously at his own wit. His arm was around a girl; she was what, all of thirteen? But he was Zeke, and the Patron let him do what he wanted, being our only doctor and all that.

The girl hung around Bob's a lot. Bob let her eat if she kept the guys happy. Like I said, you had to be useful to survive.

"Bike's ready," I told him.

He smiled up at me and patted the seat next to him. "Sit, have a beer Hales. Come sit down."

"No thanks," I said. "Still got a transmission to get working for the Patron's new truck. Didn't you need to go see him?" I stared pointedly at the arm around the kid.

He glared at me. "I'll be over," he snarled, his good mood disappearing. "Make sure it's ready to go."

I turned and left, nodding to Bob on the way out. He was dishing out bowls of venison stew to a line waiting. "You want to take some back to Jimmy?" he asked.

"Sure," I said.

Never turn down food. Especially if it's hot and mostly fresh. And not rat.

Bob got two bowls and filled them, covering them with a cloth.

"Just drop 'em back tomorrow," he said with a wink.

We weren't really meant to get extra food, but myself and Jimmy had spent a few hours the week before helping Bob get his heating working properly. His tiny room in the back had iced over in the mornings until we replaced some rusting pipes and gave him heat. I rushed back once I got out, trying to get home while the food was still hot.

Jimmy was delighted. He was such a nice old guy, and I liked when I could bring him stuff. He'd always been good to me, made sure I'd gotten a warm place to sleep and taught me all he could about cars. Never was a leering old jerk like most of the men here. Not that he was too old. He'd been seeing a "younger woman" as he called her. Dolly, who cooked for Bob and cleaned for the Patron, was all of sixty-three. He told me of his younger woman, and she called him her sugar daddy. They'd go walking in the evenings, hand in hand down the street, and sit together playing cards in Bob's. Company at the end of the world.

We ate while it was still hot. Filling ourselves was such a good feeling. Most of the time we were hungry. We took what we could, hunted or fished if we had time, but we weren't good. We'd get extra now and again if we did a job for the Patron, or when we helped out the hunters, they might drop off a rabbit for us. Though often we were hungry.

The door slammed open again. The cold air rushed in and Zeke was standing there, drunk as a lord and pissed with me.

"The bike ready?" he yelled, all volume control gone with the booze.

"Yeah," I said, standing up. "Tank's full, carb's clean, and she's ready to go."

Zeke stumbled, almost knocking the bike over as he tried to get on it. He shoved at the kickstart, but it didn't catch.

"Hey, maybe take it outside," I yelled. "There's no room in here."

"Shut up, Haley," he said, kicking at it again but it still wouldn't catch. "I thought you fixed it," he screamed, getting off and shoving the bike away from him.

Jimmy calmly picked it up and turned it around. "Flooded," he muttered.

"Like fuck old man, you didn't fix it."

"I'll get it," I said, getting on and kicking the starter a few times. It caught, and I revved it once or twice before cutting it off. I got off and pushed it towards the door.

Zeke was fuming. He hated being shown up. He pushed at me, almost falling over as the booze tripped him up. "You did that on purpose." He was ranting now, all reason gone. Just the old grudges left.

I tried to ignore him, to walk the bike outside, but he didn't like that. He swung at me and I fell, as I ducked to avoid the blow.

"Hey," yelled Jimmy, coming up to push at Zeke.

Zeke was probably a foot taller than Jimmy and forty years younger. "Get off old man, she fucked with me once too often," he said, still trying to shove me.

Jimmy swung. Maybe a long time ago he would have knocked Zeke out. He was still strong, the work we did was heavy, but he was no match for Zeke who swung right back. It didn't matter he was drunk and slow, Jimmy was old and slower. I heard the crack of a nose and then he fell, his head hitting the concrete floor behind him. A small pool of blood started to form under him.

I screamed and jumped on Zeke, pummelling him with my fists. He tried to swing me off, tried to hit back at me, and then he jumped back, knocking the breath from me as I was pounded against a wall. He turned, fury on his face. I tried to stand, and he swung, but I stumbled, and he missed.

Jimmy was still on the floor. He wasn't moving.

Zeke was roaring at me. I grabbed at the tools on the bench beside me and swung. A heavy wrench connected with his head. He half fell and then stopped, grabbing at the bike for support. His nose was out of shape, a zigzag gushing blood. He made to stand straight, wobbling, and I swung again. That time I connected with his arm and he fell, his head cracking against the concrete floor. He jerked and then stopped.

Jimmy's breathing was faint; I could barely make it out. I tried calling his name. I got some water and held the cup to his lips. Splashed it on his face. He opened his eyes and looked at me, a wan smile, and then he stopped. He just stopped.

His colour sank as gravity pulled the blood from his face. He became that dusty white that I remembered from Granny's wake, his pale blue eyes still staring up at mine. The start of a smile still on his lips, a waxy sculpture of the man I knew. That's all that was left.

I don't know how long I sat there. When the world was lost, Jimmy had kept me going. He made sure I had a place, kept me safe, gave me purpose, made me useful. He gave me hope and now he was gone. One moment there and the next he wasn't.

The emptiness inside me gave way to rage. The tiredness of a long day disappeared, and anger fuelled me as I kicked at Zeke's head. He was still out of it, the booze hitting him harder than my wrench, making loud rumbles as he snored through a broken nose. Jimmy was dead and Zeke was hurt, and I'd get the blame. Without Jimmy to protect me, I'd be in trouble. Sure, I was useful, I was the only mechanic left, but a few others knew a little, perhaps enough. The hydro power and the solar farms were already working. Zeke was a doctor and much more valuable than me. I would be a lesson on who not to mess with.

The Patron might kill me. He'd killed others. At the least I'd be beaten, maybe attacked some night walking home. They'd make sure I learned my place. Zeke wouldn't take it well either. He'd do something humiliating. Personal. It had happened here before; New Seattle was a tough place with tough people, and the Patron ruled with much more of the stick than the carrot.

I had nowhere to go and nothing to stay for.

I couldn't stay. So, I chose.

I chose home. I'd cross a continent and an ocean to find Marley. If every direction was impossible, I was going for the most impossible, the only one I wanted. I'd missed her every day since I walked away at the gate in Dublin airport. It was only supposed to be six weeks. An opportunity. A future so bright we'd have to wear shades. We could move to Seattle and I'd work at Amazon and she'd be a singer in a city with real culture. She'd be the next Nirvana, Pearl Jam, the new wave of grunge. Only six weeks. Love you, see you soon.

Four years later and I was standing over a dead friend, a bloody wrench in my hand, Zeke out of it at my feet. There was no communication. Radio worked here only at random and definitely not over thousands of miles. Too much crap in the atmosphere. No TV, no radio, and no phones. I didn't even know if home was still there. Maybe the whole place sank into the Atlantic, just as St. Patrick and St. Colmcille had promised us would happen.

I kicked Zeke once more in the head and decided to go.

The bike was still on the floor where I'd dropped it. I picked it up and checked the panniers. The top one was locked. It was a big heavy steel one we'd made for it. Zeke's small stash of drugs probably. Or a bottle or two of whiskey, the good stuff, the real stuff, made before the Fall. The side ones had some spares and, jackpot, some food.

I crammed in my things, which didn't consist of much — a bottle of water and two old apples. I grabbed some tools. I took Zeke's leather jacket, put it in the pannier, and put my coat on. His jacket would be better, but I couldn't wear it through town.

I thought about opening the top box but searching Zeke's pockets, I didn't find the key and didn't want to waste time. There were some full jerry cans in the shed, so I took those and strapped them to the bike. I rolled up my blanket in an old tarp and strapped it on, too. I took Zeke's leather helmet, an old football one he wore on the bike. It would cover my ears.

Then I kicked him in the nuts, closed the door behind me, started the bike, and left.

Chapter 6

N ow I was staring at the bike, the open top box, and realized why Zeke would never quit. He had to find me.

The box was full of drugs. Not just the few pills I'd expect him to have, but full. Packed tightly. Penicillin, aspirin, codeine, stuff I didn't know, bags of pills, and vials of liquid. A box of Viagra. If the world still used cash, then I was looking at millions. This was the currency the Patron used. Threats and violence tempered with hope, a chance to live, doctors and drugs. If Zeke had lost this stash, then he was in trouble too.

When kids died from scratches and the common cold killed everyone, these pills were gold dust. The most valuable trade. Now I understood why Zeke had come so quickly, with just one guy. He could have radioed ahead. There was some service to Othello. The patron could have sent men everywhere. But Zeke hadn't told him.

He could have just told the Patron that I'd killed Jimmy and attacked him. Then I'd be hunted down. But he didn't. Because he'd have to explain the pills. No, he went back with the pills or he didn't go back. The Patron was expanding his reach. This haul would bring in towns. The promise of law, of order and of civilization with doctors and medicine. That would bring in communities.

Everyone knew the Patron was looking for a pharmacist, but none had survived. Zeke had two people making batches of some things, but simple salves and balms. Not industrial grade pharmaceuticals. He knew the theory, but not the practice. There were no chemists left. It hadn't been a useful skill in the first few months. A degree in biotechnology wasn't going to keep you alive. Knowing which mushrooms to eat and which to avoid was better. Being able to start a fire, fix shelter, run fast, these were the skills that kept you going.

I had to run. There was no stealing from the Patron, and stealing was what this was. Even the slightest hint of theft was dealt with harshly. Everyone would be looking for me. I'd seen what had happened to others who broke the rules.

I was sitting. I didn't remember sitting down. The sun was maybe an hour over the horizon. I had to go. I tried to think, to calm myself enough to think of how to do this. I had no way to start the bike. Not pushing it over the rough ground like this. The kick-starter had snapped about halfway down. The top part, the peg that swung out for my boot was lost.

Without the bike I was lost. I wasn't far enough away yet, couldn't get far enough and fast enough on foot. Think. I had to think.

I got my wrench, caught it as tightly as I could around the starter, and tried to kick. The wrench just twisted as the kick starter went down. Much too slowly. I looked around, desperate for something I could use. Oh, for a clamp or vice grips instead of an adjustable wrench, anything.

There was nothing to fit the broken kick-start. Pliers wouldn't hold, the spanners had no way to catch.

"Think Haley," I told myself. "Levers, it's all about leverage. All we need is to turn the motor."

I stood up the bike and looked around. I found pieces of rubble and chocked the wheels. Then I found a long length of wood. Maybe a yard long. I hacked a notch out of it with my knife. I was taking too long, but I got there. I held in the notch against the kick starter, took the other end of the wood in my hand, then jumped and came down with everything I had.

The kick starter moved, the engine turned, the notch came off the end, and I fell in a heap. I tried again. And again. And on the fourth time it caught, and the bike started.

Only then I realized I hadn't filled the tank. I quickly did that, put on all the clothes I could against the chill – Zeke's coat over my own – and swung the bike south and east.

I rode, fast as I dared, away from the road, not far but a little ways from it. When the road swung north away from the river, I crossed it, now close to the water, to the no-man's land that was the Hanford facility. I saw no one. Even when I swung south with the river, I saw no one.

I pushed the bike as fast as I could. Radiation is cumulative. One x-ray won't kill you, won't do much except show your bones. But dozens build up. Hundreds and thousands do damage. I was sure I was getting hundreds a minute. I could almost feel the decaying plutonium and uranium and all the other iums shooting through my body, each causing miniscule damage. Death by a thousand cuts, death by billion microscopic tears. DNA breaking down as I rode, cancer getting ready, cells giving up.

The landscape around me was sparse brush, wild plants and thorns in strange and awful shapes, slowing my progress, making me detour around them. Were these plants normal for where I was, or was their strangeness a mutation from the radiation? Was it even now soaking my bones? With these thoughts pushing me on, I urged the bike faster still.

By noon, I hit another road. It came right up to the river but didn't cross. I could see the remains of what might have been a town. I checked my map and figured I was near Kennewick, fifty or so miles from Othello.

I should be safe. I was miles and miles from Hanford. I hoped. No one would come here, downriver from that mess. But I wasn't sure, not yet. I rode on, into the flattened town, and crossed another river. The small bridge crossing this one still stood. Mostly. Enough to take across a motorcycle at least.

When the river turned west again, I didn't. I kept going straight, south. Away from the Patron's lands. Away from the towns that were his. Into the wild lands.

The bike ran out of gas, and I filled it again, then started it the same way again. It should have run two hundred miles on a tank, but I was getting less than half of that. I kept going, a steady thirty-five miles an hour, fast for the rough road, too slow for me. The remains of a highway appeared; a sign hanging forlornly from a post proclaimed it to be the I-84. I kept on it. Empty vastness surrounded me. Occasional cars, abandoned. Farmhouses, or what was left of them. Little was standing. Some burned to the ground, some pummelled by storms. All empty.

Once, I saw signs of people. A car abandoned in the road and near it, the circle of a campfire, a few stones around it, maybe to balance a spit on, or a grill. It looked days old. I sped around it in case I was wrong.

The road was empty. There were no animals, though I'd heard tales of the wild animals taking back the country. Wolves unchecked, bears with nothing to fear in towns, a tiger escaped from a zoo. But there was nothing. I wished there was. Something I could maybe catch. Food.

Another town, a nest of roads and half fallen buildings. Most had been destroyed by fire. Once the fires started, there had been no one to put them out.

Miles further on, a city. Boise, I guessed. There could be people finding shelter in the places that still stood. I weighed my choices and knew there were few. I was low on gas, out of food. I paused by a shell of a 7-11, but I didn't need to go in to see it had been looted.

I was terrified that there would be others here, more people, desperate like me, so I kept going, slowing only to peer at broken windows and doors for signs they weren't looted. I got off the main highway, away from the larger towns. I saw the sign for Twin Falls, but there was smoke rising in the distance, so I took the first turn and went south. Smoke meant people, and I wasn't ready for that yet.

Miles on, and I was running on dregs when I saw shelter. A collapsed awning of what had once been a gas station. The heavy concrete building was still there. Windows broken, door gone, but it was somewhere. I might have passed better, but I needed the distance from Zeke. There might have been a luxury, abandoned hotel just a mile on, but I was also out of gas.

I rode around the building, the motor spluttering, and it seemed deserted. I parked out back. Taking my wrench I went in, almost on tip toe, weapon held high. Ready to fight. Ready to run. But it was empty. There were signs someone had stopped here, but a long time ago. The remains of a fire were old. Very old.

I pushed the bike inside, found a corner, and sat with my back against a wall. I'd tried and done everything I could. I'd escaped and was hundreds of miles away. Whatever else I could do would have to wait for tomorrow. I slept a little and woke just at sunset. I searched the place again, but it had been thoroughly looted. Nothing left that resembled food. Nothing like water. Problems I would need to solve soon. I pushed the remains of a shelf to the doorway to give me some protection and curled up in the corner, still wearing everything I had, and slept.

It was freezing, well below zero, when I woke with hairs of frost covering the blanket I was huddled under. Outside the broken window I could see the stars, clear and bright, my breath forming mist in the clear still air. I was shivering; that's what woke me. Wearing everything I had, it was still too cold. I needed heat, but I had no idea what the time might be, how long I'd have to wait for the sun.

The place was full of litter, anything useful was long gone, but the broken shelves and piles of junk were still there. I pulled some into my corner – the scraps of paper, of card, the small pieces of wood – and fumbled with my lighter. It was long dead, but it still made sparks.

I got up and fumbled with cold hands to roll some paper into a tight wad, dipping it into the gas tank and scraping it across the sides. The tank was empty, but I hoped for a drop. A wisp of vapor. Just enough to catch a spark. There was enough.

This time the flame caught quickly, and I had fire. Most of my fuel was damp, but there were enough scraps of paper to build a fire to catch the wood. In minutes, I had a small fire going, one with enough heat to stop my shivering.

I sat in front of the fire in the corner, my blanket out wide, hoping to shield the light from anyone or anything that might be outside. I sat for the rest of the night like that, getting up only to gather more fuel, coughing in the smoke if I stood too high. I moved a wire rack over to hang my blanket on, to have a proper screen, hiding me from whatever might be outside.

When dawn came, I let the fire die. My limbs creaked as I stood stiffly to go face the day. I went for the door to see what might be outside. In the doorway, I found a King.

Chapter 7

Two months earlier

It had been the tail end of the short summer, a few days warmer than the rest. I'd been up on the mountain with Jimmy, checking out a stream. New Seattle was growing, and we needed more of everything – power, water, food. This stream, so the hunters had told us, was clean, they drank from it all the time. It passed close to the town, maybe a few hundred yards horizontally, but a few hundred yards vertically, straight up a rock cliff. Our winding route there had taken us two hours to walk.

We could see the town. The water fell a stone's throw from the cliff before it curved back in and away from us. Someone had told the Patron about the stream and he'd come to us personally.

"We need the water," he told us as he sat down, brushing back his comb-over. "And power. See if you can redirect it, pipe it maybe. I'm told it's quite close to the cliff and it's all downhill from there. Should be enough to drive another turbine. What did you tell me about our one in the river, Jimmy? Not enough drop? This has lots of drop."

Jimmy nodded.

"We'll need a truck," I said. "It's too far."

"None available." He almost sounded sad, sitting there holding his hands up in a helpless shrug.

"We'll be fine, Haley," said Jimmy.

"Of course, I don't need you to do it, just look at it. If it will work, I'll get you help. Digging and such. But just look for now." All helpful.

"I can go on my own," I said.

It was a long hike and Jimmy had been sick, a summer cold that lasted too long.

"No, I need both of you," he insisted.

He was like that sometimes, pushing us for no reason. I would have been fine on my own, but he wanted Jimmy to go, old as he was. Some power thing, to make sure we remembered who was in charge. All reasonable and nice but underneath you knew there was no choice.

"We'll go in the morning," said Jimmy. It was already afternoon.

"No, now. We need this yesterday."

"Tomorrow," Jimmy pressed. "It'll be dark by the time we're done. The Ford needs a new gasket, and we won't get it done tonight if we leave now."

The Patron considered this. The old F150 behind him with the hood up was a workhorse, the most used truck in town and badly needed. It had been brought to our shed that morning.

"Okay, tomorrow," he said. "First thing."

"Sure," I agreed. "First thing."

The Patron left, and Jimmy made tea. The Ford sat where it was.

"Maybe we'll jack it up, so it looks like we're working," said Jimmy.

We'd replaced a spark plug earlier, but that was all that was wrong with it. The gaskets leaked, but then what didn't?

"Too late to go hiking in the woods anyway," Jimmy muttered.

***

The stream was big. Not a river, but not a small trickle. Maybe twenty feet wide, a foot deep at the most. Slow moving where we were on this plateau but much faster further uphill. We could work with it. There'd be a lot of digging to get it over to the cliff, but as the Patron had pointed out, it was all downhill from there.

"Will it work?" Soren, the hunter who had led us here, asked.

"Oh, yeah, no problem," said Jimmy. He was staring off into the trees.

"Yeah," I agreed. "We'll need to dig out quite a bit to get it to the edge of the cliff, and it's all rock, but from there it should be easy. We'll need to find a lot of pipe as well so we can control it when it goes over."

I was planning it all out in my head, could see the lines and where the pipes needed to go, the ledges on the cliff we could use, where we could drop it through a turbine, a small water tower to store it...

Jimmy held up his hand. "Shh."

Soren took the rifle from his shoulder and pointed it into the trees. "What was it?" he hissed.

"Thought I saw something out there," Jimmy whispered back.

"Something?" I asked.

"Someone," said Jimmy. "Maybe."

We waited, all staring into the trees, but nothing moved.

"Must have been nothing," Soren said at last, dropping the butt of the rifle to the ground. As he did, there was a hiss, and an arrow flew by his head. He dropped to the ground, swinging up the gun, and a moment later, I dove too. Jimmy was already heading for shelter behind a rock.

Another arrow narrowly missed Soren as he tried to find someone to aim at. I ran, crouched down to shelter beside Jimmy as Soren found his mark and fired. Then all hell broke loose as five Kings came running from the trees. Two carried bows and loosed arrows as they ran, one catching Soren in the shoulder as he tried to aim. One carried a huge axe, the other two wielded large knives.

He fired another shot anyway, and a second King fell. They were running right past us, aiming for Soren, so I grabbed at Jimmy and we ran for the trees. Another shot and then a scream, cut off. We kept running.

We ran blindly, back down the path we had taken.

"You go on," panted Jimmy.

"I'm not leaving you here," I said, half dragging him.

"No, go, get help. Get someone. I'll hide. I'm just slowing you down."

It made sense, but I wasn't leaving him. I didn't want to run on alone. I dragged him on.

"We go together," I told him.

Behind us, a shout. I looked back and behind us, a tall King was gaining. He had long matted hair and a beard, scraps of leather clothes held together with twine, red bandana around his neck. Chains and spikes decorated him. Something like a homeless punk rocker. Except for the axe in his hand and blood on his face.

I barely paused, and, in that time, another came behind him at a run.

"Run," I yelled at Jimmy. "Run."

Chased by the yells and screams behind us, we ran, ignoring the rough ground. It had taken us two hours to get up the hill, walking slowly with lots of stops for Jimmy to catch his breath, and now we were halfway down.

I tripped. Or Jimmy tripped. One of us went down, and the other went with them. I could hear triumph in the yells behind us. And then I heard salvation. The whine of a motor. A 200cc engine I'd taken apart and rebuilt. The tinny horn of the Yamaha whined.

"What are you doing here?" Zeke demanded, shouting up at us as we pelted downhill.

"Kings," I gasped. "Take Jimmy. We have to run."

"What are you doing here?" he repeated. "You should be at home."

An arrow whistled by. I glanced back; they were still running headlong at us.

"Stop," Zeke yelled at the Kings running down the path behind us.

"Take Jimmy." I tried to help Jimmy onto the bike.

An arrow brushed my shoulder.

"Stop," screamed Zeke, as if they would listen.

Another arrow, this time clanging off the tank of the bike.

Zeke swung his head, wildly, as if just now seeing the bandits and twisted the throttle, jerking the bike forward before I could help Jimmy on.

"No, you have to take Jimmy," I tried to say but he'd taken off, further on the road.

"Run, Haley," he was yelling, trying to control the bike and reach for a revolver in his jacket. He almost fell as he twisted, and a shot rang out.

I looked back. The Kings had paused at the shot, and in a moment, they were gone, melted into the trees like they'd never been there at all.

"Quick, we need to keep going before they come back." I tried to pull Jimmy on.

Zeke was still on the bike; he didn't come to help us. He was just twisting wildly, trying to look in all directions, waving his gun around. I helped Jimmy up and we hobbled over.

"What are you doing here?" he screamed at us.

"Take Jimmy on the bike," I said.

"No, he'll slow us down," he was still yelling. "We have to get out of here. Get on the bike, Haley."

His eyes were wide, face pale, as he scanned the treeline. I pulled Jimmy over to help him on the bike anyway, but Zeke turned it around too quickly and took off down the trail.

"Come on, Jimmy," I urged him on.

The trail was still steep, and we slipped and slid as we ran. Zeke was there, on ahead of us, frantically looking everywhere, gun out and waving in all directions. We hurried on, trying to make it back before another attack.

I kept looking back. I could see movement in the trees far behind and knew they were still there. Zeke was too far ahead to help, and he was the only one with a gun.

"Come on, Jimmy, we need to keep moving," I told him. "Not far now."

An arrow thudded into a tree near us. I looked behind but could see no one. Jimmy pushed on, but he was panting and limping. He must have hurt something when we fell.

"Leave me. Run for it, Haley," he wheezed.

"Come on, Haley," Zeke shouted from ahead.

"Get back here and take Jimmy," I yelled back.

We hobbled on and met what had once been the road to Seattle. The road ran level here, but our path came down a steep slope to meet it at a sharp angle, forcing us to an almost U-turn to get back home. Meanwhile, above us on the slope and hidden in the trees, our attackers were still moving.

Zeke had slowed a little. Now he had a clear run if he needed. We stumbled on, but he stayed just out of reach. An arrow came out of the trees, not to Jimmy or me but aimed at Zeke who almost fell, but then shot forward, giving it too much gas and losing control. As the front wheel lifted, he fell from the bike.

He jumped up, scrabbled for his gun, and fired off three shots into the trees. We caught up, and I pulled the bike up and put Jimmy on it.

"That's mine," he yelled.

"Go Jimmy! Go get help," I screamed as I kept running. Zeke ran after me, and Jimmy sped on, wobbling on the bike as he picked up speed.

"That was my bike" Zeke screamed at me. "We have to get out of here."

"Run faster," I panted.

We ran on.

We were met a half mile from town by a group of men with guns. I knew most of them. They'd seen Jimmy and were ready for an attack. They closed in around us, guns pointed out, but as we caught our breath, we could see that there was nothing moving behind us. We moved as a group towards the town. Some peeled off and took up positions in the two pillbox type huts that were there for just this. Built with heavy timbers and sandbags, open at the back, they sat each side of a heavy tree trunk

The barrier was dragged into place on wheels I'd taken from an abandoned Porsche a year ago. More people ran ahead to do the same with an old school bus on the other end of town while the shouts continued.

"Kings," the voices cried. "An attack is coming."

We were led into the bar, and Bob poured us shots of his best whiskey, a six-month-old rotgut brewed in a bathtub, distilled in a garden hose, and aged in a bucket. As I sat, I saw Zeke pouring himself another shot with shaking hands.

Half of the town were gathered around us to find out what had happened. Some crowded around for more information, some left to get ready, some already had guns and went in groups out on the street.

"Kings, was it?" demanded a woman I didn't know.

Then there was a commotion near the door and the Patron himself came in, all puffed up as he pushed his way past everyone.

"What happened?" Short, curt, in charge.

"Kings," blurted Zeke. He was on his third shot. His eyes were still wide. "I was coming back when I saw them chasing Haley. I shot one, and the rest ran off. What was she doing there?"

I didn't remember seeing any blood. I was sure he'd hit nothing.

"Are you sure?" a voice at the back asked.

"I saw them," Jimmy said, calmly. I noticed that his whiskey was untouched. "All of them wore the red. They were Kings alright."

"Where's Soren? He was with you to keep you safe," the Patron asked.

I hadn't thought about him in the headlong flight.

"Dead," I guessed. "They came at us at the stream. Came for him first; he was the one with the gun. He shot two of them, maybe three. We ran while we could."

The Patron stared at us. The look said the wrong people had lived, but aloud he said, "Well, I'm glad you're okay. We need to prepare in case they come here."

Zeke looked as if he wanted to say something, but he thought the better of it and grabbed the bottle to fill his glass instead.

The Patron left. That was it. He'd gotten his information, and that was all he wanted from us. The limits of our use.

Everyone crowded around. Full of questions. How many? What were they armed with? What did they do to Soren? I didn't like to think of that. It was a tense afternoon that became a tense evening. I helped Jimmy back to our shed before it got dark, made sure he was okay, but then I left again. I couldn't sit still. Fidgety and restless, I went back out.

On the road, there were small groups. Ready for an attack. I knew at the bar there would be more waiting, weapons to hand, for any cry out.

"Were there really Kings?" the woman from earlier.

"Yeah," I said. "I saw five of them at least."

She shuddered. "We saw them before we came here. Attacked a group of us travelling up the coast. Just attacked us, no cause. It wasn't like we had much. Shouting about Revelations had come. Like they were preaching to us as they mowed us down. Their holy crusade. The preacher with us said some men just gave up."

Some did, I knew that. When everything fell apart, some tried to rebuild, like the Patron, promising law and order. Some felt it a punishment from God and tried to repent. They formed communities of ultra-strict groups to do penance in the wilderness or blame the gays or the women or the strangers or the technology. They passed through, now and again, to warn us of our sinful ways. To beg us to repent and threaten us with the fires of hell. Some just gave up and ate a bullet or jumped from a bridge.

The Kings; they were ones who gave up, but then found something new. It was like they lost all humanity. They followed a strange leader, an almost mythical figure called Ted who was their King of Kings and priest and everything in between. Leading them now as Kings of Revelation, a precursor to the Four Horsemen to come. We heard horror stories of the excesses, of the monster that Ted was. A giant who ate babies and farted lightening. But we'd seen what the Kings left behind, and the descriptions of Ted couldn't be too far from the truth.

We'd seen them before. They'd come close but never this close to an attack. Every few months, a single King might arrive to trade. They'd be greeted with an honour guard of loaded guns. The Patron would meet with them and offer to trade or not. They brought a tanker half full of fuel once. Some pills another time. In exchange for food usually. Then they would leave and go back to their group, watched all the way.

Away from the town, though, they'd attack anyone. Lone travellers, smaller groups. Even if they were outnumbered, the Kings might attack, killing everyone. Not in the Patron's lands, though. The communities under his law had his protection, and there were no attacks here.

"They eat the dead you know," the woman interrupted my thoughts.

"I heard," I said.

"Do you think they'll come?" she asked.

"No."

As I said it, I knew I was right. I'd been waiting for an attack, but now I realized there wouldn't be one.

"There weren't enough of them. If there were more, I'd be dead. Jimmy would be dead. There's not enough to attack New Seattle."

She started muttering, casting glances up at the cliffs where the attack had happened. Praying, I guessed. For Soren or for herself, I didn't know. I left her and went to Bob's.

The place was packed but quiet. Everyone was waiting for an attack; no one wanted to be alone. I was pressed for answers, but I had none. They crowded in on me, sure I knew something, but I didn't, and I left to escape the noise.

Across the road I saw two figures. Zeke and the Patron. They seemed to be in a heated discussion. They saw me, and the Patron patted Zeke's shoulder, then turned and walked off.

"So, Haley," Zeke said, crossing the road.

"Zeke," I replied.

He was drunk. He held it well, but he was leaning against a wall in a way that said more about support than acting casual.

"Aren't you going to say thank you?" he asked.

I said nothing.

"I mean, I did save your life. I chased off those Kings."

There was something in his eye that told me not to argue, not now.

"Thank you, Zeke," I said. "Your arrival was timely."

"You could say it like you mean it," he retorted.

"What were you doing there anyway?" I asked.

Subject change. Let him talk about his favourite thing. Himself.

"I have a sixth sense for a damsel in distress," he said.

I stared at him. He stared back.

"Someone got hurt up at the logging camp," he said finally. "Yesterday. They needed a doctor. I'm a doctor."

Med student, I thought.

"So, I saved his leg, and then came back to save your ass, Haley. Aren't you grateful?"

"So grateful, Zeke, but I better go check on Jimmy," I turned to walk away.

He grabbed at my shoulder. "How about showing a little gratitude?"

"I said thank you, Zeke. But I really have to check on Jimmy."

"What's up, I'm not good enough for you, Haley? Little miss prim and proper and too good for everyone. What's a guy got to do for you? Saving your life not enough?"

"Thank you for today, Zeke," I shrugged out from his grip and walked away. As I did, I saw the woman from earlier staring at us. Zeke must have seen her, too. He didn't follow me.

Chapter 8

Present

N ow I faced a King alone, and he was blocking the doorway. He filled it, his mohawk touching the lintel. He wore a red patch on a long and ragged overcoat, which flapped behind him, pushed back to give freedom of movement with the large knife he held out. I tried to look around him, out the broken windows, to count how many were out there. One. There was one.

"Food," he said.

"I don't have any," I said, backing away, towards the bike, reaching for the wrench.

"I saw your fire. You have food," he said.

"We had. My husband and his brother, they went for more. They're hunters. They'll be back any minute," I tried to sound convincing.

"You're on your own. No one's left here for hours."

He started to advance towards me, the knife held low and to the side. It was then that I noticed that he was injured. His right hand held the knife, but his left hung limp and useless from his shoulder. The hand looked wrong, scarred and twisted. A leather strap above the elbow kept it from moving and he'd tucked his coat behind it.

I raised the wrench.

"Don't come any closer," I warned.

He came on.

"Give me your food," he said. "Maybe I'll let you live."

"I don't have any."

"Then better hope I let you die," he screamed as he lunged.

He was clumsy, stiff with the cold, but this wasn't his first stabbing. He'd practiced this before, and the knife came so fast I couldn't jump fully away.

I swung hard and caught him on the left shoulder. He winced in pain, but still tried to skewer me without pausing. I jumped aside, swinging again. The knife clattered to the floor as my wrench caught his good wrist. He yowled, and I didn't stop. I couldn't stop.

He was still coming for me and I dropped to one knee as I jumped aside and swung all in one move, smashing his knee cap. When he went down, I followed up with a blow to the head as I rolled away.

He stopped moving. Still breathing, but not moving. I stood there, panting, trying to suck in all the oxygen in the room. Then I came to my senses and ran for the door to check outside. There was nothing stirring, so I went back in. He was still unconscious on the floor.

Part of me wanted to finish him. Part of me couldn't. In the end I satisfied myself with the thought that he couldn't hurt me. He couldn't walk, and he had a broken wrist, a useless arm.

I felt pain now, a sting across my ribs, and looked down to see a trickle of blood. I was covered in layers of clothes, and that's what had saved me from his knife. His swipe had cut through the leather jacket, my old coat, and a t-shirt to scratch a thin red line. I pulled my clothes tight for now and held my hand to my side to stop the bleeding. I knelt to check him.

He was unconscious, definitely, but to be sure, I grabbed his fallen knife and poked him, hard enough to draw a trickle of blood. No movement. I should have put him out of his misery, he had no chance to survive in this world that injured, like a horse with a broken leg, but I couldn't do that. I flipped open his coat and searched him, all the while watching for movement, ready to stab. He had no food, no water. Only the knife, an old lighter in a pocket, a wallet with pictures of a man and woman and kids. I tried to compare the happy smiling faces to the ragged pockmarked face before me. It could have been him once. I couldn't be sure.

I went back to the bike and filled a bag and my pockets with everything I had. All the drugs, my empty bottle, everything. Then I left.

But as I went through the door, something nagged at me. Something was off. Something I was missing.

No one's left for hours. That's what he'd said. He'd been watching. For hours. He'd seen my fire. So, he had a camp somewhere close by. There could still be food or water there.

Or all his friends. The thought scared me. But no. If he had friends, they would have been with him.

Unless he saw me first and snuck out for food, fear told me. *Kept it all to himself.*

I'll be careful, I promised myself.

In the early morning frost, I could see his tracks. With nowhere else to go I followed them, my new knife ready.

It was maybe a half mile off, behind a dip in the landscape, a few trees hiding it from the road. A rusted panel van, wheels flat, windows broken and stopped up with wood, marked the location. It was surrounded by junk – piles of wood, old barrels, a bicycle with one wheel, two shells of Harleys.

I crept up and tiptoed around. There wasn't a sound. I pulled open the back door of the van and jumped aside. Nothing. I peered in. The smell was a kick to the head and it was a mess, full of filthy clothes and junk that he'd found wherever.

There in the back, though, I saw it. The holy grail. A small generator. Old and rusty but obviously used, wiped clean of dust in places, covered in grease everywhere else. I tried to not breathe in the fetid odours as I checked it and found what I was looking for. There was a half full jerry can connected to it. I grabbed the can and took it outside.

I opened it and sniffed; it smelled like gas. I hoped it was. I took some time and searched the rest of the junk. I found water; a tarp was set up in the trees to catch rain and fill a bucket. I drank all I could and filled my bottle. I found another five jerry cans hidden around the area, but only three had gas and none of them full. When I poured all together I had just under two cans, maybe eight or nine gallons. Enough to get me much further away from here.

Delighted with my find I almost ran back to the bike I'd left behind. I saw nothing on the way back, slowing as I came close to the road, checking all around. When I got to the gas station, he was gone. A trail of blood led to the door and towards the back, but I didn't wait to check. I hurriedly put some gas in the tank, tied the cans to the bike, and went through my ritual of starting it.

When I was safely away a few miles I stopped and looked back. Still alone. I emptied my pockets and tied everything down properly. I took my time, did it slowly, did it right. I looked ahead, looked back. All around me was empty.

I was far enough away from New Seattle, my tank was full, and I was free.

Chapter 9

I drove for miles on empty roads. Slower now, careful with the bike. I could take my time. Further east there were small communities, little pockets of people surviving, but here it was barren. When the world fell, everyone had fled the coast, crossed the Cascades, and kept running until they hit the Rockies. New Seattle was the exception, still close to the memories of the nukes and the floods.

I watched but saw no one. My only fears now were wild animals and the Kings. And starving. I was hungry, hadn't eaten in a long time. When I came to an area that was greener than most, I stopped. Hidden by some trees, I found a small river. The remains of a house were nearby, long ago fallen to rubble.

The water looked clear, and it was running quickly over rocks and sand. A natural filter. I saw tracks around. Animals, nothing too large. They drank here, so I drank my fill too, hoping it was safe.

It took me an hour to set up traps, hoping the animals would come back. I'd seen snares on tv, one of those survival shows. I knew in principle how they worked, but it still took me a long time to figure one out and set it where I hoped to catch something. A rabbit, maybe. I also made a small net, tearing through one of my t-shirts and slicing it to small strips to set in the river. Maybe there were fish.

I moved upstream a little and into the woods, away from any tracks, and in the shelter of two large trees, I burrowed into the undergrowth to make a tiny den. While I searched for anything edible, I gathered firewood. There was nothing I recognized as food, but I could be surrounded by the most delicious foods in the world and not notice. I could also pick the wrong mushroom and poison myself. I'd seen food in the wild around New Seattle, but there was nothing familiar here, nothing that would grow on a farm in Monaghan. I'd have given anything for a half hour on Google right then, searching for 'edible plants.'

In the morning, my snare had something. A small mouse. I'd eaten worse. My net was empty, a hole as if something had ripped right through it. I cooked the mouse and set off again, still starving.

I didn't know where I was when I found them. A small community. At first, I thought it was another ruined and deserted crossroads. I wanted to stop to search but decided to be careful. I drove through and hid the bike in the trees a half mile on. I buried my stash of drugs in the roots of another tree, taking only a few painkillers just in case. I passed a sign on the road as I hiked back, faded and rusting. Sanders, Nevada.

Sanders was tiny, a side road off a back road. A church, collapsed; a school, I think once, was burned and in the middle of a slow collapse; a broken-windowed post office and a scattering of houses about to fall down; grown over tracks railway tracks led past a station. That was it. Even before the Fall, I doubt more than fifty people lived in this town. The buildings were well spaced, it wasn't so much a town as a cluster of houses in the middle of nowhere.

With my knife ready, I walked back. The first house was a pile of shingles and wood. The next was burned to the ground. A sign crunched under my feet where it had fallen; Goshute Mercantile, it read. The building still half stood, so I decided to begin my search there and maybe find food. Low chances I knew, but I had to try. I crawled under a precariously leaning wall to get inside.

"Don't move," a voice behind me said, followed by the click of a gun. Safety catch, a bolt being cocked, a bullet being loaded. I don't know. A gun sound. Years without a television, but this sound was wired in my brain from the movies.

"Come on out now. Slowly, hands in the air," the voice said. "Nice and easy now."

I raised my hands as much as I could and hobbled out, bent over. A man with a rifle and two others, one carrying a baseball bat and one holding a crossbow, stood in the street. They were spread out, blocking any chance for me to run.

Chapter 10

"Drop it," one man yelled.

I dropped the knife; it was no use. I wanted to run, away from the guns and the threats, but I knew I wouldn't make it more than a few feet.

"What do you want here?" the tall man with the gun asked. He was tall, skinny and fair haired.

"I thought the town was empty. I saw no one. I need food. Gas," I replied.

"There's nothing here for you," he told me.

"I can trade," I said.

"We still got nothing to trade," he said, lowering his gun slightly.

"Just some food," I pressed.

"You alone?"

"Yes," I said. I was sure they already knew. They must have been watching. "Just me, but I can be useful. I'm a mechanic. I can maybe work for some food."

"Nothing here to fix," he said, and pointed back up the road with the gun. "Get going."

The guy with the baseball bat moved aside to let me go, his bat still held ready to swing. He was shorter, balding, and looked nervous.

They hadn't killed me. They hadn't tried to rob me. They just wanted me to leave. I took a risk.

"Please," I said. "I haven't eaten in days. I can work."

The leader shook his head.

"I have pills," I told him and reached slowly into my pocket to take out the small bag. "Three aspirin."

It was a risk. They could just rob me, but I needed the food. I hoped the nervous guy hadn't done this before, but since the Fall, everyone had. No one was innocent anymore, but he looked less guilty than most.

A glance around. An easing of the shoulders. A slight drop in the gun.

"They real?" the guy with the bat.

"Still in the foil pack," I said. "Three aspirin for a few days' food. It's a good trade."

"You sure you're alone?" he asked.

I could see what he was thinking, but I gambled and said, "Yes. I don't want trouble, just a trade."

"We could just take it," the guy with the crossbow said.

"No," the guy with the gun snapped. The leader.

"She's alone, there's three of us," he insisted.

"We're not like that," the guy with the gun told him and then swung back to me. "We won't hurt you. We can trade for the pills. You got anything else? That bike maybe?"

"It's not for trade," I said.

"You got any other pills?" he asked.

"Nothing," I lied. "I just need food and gas."

"For three aspirin, we'll give you a meal," he said.

"One meal? They're worth way more than that."

"It's a buyer's market here," he told me. "We could always just take them."

"It's worth more than a meal."

A woman came out from behind a wall. "Give her what she wants," she said. "Eric, let her in. "

The guy with the gun looked at her as if to argue but conceded to a stare.

"Come on in," she told me. "I'll get you some food now."

I walked in slowly. I could feel more people, appearing from hiding, behind me. I knew I was in danger, but I had little choice. Following the woman with the armed men behind me, I went into what had once been a train station, just a tiny, weathered building beside overgrown tracks.

They're not going to hurt you, I told myself, trying to walk calmly and not look around or run. I could feel the gun behind me. The crossbow. All those nervous fingers on triggers.

The woman got me a plate, a little meat, some vegetables. A tiny portion that I wolfed down. It seemed like the whole community was watching me. I gave her the aspirin and she held them up to the light like checking for counterfeits but seemed satisfied. She handed them to a girl, maybe fourteen or fifteen, with dirty blonde hair.

"Give them to Sis," she told her. "She's with your brother."

The girl snatched them and almost ran out the door.

"Where'd you come from?" Eric asked.

"West," I said.

"New Seattle?"

"You know it?" I asked.

"Biggest place out there anymore," he said. "You steal these pills? Are we going to have trouble with the Patron?"

"No," I lied, worrying that they worried about that. I had thought I was hundreds of miles from where anyone would know him. "They're mine."

"Are you really a mechanic?" he said. "Don't get much girls doing that."

"Yeah, I am. You need something fixed? I'll trade work for gas."

He thought about it but said nothing.

"You've been to New Seattle?" I asked him.

"No, we came from east of here," he said. "Denver originally. Before it fell."

"Denver…I never heard anything about that."

"Finish up your food," he told me.

"How'd you hear about the Patron?" I asked.

"Everyone knows the Patron," he said with disgust.

The conversation was over. I finished my food, and the woman brought me some more to take with me. A small amount of bread, some chicken, and three eggs. I thanked her. I wanted more, much more. The pills were worth that.

"That's all we have," she said, as if reading my mind.

If they knew of the Patron here, then I needed to get farther away. I needed gas.

"You sure there's nothing you need fixed?" I asked.

They looked at one another. The guy with the bat shrugged as if to say 'what's the worst that she can do?'

"Jon, bring in the generator," Eric told someone standing at the door.

A guy with long brown hair, tied back in a tail, left for a minute and then came back pulling a small electric generator on a cart. I guessed that it had been in the small shed just outside.

"You fix that, and we can give you more food," he told me.

"Gas, I need gas," I told him. "And food."

"We don't have any gas," he said.

"Then what use is a generator?" I said. "I don't need much, a few gallons."

"Fix it and we'll see," he told me.

I asked if they had any tools and they brought out a rough and rusted selection. Everyone watched as I started to work. I pulled the starter cord and it turned over but wouldn't start. I checked the gas. What little there was seemed clean. Nothing was blocked when I checked the line. I started to take things apart, and when I was testing the spark plugs, only one fired and it only sparked half of the time.

I picked at it, cleaning it as best I could, checked the caps, the wires, sanded the terminals down. I now had one firing all the time and the other not at all.

"You need a new plug," I told them.

I showed them what I was doing, the spark on one, the other dead.

"Where do we get one?" Eric asked.

"Another generator," I said. "Or any small engine. Lawnmower maybe. If not, then a car one will probably work."

"How about your bike?" the guy with the stick asked.

"No," I said.

"There's a lawnmower at the Miller place," one of the kids said.

The woman who had given me the food rounded on the kid, looked ready to beat his ass. "Elijah, what are you doing at the Millers? I told you not to go around there."

"Whisht," Eric said. "You go on Elijah, take Jon and show him where."

"You really think she can fix it?" The question came from short guy with the stick again.

"Did you know that we needed plugs?" Eric asked and the guy shrugged. "Nothing lost trying."

"How did you come to be here?" I asked. "The place seems…well, unprotected. The Kings and such. And you're from Denver. You're not farmers."

"The Kings? Ted's gang of crazies? They don't bother us much," Eric told me. "Mostly no one comes by here. Too far out of the way. We hide well."

"You hid very quickly," I said. "I didn't see anything."

"There's a shack up on the hill behind us," Eric told me. "Highest point for miles. You were spotted coming in. We had time."

They saw me hide the bike, I knew. Did they see the pills?

"You have someone on watch all the time?" I asked.

They looked at each other. There was something else going on there.

"Just fix the generator," he told me. "We'll see about gas."

"What did you do before?" I asked.

"Lawyer," he told me. "All of us, not a useful skill between us. So now we're here."

I nodded. Lots of people suddenly discovered that they couldn't survive in the After.

"How'd you become a mechanic?" the woman asked.

I told her how I'd studied engineering and robotics. "It was easy to pick up after that," I said.

Elijah and Jon came back just then, dragging an old lawnmower behind them.

"Any trouble?" asked Eric.

"Nothing stirring," said Jon.

"Will it work?" Eric asked me.

I was already on my knees, removing the spark plugs. They were old and rusted but so was everything. I sanded them down and tested them. Both worked fine.

It took a few pulls, maybe more than a few, but the generator caught and sprang to life. A cheer went up.

"Looks like you know your stuff." The guy with the bat extended a hand. "Jake, Jake Thompson, CPA."

I shook it. "Haley," I said.

The others were looking at each other. An unspoken conversation. A silent debate. It went on.

"So," I pressed. "About that gas…"

"Why don't you stay the night?" the woman said. "It'll be dark soon, cold. Stay, have a meal with us, and set out in the morning. Eric will get you some gas."

I wanted to be gone, but the prospect of more food and a slightly warmer place to sleep had me. Also, I might get information. They'd come from East, and that's where I was headed.

"Yes," I agreed. "That would work."

"Great," said Eric, clapping me on the back like an old friend. "If you worked on robots, how are you with wiring? We have a few lights you could look at."

I nodded. In the After, the more useful you were, the more you got. There was something else going on, but I didn't feel unsafe, so I would help for trade.

I was led out the back door and to a stairway hidden under a fallen roof and overgrown with weeds. It led to a small basement, more a high crawlspace, that I would never have found, but I suspected that if I looked more carefully there would be more of these. There wasn't room for all the people that I had seen, so I guessed the rest were somewhere else.

This place held a few car batteries and some wires. "There's a solar panel up on top of the house," Jake told me. "You can't see it from the road. We managed to get a few lights running, but they stopped working."

"You got a multimeter?" I asked.

He stared at me like I'd spoken another language.

"Any tools, voltmeter, any kind of tester?" I tried. Blank incomprehension. I tried going simpler. "You got a bulb I can use to test?"

He fished around in a box and found me one.

I tested the cables. A weak light told me that there was power coming in from the panels, but the batteries were all flat. I told him this.

"You get the lights working in the daytime?" I asked, and he nodded. "But not at night?"

He nodded.

"These batteries aren't any good for what you're doing," I said.

"Can you fix it?"

"No. They're sealed acid." I could see the confusion on his face. "You need new batteries. Deep cycle, a kind of battery designed for this. Charge it fully and use it completely and same again."

"But aren't they all just batteries?" Eric asked.

"No, these are car batteries. They get fully charged; you use a little to start the car with a big jolt, and running the engine tops it back up. You don't drain it completely. You just take a lot of power for a very short period and then recharge it. You need to get deep cycle batteries. Slow use, slow charge. Drain them fully and start again."

"Where would we get them?" the woman who had now introduced herself as Claire, Eric's wife, asked. "And how would we know them?"

"Where'd you get the solar panels?" I asked. "There would have been some on that system."

They looked at each other. It was one of the questions that they're weren't going to answer. Was it just fear of a stranger, or were they hiding more?

"An RV, a caravan?" I saw a blank look and corrected myself. "A trailer, I mean. Something like that would have deep cycle batteries for the inside lights and stuff. Or a golf cart, an electric car. They all have something you could use. You know where there's one of those?"

A lot of head shaking.

"Then a car battery. Not as good, but it will work."

"We tried that," someone said. "Didn't work."

"Charge it first," I said. "Leave it on for a few days and don't run the lights. Let it charge fully."

Eric nodded. "We can get some of those. I'll bring some over later," he said as he turned to leave.

I went to follow but Jake stopped me.

"Why don't you stay here?" he suggested. "It's probably safer for everyone. I can stay, and maybe you can teach me about these deep batteries. Hey, how about a cup of tea? You English love your tea, don't you? Now it's not Earl Grey but we have something."

"Irish," I corrected automatically. "But yeah, I'd love a cup. And hopefully some food," I added, just to myself.

He seemed more talkative now that I'd fixed something. I needed information as much as I needed everything else. Food, water, shelter, gas, information, pills. All things that were worth something.

He left me there, sitting in the small light from the bulb overhead, and closed the door behind him. I looked around. The space was a storeroom, neatly kept. Shelves on the walls held short lengths of wire, some old car batteries that I guessed they'd already tried and some empty gas cans. No food, nothing of much use, just things that they thought at one time they might use.

I worried a little that they might steal my bike, but I didn't think that they would. I was just being kept where I wouldn't see too much. They had something to hide. Then again, so did I. But they seemed to be safe. Just in case, I was glad I'd hid the rest of the drugs. I dug around in the corners while I waited. There was little here. I found no food, no water, no gas.

Jake came back carrying mugs and a well battered thermos, with a kid in tow struggling under a roll of blankets.

"Just put them over there," he told the kid who dropped his load and scurried off.

Jake took a seat on a crate and poured out two mugs of a brown liquid. I joined him and took a sip.

"Holy shit," I said, taking another sip, and then another. "This is actual tea. Actual honest to fucking goodness tea. Where'd you get it? I haven't seen a tea bag in two years."

I drank more, savouring the flavour of home, of mornings before school, of evenings in front of the TV, of funerals and weddings, a cure for everything. For a moment I wasn't sitting on a crate in a basement in the middle of nowhere America. I was in the kitchen on the old wooden chair with the dodgy leg, warming up by the Stanley range in the middle of nowhere Ireland.

"Thank you." He smiled and reached for the thermos to top up my cup. "I grew it myself. Or to be honest I found the plant it was growing on myself. Then I watered it now and again. Found it in a teashop, miles from here. We were searching for food and found none but I recognized the half dead plant in the window and took it. There for ambience and authenticity I would guess, but now it's turned to its full use."

I drank the tea, it was wonderful.

"So, Haley," Jake said. "What brings a girl on her own to our little community?"

It seemed a polite question, but like lots of questions over a cup of tea, it was loaded. Who was I? Would I tell people about this community? They hid for a reason; was I a risk to them? I went with the truth.

"I'm going home," I told him.

"And where is home?" he asked. "Chicago? Boston? New York? I'm afraid none of those places exist anymore. At least as far as I know."

He looked away for a moment, lost in a memory. I knew that look; everyone knew that look. Someone he knew had been in one of those places, and he hadn't seen them again.

"Ireland," I said, and an eyebrow rose in response. "Monaghan, a little place in the middle of nowhere."

He blew out a breath in a half whistle. "That's a long way."

I didn't deny it, didn't say anything.

"No one crosses the Atlantic anymore," he broke the silence. "Or so I'm told. And coming from the west coast, you'd know that no one crosses the Pacific anymore. No one goes out on the ocean at all. Crazy weather, huge storms. So, while I would be loath to question your honesty, it seems a little...well, a little far-fetched."

"Still," I said, sipping at my tea, the aroma of home strengthening my resolve. "That's where I'm going."

"And how do you intend to get there?" he asked. "You still have some two thousand miles to get to the coast, and the whole east coast is a radioactive nightmare. All the nuclear power stations melted down. The cities got hit with nuclear bombs. You must have heard of them, but if you missed it, I can tell you. I've seen the people that fled from there. Burns, skin peeling, hair falling out, bleeding from their ears."

He stared at me. I didn't say anything, so he continued.

"The chemical weapons, the plagues, the death. Everywhere. No, you must have heard, Haley. There's no going east. And even if you get there, there's an ocean to cross. I know we have no TV news, no internet, but enough people travel what's left and you'd have seen them in New Seattle."

"There's less radiation further south," I said. "And I'll cross that ocean when I come to it."

"Why the push to get to Ireland? Not that it's not a wonderful place, of course, but near impossible to get to and just as likely destroyed as the rest of the planet. I mean, I was there myself, many years ago. Dublin and Galway. Cliffs of Moher. Lovely place, I understand, but impossible."

"There's someone there," I confessed.

"Ah, a young man," he nodded. "But it's been what? Four years, Haley? Why now?"

I didn't correct him.

He changed tack. "You were in New Seattle. Why leave?"

"It was just time to leave," I said.

He nodded. There were questions he wouldn't answer either. We were still feeling each other out, who was a threat, who could be useful.

"How did you end up here?" I asked, sipping my tea.

"Here? Well, I guess there was nowhere else for us to go. Our homes were all destroyed and heading west seemed to be the best option. The whole east coast being as I just described."

"Why not further? There are bigger communities further on. New Seattle, you must trade with some of them."

"We were there for a while, but there's little room for lawyers, accountants, and hairdressers. Teachers, we thought they might be welcome. Claire taught primary school for years and Jon at least taught science, something that might be useful, but more and more we weren't welcome. We got pushed to the edges. Then the bikers came."

"The bikers?" I asked. "You mean the Kings?"

"Yes, the self-styled Kings of the end times. At first, they weren't as organised, just armed groups roaming and attacking. Then they all came together under Ted, who led them to new depths of butchery and depravity. They started wearing their red. Some marker of rank. They became more organized. Came out of nowhere to band together all the small gangs. They were picking people off, and we decided it was better to find somewhere else. This group is all from Denver and we ended up on the outskirts of Moses Lake, but the Patron pushed us out further and the Kings were closing in, so we left and found here."

"Moses Lake? That's not one of the Patron's towns. Othello, yes, but not that far."

"Not officially, but he has a lot of influence. Most of the west answers to him in one way or another. He had more people who were built to survive. Hunters, farmers, survivalists. Men with guns, I guess. And with them, more fuel and guns and food and everything we needed. When the Kings grew stronger, he was the only one who could stop them."

"But not here?" I was getting worried.

"No, we...well, no one bothers us here. No one knows we're here really. We travel occasionally to trade but not often. North and west, it's the Patron and radiation. South and east there are the Kings, pollution, chemical spills. Not often someone comes this road. You're the first in months."

I nodded.

"Which leads us to my questions, Haley," he continued. "Where are you really going? You could stay. Your skills with all these," he waved a hand at the batteries, "would be of great use to us. It's a safe place, and truth be told we are desperate for the help. We were not looking forward to a winter without power. It would be very dark and cold and difficult. Your timing is excellent. But we can't have people find us here; we've put too much into our little community."

I'd made up my mind somewhere on the road the first night. I was going home. I'd always known I would. When I kissed Marley goodbye on a wet morning at Dublin airport, I was sure I'd be back. After the Fall, it was what kept me going. I was going to get home.

"I'm going south and east," I said. "Down past the worst of the east coast. I'll work for trade, but I got to go. I'll keep your secret."

He said nothing, just sipped at his tea, so I pushed with questions.

"What's east of here?" I asked.

"Nothing. Large toxic areas with a few safer spaces. Of course, those safer spaces are full of people who aren't safe. If you go far enough, every nuclear reactor melted down from the Chicago onwards. You really can't go east, Haley."

I wished I had my map so he could point out these areas. I asked if he had one. He didn't. I made a note to get him to show me before I left.

"You can go south. There's a large no-go area just south of here. A nuke hit the middle of nowhere, a ten-mile wide circle that the Giger counters go bananas at, but you could avoid it. Also, it will snow soon, and once it does, you'll be stuck. If it's anything like last year it won't clear for five or six months. Nowhere for you to go on your little bike."

"What can I expect there?" I asked.

"There are communities," he said. "A few, but none close to here. Some nuts who predicted the end of the world and already lived out in the desert. Some of the more religious preaching the next end of the world who were kicked out of everywhere else. Nowhere big. Just small groups of people. More of the Kings. Dangerous and lawless.

Which is why we need to know what you are going to do," he added. "You would, I am sure, be welcome here. A good fit with our community. If you want to go north again...well, that's trouble for everyone. If you go south, then you risk us, too. We both know east and west is no good."

He looked at me and pressed, "I don't think you want to go back anyway, Haley. You're running from somewhere and here...well, here is a good place to hide."

The door opened, and a young girl came in, she was all of twelve, maybe thirteen. I noticed she was wearing a t-shirt from The Who, and I wondered if she ever heard their music. She struggled down the stairs under the weight of a heavy battery which she dropped at my feet. Behind her, Eric carried two more. She stood, staring at me as she pushed dark hair behind her ear.

"These do?" Erik asked, as he dropped his.

I looked at them. Two were sealed acid car batteries, the other was serviceable. I checked it, prying off the cover. The girl hunched down beside me, watching with interest and chewing on her bottom lip.

"We need to top up the water on this one," I told them. "What are the chances you have distilled water around?"

Blank looks answered me. I wondered how they'd survived so long. They knew nothing about anything.

"We have distilled water," the girl piped up. "Claire uses it. Jon makes it."

I was surprised. Maybe someone knew something.

"Can you get me some?" I asked her and turned to the others. "Also, this will need a vent. We need to put it outside or have a vent to outside."

"Why on earth would you need distilled water?" Jake asked. "And a vent? Oh, wait, it doesn't matter. I'm probably not going to understand anyway."

"We need to get Jon in here," Eric said to Jake. "Maybe he'd understand this."

"He's probably..." Jake paused. "Busy. We can have him look in the morning."

The young girl came back with a bottle of water. She watched closely as I topped the batteries up and asked me about them. She asked me more as I hooked them up to charge, about the solar panels and how long it would take to charge and how long it would last. I had no idea. She was the first one here who might understand any of this, I thought, though it was all pretty simple.

She ran to get more wire so we could move the batteries closer to the ceiling where small holes could be made to vent the gas.

Jake and Eric left but sent a kid back with the thermos, filled again with tea. I sat with the girl for a while who introduced herself as Addy. Just Addy. Never Adeline, she told me.

She was interested in everything, how to fix the batteries, how they worked, how I got a bike running, where I'd come from. Her questions flitted from subject to subject, eager for someone new to talk to.

I asked her about herself too, but she avoided the questions easily. Her parents were dead, and she'd stumbled in here. I couldn't get anything more from her. I tried asking her about the town, but she avoided those questions, too.

Claire came by as it was getting dark, bringing some food. She sat down, and Addy left. I guessed I was going to have company for as long as I was there. Someone would make sure I didn't stray to the wrong area. She didn't talk much. We just sat in silence as it got darker and darker.

"Who's sick?" I asked, desperate to break the uncomfortable silence. "The aspirin? You used them straight away."

A pause.

"My son, James. He's... he's not doing well."

"What's wrong with him?"

"A tree fell on him. A group of them were cutting wood. He shouldn't have been there. He's just fourteen. But he insisted, wants to be a man. And in these days, we need every hand to help we can get. Broke his arm which I can fix. The cuts and scratches weren't anything at all, but then they got infected. Nothing we can do. I've washed them and washed them but they're just getting worse. We made a poultice but I don't know if what we tried helps. The few books we have are years old."

She looked away, tears in her eyes while my mind flew to a tree a half mile away. There were antibiotics there. Lots of them. Enough to clear up an infected cut. Worth a fortune. Worth a kid's life. I couldn't go, not now when I was being watched. But I knew I'd have to.

"Did they help?" I asked. "The aspirin?"

She nodded. "A little, for now. His temperature is down. What he needs are antibiotics. And a doctor. Or at least a book on medicine published sometime after the nineteen twenties. You see any of those around?"

Antibiotics, check. Doctor, check. Yes, I'd seen those. Books, I had no idea. I think Zeke had some and the Patron had a bookshelf, but I think his were there more for to complete the look than anything else. All so impossible to get that they might as well be on the moon.

I finished eating in silence, thinking and planning. I needed to get her the antibiotics, there was no question of that, but I couldn't lead them to my stash. There was no way I'd get away again. No one could let that go.

I couldn't sleep, so I lay awake, thinking of what I was doing. Ireland, was, as everyone told me, impossible. Behind me, though, was certain death. A lesson to anyone else who might cross the Patron.

I thought of all the miles between us, the wastelands and the ocean that kept me from Marley. This wasn't the first time I'd tried to get to her.

Chapter 11

Two years after the Fall

It was summer in New Seattle when the Wanderer came through. Life hadn't been easy for any of us. New Seattle was getting rougher. There were more attacks on outlying places by the Kings, and Alfred was now fully the Patron, running a small army. Everyone had given up their guns for a militia. At first, we were all drafted in, to stand watch one night and two days every week, but then it became the same people doing it and they stopped doing anything else.

Without realizing what had happened, we had a full-time army, a group of heavies and thugs who had all the guns, did just what Alfred told them, and they got away with everything. A girl was raped in the spring; she was just twelve and everyone know who did it, but he was one of those thugs, and nothing ever happened. She moved with her family soon after and we never heard from them again.

I was missing home. More than before, more than ever. The first summer we'd worked so hard just to get food, to build the town, to stand watch and protect ourselves, to stock up for another winter. Cutting trees, chopping firewood, rigging solar panels, building wind turbines, just enough for a little light. Fixing cars and figuring out how to make ethanol. After the first winter when so many had died, we worked dawn to dusk and often more trying to make sure we'd survive the next one. There was no time to miss anything. Marley was in my dreams, but the days were too long and hard for thought.

That summer though, we were better prepared. We had two tractors that worked, and farmers had planted fields. We had a sawmill running off a water wheel and a constant flow of firewood and timber for building. We had our army to protect us, in their own way.

We had ethanol and a few trucks. We had some electricity. Yes, there was still more to do – we had plans for more wind power, we were building a small dam for hydroelectricity. But we had a routine to settle in to, and while I wasn't safe, I was safer than most. I was useful.

So, I was bored when the wanderer came through. Time to myself, to think of home, to dream, to miss. We'd seen more wanderers the first year; the second winter killed them off or they gave up and joined a town. They were the ones who when they'd given up they had run from the wreckage and just kept running. Some shunned the new communities, targets of destruction, afraid of the next round of nukes. Some fled the coast, afraid of the next tsunami. Some just quit.

They were the new nomads, surviving on what was left. Hunter gatherers that lived off the ruins of civilization. Hunting what animals survived, looting deserted cities, living in whatever still stood. Travelling by foot or bicycle with backpacks full of small things to trade.

Marcus had been a farmer in Prince George, somewhere way north in Canada he told me.

"That's why I survive," he said. "Not like those other idiots. I grew up hunting and fishing."

He came in on a battered mountain bike, towing a small trailer. The kind that hipsters had towed their kids in way back when. Jimmy saw him first, and he told me all about it later. He'd brought a turkey and two rabbits and exchanged them for bread and grain.

"The Patron offered him a place here. He won't stay though," Jimmy told me. "One of those who'll never settle. I'm surprised he lasted this long."

Marcus came to me that afternoon to see if I could fix his brakes. It was just a cable, so I swapped it out for him in exchange for half the sandwich he'd brought from the bar.

"Where are you off to?" I asked him.

"South," he said. "South and east. Winter will be early this year, I think. South, away from it. East, towards Genesis."

"Genesis?" Jimmy snorted. "A myth. That place doesn't exist."

He stomped off to Dolly's.

Genesis. That mythical place we all talked about and hoped for. It was the holy grail, like stumbling across a bunker prepped by some billionaire who never made it. Food to last for fifty years, nuclear power forever, clean beds, water, and a wall to wall and floor to ceiling rack of DVDs and CDs and books and everything you could want. Plus, a small armoury with enough guns to take over the Dakotas.

We'd all heard of Genesis. Some said it was a network of bunkers for the Silicon Valley elite and their families, the ones who were sitting drinking fifteen-dollar lattes on Nob Hill when a nuke vaporized them. Now the bunkers sat empty and waiting.

Some said it was a military base. Area 51 maybe. Or wherever the president was meant to run to. Huge stores of food. Enough for a million people for a hundred years. Laws and doctors and safety.

One guy told me it was an ark; a secret ship built by the government that could house fifty thousand and survive the worst of the storms. An undersea lab. A secret island off Mexico.

No one knew what it was, or where it was, but everyone agreed. It was Genesis. That was the official name. It was empty or had just a staff of doctors and cops or something and a whole host of empty beds just waiting for us. It was safety and normality. The old world just waiting to welcome us back.

"I heard it's down in Louisiana," Marcus said. "If it's there, I'll find it. Civilization, proper civilization. A place I can settle in. You ever play video games? Gods, I miss video games."

"I thought Genesis was in Montana," I said. "That's what the last guy said."

"I heard that, too," said Marcus. "There's not much left of Montana. Anyone who went there got sick real quick. That's where the ICBMs were launched from. Half them never got more than a few feet off the ground before they blew. Fifty-year-old tech they thought was built to last, but it didn't survive. No, Genesis is in Louisiana. I'm sure of it. I picked up a fragment on a radio, a few weeks ago. North of New Orleans. That's where it is."

"It's a long way," I said. "Dangerous, with the Kings all over."

"I've seen them before," he said. "I've avoided them, too."

"When will you leave?" I asked as I tightened the cable and adjusted the play.

"In the morning," he said. "Bob promised me a dinner and a place to sleep. I'll start at first light."

"How far is it?" I asked.

"It'll take more than a month to New Orleans. Probably two. Then I'll find Genesis. Or spend the winter at least somewhere warmer. Gulf coast."

"New Orleans is on the coast? My geography was never good. I thought it was south."

He laughed at that as he rummaged in his trailer and pulled out a battered Michelin Road Atlas and flipped to the right page.

"Just there, south coast. Florida sticks out east of there, but yeah, the Gulf."

"Are there boats there?" I asked. "I mean, can people still go out in the water there? They don't here."

"I don't know," he said. "I've never been there."

"But if there were, they'd be there, yeah?"

Zeke came barging in to interrupt us. "This guy bothering you, Haley?" he demanded, squaring up. Marcus didn't move.

"Thanks for fixing the brakes," he said, ignoring Zeke.

"Anytime," I told him.

"You shouldn't be hanging around with them, Haley. Those people have no place here, they contribute nothing, they're not like us."

"Oh, fuck off, Zeke, I was fixing his brakes. It's nothing to do with you."

He stormed out. As he slammed the shed door, I saw Marcus outside, adjusting his trailer. Zeke made as if to go at him, but then decided against it and veered away.

I couldn't think about anything else the rest of the day. As I was working on the propellers for our turbine all I could think of was a way home. A path, a whole map showing a route out of there. I wanted to ask him more. If it was real, if it was actually possible.

What was there here for me? Nothing more than a hard life full of risk and deprivation. It was the same everywhere. But I could be home. With the ones I loved. If Ireland even still existed.

That evening I went to Bob's, determined to find out. There was food, a little soggy turkey, badly cooked that I was chewing on and waiting for Marcus when Zeke came in.

"You seen the Wanderer?" he demanded.

"No, he's not here."

"You shouldn't be hanging around with people like him, not here. You'll only get in trouble," Zeke started. "The Wanderers are just a step up from Kings."

"Oh, leave off, Zeke. I'll talk to whoever I want. It's none of your business."

I stood to leave, and he pushed me back down.

"I won't allow it," he said. "You don't hang around with shit like him."

I pushed his hand off and stood up.

"It's none of your business," I repeated.

"Yes, it is. I'm responsible for you here and I'm not going to let you make a fool of yourself." He was redder in the face now.

"Hey, you looking for Marcus?" Bob called as he came over.

"Yeah," both myself and Zeke answered.

"Was in earlier and left already," Bob told us.

Zeke stormed off. I finished my food and left, too.

That night, I lay awake. A month or two to the coast. A place where I could get a boat. Home. Marley. I could picture a long open highway, a gleaming black tar road leading all the way. A shining blue ocean on a white sand beach. Ready to take me home.

The next morning, way early, before the sun was up, he came by the shed. Jimmy was still away at Dolly's.

"So, you coming?" was all he said.

I said nothing.

"I saw it yesterday; you want to go with me. You're a Wanderer, Haley, you just don't know it."

"I just want to go home," I told him. "East is the general direction."

"Well pack and come with me," he suggested. "We'll go east. Safer in pairs. And you seem like you're someone who'd be useful. You know your way around fixing things, I know my way around finding food. We'd be a good team I think."

"I don't have much to pack," I said. "And I don't have a bike. I couldn't keep up."

"I saw bikes all around, take one."

"I can't," I said. "I'd be caught. It's – "

"I understand," he said. "We'll walk. We can find a bike. There were three hundred million people living in the USA two years ago. Now I doubt there's three million. There's a whole lot of bikes out there that no one owns. There's something about you, Haley. I don't know what it is, but my instincts tell me I should take you with me, and I trust my instincts. They've kept me alive this long."

I looked at him and thought of Marley. An image of Zeke ordering me to stay intruded on my thoughts, but I pushed him away and let Marley fill my mind. I grabbed my coat, filled a small backpack, and left. No one saw us go.

We went south on an old logging road. The farmers would have gone east, the hunters I knew were looking at a river to the north. Expecting a salmon run. The trees swallowed us quickly and we were gone.

"Didn't you say you were going East?" I asked him later.

"Instincts, Haley," he said. "Told me not to. What did yours say?"

"To not go east, I suppose."

"Why?" he asked.

"If you weren't staying, then you weren't useful to Alfred. Your bike and whatever else you might have is though. And you pissed off Zeke. You might not make it very far."

"That's what I thought, too," he said. "I've gone through a whole lot of small towns. Some I traded in, some I went miles out of my way to avoid. Some I felt fine trading and riding on out, but I'd rather not have anyone know where I've gone to. Anyway, there's some stuff just up here."

He stopped the bike and got off, then pulled a pack from behind a tree and dropped it in the trailer. "Lesson one, Haley. Hide the stuff worth stealing."

He told me to get on the bike and he'd walk a while.

We went on like that, swapping over every few miles, one on the bike, one walking, maybe both pushing up a hill. Me on the crossbar for the downhill while he tried to steer.

We went faster than I thought. By evening he guessed we'd done over twenty miles. We found a house not too badly damaged and hid for the night. He'd been grand all day, a gentleman, but still, I fingered the knife at my hip, ready to use it.

He saw it, the small movement in the half light.

"Don't worry, Haley," he laughed. "I won't be hitting on you. I'm guessing I'm not your type."

I said nothing.

He pulled a gun from under a blanket in his trailer. A small one, revolver, and I looked for an escape.

"You know how to use this?" he asked me.

I nodded. "Point and pull the trigger."

"Pretty much," he handed it to me. "Just remember which end is which. It's no use unless you're close. Like, really close."

I nodded. Jimmy had said something similar when he'd shown me how to use his old colt. Back before it was taken for the Patron's army. To protect the town. To keep us down.

Marcus pulled out a shotgun from the trailer. It was in a sling underneath the trailer, easy to access but I hadn't noticed it. Short and ugly, the barrel cut down.

"We'll need to keep watch," he said. "How about some food? See what we've got, and I'll go see about water."

He took our empty bottles, a water filter, and the shotgun, then walked out and left me a revolver. It was like an open invitation. I checked his trailer, his bags, but there wasn't much. The Road Atlas. Another bottle of water, some clothes, a Leatherman multi-tool, and a folding knife. A half dozen Bic lighters. A naggin of vodka. Two well battered tins of beans and the food he'd bartered for in New Seattle, a quarter loaf of bread, and a few carrots.

Beneath it all, I found a photo. Marcus and another guy, both with beers, standing under some monument I didn't recognize. A brother, a friend maybe.

"Matt," a voice behind me.

I almost dropped it.

"I was looking for the food," I said.

"It's okay" He came in with the two bottles full, and nodded at them. "Stream out the back seems clean. I ran them through the filter just in case."

"Who was Matt?" I asked, handing him the photo.

He took it, sitting down, staring at it a moment. "He didn't make it," he said.

Silence.

"Boyfriend?" I asked.

"Husband. We were married six months before it all happened," he said, getting up and putting the photo gently back in the trailer, folding it in a pair of jeans.

"I have a girlfriend," I said suddenly. I hadn't talked about it to anyone. Not really.

He nodded.

"Back home, in Ireland I mean. It's where I want to go. East coast and then try to get home," I said, all in a rush.

"Wouldn't be easy," he said. "It's a long way and there's a whole mess out East. A whole big mess."

Silence.

He turned with his gun, staring out.

"We could get you there," he said, standing to walk out. "First, we find Genesis. We'll be closer to the right coast for you. If anyone can get you to Ireland, it would be the people there. Get some sleep. I'll wake you in a few hours."

In the morning, a few miles on, we found a pair of bicycles in a half standing school. It took little effort to get one fixed, just air in the tyres really, and tie some of our load on.

Soon afterwards, we hit a road. A proper paved road. Full of pot-holes but much faster than the tracks we'd been on. South and on. Forty, maybe fifty miles. Freedom like I hadn't had in a year.

I started to notice where I was. Towering mountains, snow-capped peaks, the smell of pine forests. The leg burning slog up the hill, the exhilarating rush of coasting down the other side.

That night, we slept out in the open by a small lake, well back from the road. A rare clear and warm night, a small fire for cooking. I was off when it happened. Taking a shit—that's why I was hidden. A genetic instinct for privacy. But I heard the roar of the bikes coming in, voices raised.

Instantly full of terror, I tried to run, tripping over my pants. My instincts screamed for me to flee, but there was nowhere to run. I'd be seen. Hiding was my only option.

Shouts, whoops of joy. A scream. A shot. Laughter.

I could see bits between the trees. Large men in leather on big bikes, silhouettes against the fire. I heard cries of excitement as they found food, a yell when they found the vodka. The screams had stopped.

I went back, maybe an hour after they'd left. They'd never come looking for me. Didn't notice or didn't care. Marcus was lying there, half in the fire, half burned and half untouched. The fire was dying, our food gone. Our bikes smashed, the little trailer upended, anything of value gone, and everything else strewn about.

I dug a hole beside him. With no tools, it wasn't deep, but I rolled him in, found the picture of Matt and put in beside him, and covered the body as much as I could. By then it was dawn, the pale pink light of a beautiful new day creeping in from the east.

By light, I could see the bikes were ruined. Wheels bent out of shape, tires slashed. Destruction for no good reason. I searched around, but there was nothing left. With no other direction, I started walking. West, back to New Seattle. Just at the edge of the clearing, where I'd missed it, a small patch of red. The road atlas, I gathered it up, smoothed it out and wiped the morning dew off, and walked on.

It took four days to get back to New Seattle. I'd searched most places I passed, but it was the second day before I found something I could use. I'd gotten lost in one of those places were the road almost disappeared and it was hard to tell what was road and what was a mud track. Off somewhere up a mountain, I found a cabin, a shack, maybe used by hunters back before. Untouched since the Fall.

Inside was a quad, painted in muted brown camouflage colours. One wheel was off and it was up on jacks; someone had meant to come back and finish fixing it. I checked; the wheel was on the ground beside it, but a shock was gone. I didn't find the replacement anywhere.

Next to it though was an old blue Yamaha DT200. I siphoned all the gas from the quad and started the bike after a dozen tries. Then I continued west. I found a road, glimpses of an ocean, and turned north.

When I got back, they wanted to kick me out. A public whipping for deserting the town. Abandoning the community. Theft, of what, they weren't sure. The Patron wanted an example. Jimmy told them he needed help getting the new turbine in and I'd be no use if they did that. In the end I got to stay, Zeke took my bike, and there were plenty of threats.

Later, after the arguments over my fate, I lay awake, staring at Marcus's battered road atlas, my finger tracing the route in the dim light from the flickering bulb. All the roads, joining page after page to go east, to go south, to go east. A path to the ocean.

A path home.

Chapter 12

Later, much later, I was lying on the bed waiting for all to go quiet. I listened, and outside there was a noise. A snore. Soft and quiet, not the rasping death rattle I'd been used to from sharing a shed with Jimmy.

I got up as quietly as I could and poked my head outside. I didn't notice the can, precariously balanced by the door until it was already falling. I caught it just as it went to rattle loudly down the stairs and held my breath until I heard another snore. It took me a few minutes to place it, but there under what seemed a pile of junk was a shape in the shadows. My guard was sleeping. I thought it might be Jake.

I crept slowly past him and to the road. The night was still, not a sound, not a rustle of wind. Around me, the ruins were dark, sharp shadows in the dim white light. I walked as quietly as I could, carefully placing my steps, until I was out of town. Then I was over the rise and in the trees.

My bike was still there, just where I'd left it. I looked around, but there was no one. I stood, hidden in the shadows of a tree and waited. The hanging half-moon reminded me of some godawful pre-baby Facebook photo with artfully placed sheets. A pregnant moon among wisps of cloud.

I dragged my mind back to the task at hand.

Nothing moved. Quietly, I dug around until I found the pills and held up the packs one by one until I saw what I was looking for. Keflex. I'd seen it before. I didn't have the box, just the blister packs. I wondered how many a dose was. I ripped off four. Then two more and another two and put them in my pocket.

Was that a noise? I froze in the act of hiding the pills. A cloud covered the moon's modesty and I waited. Nothing moved, but I waited longer. A hint of belly peeked from a cloud and then, out on the road, a footstep. I shoved the pills back where I'd hidden them and pushed whatever I could over them, then crept away as the moon retreated behind the sheets.

I moved away from the road and doubled back. I saw her there, peering between the trees as the clouds left completely and the moon just flaunted it all.

"Addy, what are you doing here?" I hissed at her.

She jumped and spun around.

"What are you doing here?" she countered. "You snuck off."

"I was checking on my bike," I said.

"No one's going to steal your bike," she told me. "They're not like that here."

'They're.'. Not 'we're.' It was more than she let slip all evening.

"Well, I had to check," I said. "Shouldn't you be in bed?"

"Shouldn't you?"

"No."

"Well neither should I. Can you show me your bike?"

"Not now" I said.

"Tomorrow?"

"Maybe."

"Are you really going to leave?" she asked.

"You're full of questions."

"So are you."

Smart-ass kid.

"We should get back," I said. "Someone could be looking for you."

"No, they won't."

"We should go anyway. I need to get some sleep."

We walked back. I hoped she hadn't seen more. I needed to ditch her and go back and move the pills. They were my currency to get across the continent. My best chance to get home. If anyone else found them I was lost.

Addy pestered me the whole way back. I tried to quiet her, she'd wake everyone, but she had questions on everything.

She did wake someone. Jake, looking sheepish, was standing by my basement door and waiting for me.

"Checking on my bike," I said quietly.

"She's going to show me it tomorrow," added Addy.

"No, I'm not," I countered, almost automatically.

"Addy, shouldn't you be in bed?" Jake said. She made to argue but he continued "Now, Addy. You've plenty to do tomorrow."

She gave in quietly and left.

"Now that you know your bike is okay, maybe you can limit your night-time walks?" he asked.

"Now that I know you're here, maybe you should just move inside. It's probably warmer," I said. "You could stand guard more easily."

It was cold outside. There'd be frost in the morning, I guessed. He grinned.

"No one guarding you, just...well, you understand, obviously. And yes, it is a little cold."

He grabbed the bundle he had been sleeping in and followed me in. It was still cold in there. I burrowed into my blankets, only grazing my shins once as I fumbled in the dark. Jake closed the door, blocking what little light there was. I heard rustling as he unrolled his bundle and set up by the foot of the steps.

In the dark, I could hear his breathing. Quiet and regular. I needed to get past him again, to hide the pills properly.

"Thank you for not stealing my bike," I said.

"We're not like that, Haley," he said. "Tomorrow, bring your bike down. I'm sure Adeline will pester you non-stop until she gets to see it anyway. It will be safe here for as long as you decide to stay. I'll walk up with you in the morning if you like."

"I'm not a danger to you," I told him. "I just want to get home."

"So, do we all, Haley. So do we all," he muttered. "Get some sleep."

Chapter 13

I slept fitfully, my mind still torn. While they were hiding something, everything else here seemed safe. They offered safety. I went
back and forth most of the night and was woken gritty eyed and
yawning by the door opening with a loud bang as Addy came in.

She came running down the stairs, tripped over Jake, and fell on top
of me.

"We can at least offer you breakfast before you run off," Jake said, as
I stood up and stretched. "Addy, why don't you make yourself useful
and let Claire know we're up. We'll be there in five."

She ran off, talking all the while, and I got up slowly.

"There'll be hot water. You can wash," said Jake, watching me try
to brush my hair into some semblance of order with my fingers. He
was already up and sitting on the roll he'd slept in.

I picked up my blankets and half folded them while he watched
before I gave up and dropped them there. Breakfast and hot water were
a good offer. I allowed him to lead me out and take me to the same
room in the abandoned station I'd been in yesterday.

Jake pointed me at a door where a basin of warm water, a rag, and a
bar of what might have been soap waited for me. I got to clean myself
for the first time in a week, and I felt a million times better with just
a slightly cleaner face and hands. When I was done Addy, my new

shadow, ran off with the muddy basin, Jake handed me a cup of tea, and Claire came in with a slice of toast and a fried egg. Heaven couldn't describe it.

"I should get going," I said as I finished the food. "I'll just take my gas."

I figured I'd leave the pills somewhere they would find them.

"It's going to snow," said Erik, coming in. "Won't last long, should clear this afternoon. Why not stay a little longer? There's a truck you could look at for us. We'd pay. A little more gas. Feed you, too."

I was still hungry. And with my night-time walk, I could use the extra rest.

"I'll go in the morning," I said. "With a tank full of gas."

"We'll can fill your tank," agreed Erik. "And give you food."

It was probably the best I could do. I could use the Keflex to trade for anything else I wanted. They needed it badly. It was a seller's market so long as they didn't find my stash.

"We can go and get your bike now," said Addy. "Can I ride it?"

She'd changed her shirt. Now it was the Clash. My question of the day. Should I stay or should I go now?

"I'll walk up with you," said Jake.

Was it a gentlemanly offer, or was he being more diligent with his guard duty? Probably a little of both. Either way, we bundled up and left. Already a light snow was falling, melting as it hit the ground. Some white patches gathered here and there. I didn't want the company, especially since I wasn't sure how well I'd hidden the pills in the dark, but I had no excuse to ditch them.

Addy ran on ahead and was waiting by the bike when we arrived. I glanced around nervously and could see plainly where I'd been digging. If the snow hadn't been melting so quickly, they would have been covered.

Neither seemed to notice anything as I roped them into helping me push the bike, steering to keep them looking away. At the road, much to Addy's disappointment, I didn't start it. I just pushed it to the crest of the hill instead. I let her sit on, showed her the brake, and let her coast back to town.

"She's so young still," said Jake, as we walked in the wake of her screams of joy. "Sometimes we forget that. Everyone needs to grow up so quickly now."

"What's her story? She isn't one of you?"

"We found her when, we were fleeing Moses Lake and hiding in some old ruin the first night. She was there already, with two others, her mother and older sister, I would guess. She was the only one who made it. The others had…" He paused, scratching his chin while he searched for the right words "Well, there were signs of a struggle. Adeline wouldn't speak for days. She came along with us; I think more for food than anything else. It certainly wasn't for safety; she was terrified of all of us. She'd grab whatever food and water we put near her and run away to eat. She'd only travel with us in the back of an open truck, never inside in the warmth. We offered her a spot behind the cab, out of the wind, but she refused. Just huddled as far from everyone as she could in the small space. So, we gave her a heavy coat and let her. Nothing else we could do."

He shrugged. "When we got here, it was still months before she spoke. Even now she wanders all the time, doesn't spend much time with anyone. Bugs Jon more than anyone. I guess she likes machinery and he's the closest to a mechanic we have here. He taught science in school for a while, I think I told you that. But she sleeps on her own and is easily startled. Quick to violence, too. I woke her once and she just jumped up and kicked me. She swung around with a knife before she realised who I was. I never saw it coming. We don't know where she even got the knife."

"She seemed very chatty," I said, watching her get off the bike and look for a stand. "She's non-stop with the questions. Not at all nervous or shy or anything."

"It is unusual, I'll admit," he said, shaking his head. "She's taking a liking to you. Like I said, she likes machines and you fixing the generator probably impressed her. Plus, you're close to her age and a girl. Maybe you remind her of her sister. If I remember right, she would be about your age. We're mainly older here. There are a few kids, but she avoids them. I don't know why she likes you but thank you for letting her ride your bike. It's good to see her smile."

I thought about it. Addy avoided answering questions, but other than that seemed like a regular kid. Like my nephews who were that age when I left. Curious, full of chatter at times, and sullen pre-teens at others. Addy was standing by the bike when we reached her, trying to lean the bike against a low wall.

"The side stand broke off long ago," I told her and showed her the centre stand.

She pulled at the bike and got it up on the second go. Not bad for all of eighty pounds and five foot nothing.

"We should move it off the road, though," I said.

"How do we start it? It's this isn't it? But it's broken." She'd found the kick starter.

"Yep," I said. "It's broken, so easier to just push it."

"Let's take it over to the shed," said Jake. "Jon may have something to fix it."

Chapter 14

The shed turned out to be a very battered UPS truck laying on its side. It was off the road, behind a burned-out house, between a few scrubby trees and a rusted car up on blocks. From up close, it looked looted and empty. Years before, someone had badly spray painted a dick on the roof, and its faded yellow balls were half hidden with dirt.

Surprisingly, once Jake held the door up, I barely had to duck my head and could wheel the bike in. Jon was there, sitting on a crate and fiddling with a small metal box. The inside was littered with old, opened, and empty UPS packages everywhere, long looted of anything of value.

Jon turned to us, a box in his hands, bloodshot eyes and a pale face, grimacing at the noise we made. "Haley," he said, offering me the box. "I don't suppose you know much about Geiger counters?"

"Nothing at all." I said. "Never needed to count Geigers."

He looked at me a moment before giving a wan smile.

"Well, this one still works most of the time. I took it from my school when the bombs started to fall. I just don't know how to maintain it, or even if I had to. If something like this broke before, I'd just get a new one. Anyway, what can I do for you? Looking for a place to store your bike?"

"It needs a starter," Addy piped up.

"Well, the kick start is broken. Jake thought you might have something to fix it," I said.

He shifted on his box and peered around me at the side of the bike. "I have lots of bits and pieces," he told me. "I think we could do something."

"I'll leave you to it," said Jake, looking at Jon.

It sounded polite, but the look they passed spoke of a changing of a guard.

"When you're done, Jon, can you show her the truck? Erik thought she might have more luck with it. Perhaps trade the bike parts for some work there."

There went the extra gas, but I needed the kick starter fixed in case I ever needed to get going in a hurry. My makeshift way took too long.

Jon nodded and led me out, Addy following. Under a random fallen wall, he lifted some wood and started pulling out pipe. Mostly old plastic pipe but then a short length of three-quarter copper pipe and a yard or so of rebar.

"They should do perfect," I said.

"I thought they would work. Why don't I show you the truck? I've tried to get it to started but got nowhere. Fixing your bike, I can do; it's a pretty straightforward fix."

He led me to an old blue Chevy. It was parked behind his UPS truck and covered in dirt.

"Keys are in there," he said. "It just won't start. Quit working a week ago. Addy, why don't you stay and help while I fix the bike? If you need any tools, Haley, my shed is full of them."

He left, and I opened the hood. Addy hauled herself up to perch beside the engine and watch me. I started at the beginning by turning the key, and there was some clicking.

"The battery is charged," Addy told me. "Jon used the generator last night."

I nodded and got out to check the starter. When I went to look for tools, I found a surprising number of them. Jon was drilling a hole in my kick-starter by hand when I went in. He pointed me to a tarp when I asked if he had a wrench. Underneath there was a large selection of older but well-ordered and clean tools. I took what I needed and left him to go work on the truck.

Everywhere it seemed there was ruin and rubble, but there was a whole community hidden under it if you just knew where to look.

It took an hour. Some wiring was messed, but I had seen enough wire in my basement the night before to know where to look, and I replaced what was falling apart. When I turned the key, the truck started on the first try. I got out to clean the carburettor, a constant job in New Seattle, and as I did, I heard another engine start and Jon came out riding my bike.

He'd bent a length of rebar into an L and fasted it to the stub of the kick-starter with the copper pipe.

"That looks amazing," I told him. "Better than new."

"I hope it holds," he said. There's another length of copper pipe ready in case this one breaks. I put it in the case on the back."

Now that he was right up close, I noticed a slight smell of booze on his breath. He looked steady and sober, but it was there.

"I filled the tank for you," he said. "You should be good for a while. Let's go eat. We'll all be glad to have that truck running."

I followed him and Addy back to the same room as before. This time Jon disappeared and came back with Erik, Jake, and some food.

"I think Claire could use some help Adeline," said Erik.

She glared at him but went.

"Jon tells us you fixed the truck. Thank you, Haley," said Erik. "And he's fixed your bike and filled it with gas. So, I think we're even."

He waited for an answer.

"I still need more gas," I told him. "I've a long way to go."

"Jake told us. Ireland...that is a long way. A really long way. You could always stay here. You're obviously the most mechanically minded here. Maybe stay out the winter, show Jon some more things, help us fix up the place. Food, a warm place to stay, and I promise that come spring we'll give you enough gas to get you where you want to go."

"That's a lot of gas," I said, noting he was the second person to ask me to stay. First, they wanted to run me off, now they wanted me to stay. They needed something, and I could use this to bargain. "I thought you had none."

"You can make gas here," he said. "Ethanol. Jon's been experimenting, and Jake told us you've worked on it before. I'm sure that there'll be enough come spring to share with you if you stay."

I thought about it. It was a tempting offer. Outside, the snow had turned to rain and everywhere was cold and damp. I could stay. If I stayed though, I might never leave, and sooner or later I'd be found.

"No," I said. "I still need to go."

"Are you sure? You won't get far on a tank of gas," he said.

"I could trade," I said. "Your son...he needs medicine."

Everyone looked at me.

"I can get some Keflex. It's an antibiotic. I know where there is some."

I tried to look straight ahead, not give away that they were in my pocket.

"I thought you already traded all you had," said Erik carefully.

"I did, but I know where there's more."

"On your bike," said Jake.

"No," said John. "There's nothing there." He'd searched.

"I hid some, back on the road," I lied.

"What would you want for these meds?" asked Erik.

"I've got enough cans to hold fifteen gallons. You can give me another, say, twenty gallons of gas and food for a week."

Erik looked at Jon. I was asking for a lot. It would get me most of a thousand miles. But it could save their kid. I was giving it away cheap.

"We'd need to make another run," he shrugged.

"We can't," said Jake. "Remember what happened last time?"

"James needs the drugs."

"She must have hidden them with the bike or beside it," said Jake. "Another run is too dangerous."

"Wait," said Erik, and he turned to me. "You are sure?" he asked. "Keflex, antibiotics. How many are we talking about?"

"Eight."

Erik looked at Jon who shrugged. "Probably enough. It's four days. I'd like a week, but it should do it. It has to." He looked at me again. "It's a lot you're asking, Haley. We don't have that much gas; we can get it, but it's risky. It would take some time. If I promise you we'll try, would you trade us now? James, my son, he can't wait. Your aspirin helped a little, but..."

There were tears in his eyes.

I reached into my pocket and took out the pills.

He took them gingerly, like they might break. "Thank you Haley," he said. Then he stood up and almost ran off.

Jake looked at me.

"You had those all along?" he asked. "Or was this your walk last night?"

I said nothing.

"What else is hidden there?"

"Leave her, Jake," said Jon. "We don't steal here."

I wondered how long it would take for someone to search the area where I'd hidden the bike. I needed to move the drugs as soon as I could. They might not steal here but when a kid was dying, all bets were off.

Chapter 15

"Come on, Haley. Let's grab a drink and you can show me how you fixed this truck. I'll get you your gas. And no one will touch anything else you've got. We're not thieves here." He looked at Jake, a stern look, not a conspiracy. "You can trust us, I know it's hard where you came from, but when we left, we swore we weren't going to be like that. We look out for each other. We share what we have and if we trade, we try to trade fair."

Jake looked as if he wanted to reply, but he said nothing.

He led the way out and over to his UPS workshop. All the way over, I worried that someone was going to find my stash. Under a rag in a corner, he pulled out a bottle of clear liquid and handed it to me.

I coughed as it burned my throat. Almost threw up.

"I distil it myself," he said, taking it back and taking another drink, wincing as the alcohol ripped through his taste buds.

"It's terrible," I said, and he handed me the bottle with a grin.

I took another drink, this time managing not to splutter as it seemed every nerve ending in my face had already died in the last assault.

"Thank you for the pills," he said again. "It's been tough. We couldn't lose another kid."

He paused a moment. I wanted to ask, but I didn't want to know.

"Let's go see the truck," he said.

He took another drink and passed me the bottle. I shook my head, so he drank again and then put it away.

I showed him the wires I'd changed in the truck. He asked some more questions, and I answered what I could. My brain was a little numb. I was well out of practice on drinking. Never was a big drinker to start with. Jon was completely steady.

"Where is the gas we need to get?" I asked.

"That's a bit complicated," he told me. "It's in a gas station. Just...well, it's also kinda radioactive. Then there's the Kings occasionally. They mostly stay clear, but they come close now and again. Last time we ran into them coming out. They shot out the tires on a truck, stole the load of gas. Killed Ephraim. I was lucky to get away. If I'd have been in the second truck, I'd have been gone and he'd be here."

He looked off into the distance.

"Kind of radioactive?" I was still stuck on that bit.

"Just a little," he said. "Trouble is that west of there is very radioactive, and the wind usually blows that way so it's not safe to go there most of the time. If the winds are from the east, then you get toxic fumes from a chemical spill. Old paint factory on the side of town. If there's no wind, you're still not safe. Now though, with the wind from the north, it's mostly clear. The area's still radioactive but you're probably okay if you're quick."

"Probably?"

"Yeah, it's bad for you. But it's like smoking. You have a pack of cigarettes, it's not good for you. Have ten packs it's worse. But you have a pack a day for years and you get all kinds of crap. This is like having a pack of cigarettes every hour. You stay a week and you're in a lot of trouble. But in and out and don't go too often, you'll make it."

"You've been already," I said.

"Twice," he answered. "But cigarettes don't always kill. Everyone knows someone who smoked a pack a day and never got cancer. My gramma swore that a shot of whiskey and a pack of Camels a day kept her alive to ninety-three. Personally, I think it was more spite than anything that kept her going. But then again, some die at forty withered away to nothing. It's a risk. Everything is.

"We're going to need the gas here anyway. We can't last the winter on solar. We'll be in and out fast. When we go, we can fill the truck and enough for your bike. Hell, you find out you know where there's some more pills and we'll get enough to take you to Florida which I guess is where you're heading. I'm serious, Haley, we won't steal from you, but we need those pills. You need the gas. Think about it."

"I couldn't carry that much gas," I said.

"Stay a bit. There's another truck around here. Fix it and load it up. You can have it fixed by spring. It will take you out of here."

"I can't stay," I said automatically, before falling silent as I tried to think it out.

Could I, though? Rest up, stay safe for a few months, leave well prepared instead of just running? This was an offer I had never considered. A truck, enough gas for two thousand miles. Probably a hundred and twenty or so gallons. Maybe barter for a gun, some kind of a weapon. Something I could sleep in.

Could I? Zeke was at least a few days behind me. If I was leaving, I needed to leave now. If it snowed when I was on the road with the bike, I was stuck. If it snowed before Zeke found me, he was stuck.

Middle of nowhere, he couldn't find me. He'd need to hole up until spring. Backtrack. I could leave at the first sign of a melt. All wheel drive, snow chains. I knew Zeke had them, but not on the truck he was in, and they must have pissed through gas. I could have a head start and be gone.

Could I risk it?

"Well then we'll get you a bigger tank," Jon was still trying to convince me. "I'll build you a trailer. It's a small bike but we can figure out something. I know where there's a bigger bike. Not sure it will run but we can try."

It was a good offer. I thought about it, numbers running through my head. A gallon of gas weighs about six pounds and I got about forty miles to the gallon. I could currently carry twenty gallons, about a hundred and twenty pounds, which slowed me down and got me only about thirty-five miles to a gallon. So, seven hundred miles loaded up. Add another twenty gallons, getting lighter as I went along, maybe another four hundred miles. Over a thousand miles in all. It would be slow; the weight of all that gas would be like having an extra three of me on the bike. If I added a trailer, then I could maybe add forty more gallons, but I didn't know if the bike would move all of that weight.

"We can work it out, Haley," Jon continued. "I've got some plastic drums that would be lighter. Take that steel box off the back and anything else that's not needed, cut down the weight and make room. Just give us some more pills. Please."

It was a golden offer. Would I ever get a better offer? I doubted it, but the fear of what was chasing me made we want to leave.

"How many pills do you need for something like that?"

"Whatever you got," he said. "All that gas? Say twenty aspirin and a couple dozen more antibiotics. Or something like that."

"I'll do it," I said.

His eyes widened, just for a moment. I'd made a mistake. I'd let my guard down. Maybe it was the alcohol, maybe I trusted him too quickly. Either way, I'd overplayed my hand. He had been ready to haggle. He'd named a stupid amount. What he asked for was a fortune, unobtainable, nothing a lone traveller could have to trade. He had expected me to bargain with him, to counter. I'd given in too quickly. I felt fear. They might tell me that they don't steal but this was so much, just sitting out there, waiting to be taken. Even a saint might be tempted by a suitcase full of cash and this was a stash of lifesaving drugs when none were available. A box of miracles. I tried not to let my face show it but I needed to move those pills now.

Jon recovered his surprise quickly. "Good, we can start now. Wind's from the north at the moment. We can go in the morning."

Addy came out and followed us around as we picked bits and pieces in the rain. Tie down straps, a hose and a manual water pump. When we moved to Jon's shed, Addy went off and came back with Claire and tea for all of us.

"How is James?" I asked.

She didn't answer, just grabbed me in a fierce hug. I felt embarrassed; I had the pills all along, but I'd held out to barter. A kid's life was on the line, but this was the new world now, everyone for themselves.

"No change," she told me. "But thank you, Haley. He has a chance now."

I said nothing. I should have given her the pills straight off. He'd have a better chance. We were better if we were in this together. They were in it together, wouldn't steal from me, looked out for each other. I felt not just the old Catholic guilt, but a deep shame at what I'd become.

"Jake tells me you're making a run," she said. "Are you sure?"

"I'm going, too," said Addy.

"No, you're not," said Jon. "You stay here."

"You can't stop me," she said. "Anyway, it will be faster with three of us."Three?" asked Jon.

"You and Haley. You are going, aren't you, Haley?"

"Of course," I said. "But you're not.

"I can help."

"It's dangerous," Jon warned. "I'll go on my own. Haley's giving us enough."

"Everything is dangerous," Addy argued. "You can't treat me like a kid forever."

"Well for now I can, and you're staying here and helping me," said Claire.

Addy stormed off at that.

"She'll be alright," said Jon. "She's just taken a liking to you. Good to see her get out a bit. She's not had it easy, that kid."

"You can't go on your own," I said. "Addy's right, it would be faster. And the gas is for me."

"You're offering us something which will keep some of us alive a little longer," he said. "That's all you need to do."

Again, there was something he wasn't saying.

"Well, I'm coming," I told him. "I got to keep an eye on my investment."

We loaded up the truck. Four fifty-five-gallon drums and a dozen smaller cans, all tied down tightly. We filled up the tank with the last of their gas, emptying the generator to get the last drop.

"How do you know about this place? With the gas?"

"Let's go have a drink and I'll tell you more."

This time he didn't lead me to his workshop but to the outside of town and into the trees. After a half mile we came on an old concrete shed. The place was filthy, and it stank of stale sweat and piss.

"Welcome to Casa Jon," he said with a grand sweep of his hand.

There wasn't much there. A bed, some dirty blankets, and a copper still. A few bottles I guessed were in various stages of ageing and an old blue plastic bottle from an office cooler full of a murky brown liquid. I guessed it was the mash. I'd seen it before at Bob's, a sugary mass fermenting into beer or something that could be distilled. I mainly thought it was a waste of good food. Or if too gone off, something that could be used for fuel.

Jon pulled an odd shaped bottle of brown liquid from under the bed, then changed his mind and searched under there again for a different one. This one had a Jack Daniels label on it.

"Actual whiskey," he told me. "Found it on my first run. A lucky find. Not too radioactive either."

"The what? Radioactive?"

"It's okay it's not radioactive. It was mostly buried under a pile of rubble, but I saw some pipe I thought would be useful. I was pulling it out when I saw this and dug it out. I checked it with the Geiger counter. Nothing past normal background radiation."

"You do this a lot?"

"Do what a lot?"

"Check your food with a Geiger counter?"

"Why do you think we're here, Haley?" he asked. "I mean, why do we hide here?"

I shrugged. "Had to be somewhere I guess."

"No, if you go west you hit a lot of toxic shit and north as well. Chemical dumps. East and south are radioactive. We're pretty much surrounded by places you don't want to be. When we ran, we had no choice. We kept going, and it was more luck than anything we found this place. It's a little safe place hidden by places no one wants to go."

He pulled two glasses from a shelf and wiped them with an almost clean rag. He gave me one and poured a shot.

"We'd been running for two days, twenty-nine of us in three trucks. Along the way we picked up Adeline, and then the Carlson's a little later. Thirty-four of us in three trucks. All out on the back roads, trying to stay away from the Columbia and all the sludge in there. Away from the coast and what's left of Portland."

He downed his shot.

"Then the bandits came, those Kings. They picked off two people before we managed to shoot one and run for it. They chased us for two days. We'd get away and then they'd find us again. And suddenly they weren't there anymore. We weren't sure why they stopped. Usually, they just let their dead lie where they fell but they pulled back. We went screaming on, full speed."

He poured another shot for himself and went to top mine up, but I had only sipped. I took another sip, still half full, and he topped it up.

"We realized soon that we must be somewhere we didn't want to be. I was driving a truck and we paused just long enough to dig out my Geiger counter. It was ticking so much it was a hum. We took all of ten seconds to decide to keep going. There was no going back. We thought we might get past the worst of it, we knew what was behind us.

"Well, we kept on and the ticking would get worse and then ease off but was still really bad. Then it'd get worse again. We found a road and followed it, and maybe ten miles from here, the radiation eased to bad but better than we'd seen in a while. So, we stopped and agreed to rest. Patched up Ronnie Carlson who had a bullet in his arm and found water for a truck that was steaming from a bullet in the radiator."

He sipped his drink, I sipped mine. He finished his and topped it up again.

"We didn't rest long, just enough to catch our breaths and fix things up before we went on. When we got here and realized the radiation had died right off, we stopped for the night. And another night to fix the trucks. Let Ronnie rest, he was in a bad way. Died a week later the poor guy.

"We ended up staying longer, hid out in the hills behind us. We kept a watch, but no one followed us, and the radiation stayed low. So, we stayed, and we searched everywhere. Like the rest of the world, there was little left to find here. No one else came though, so we worked on the ruins of the houses, converted basements to be useable, and then we hid them. Dragged junk over doorways, burned the one house that was almost still standing. No one would stop too long, we thought. We were still terrified and still wanting to run and hide."

"We planted small crops in areas. Here and there, a small clearing and a few seeds. Everything was set where it would look wild. Everything was hidden. The longer it went, the longer no one came near, the safer we felt, the more we could do, as long as we could stay hidden. We were here, five, maybe six months before someone came through. A truck just blasted by the road, didn't even stop. We were all hidden, weapons ready, trucks hidden. Fight or run. But they just sped through like they were running. I guess they thought this place was as toxic as everywhere else."

He finished his drink and sat, rolling the glass in his hands.

"We found some cattle running loose, a few chickens. We knew we were in a good place. If you keep going east you hit a huge barren area, maybe forty miles on. Not sure what hit there, but it's scorched earth. Probably a nuke, but there's no crater. Anyway, the Geiger counter goes nuts there. South and it's iffy, toxic spills and the like, and north is the same. So, we're protected in a way by it all. We've got an area of maybe two, three hundred square miles that's clear enough. Maybe fifty square miles is actually pretty good. Around here, levels are low. Way higher than the before times, but a little less than New Seattle when I was there."

"How?" I asked. "I mean, apart from places where everything leaked or got hit, isn't it all in the air anyway?"

"No idea," he said and poured us another drink and clinked glasses. "Here's to the freak of nature. Well, I guess I have some ideas. East is like a desert, and I am guessing the thermals off there redirect some of the wind. Not sure why, but it's just a little better than most places. I guess what I'm trying to tell you is that this is a good place to stay. No one comes here, you can hide out pretty well. We got food, we got the start of things here. You could stay here."

I didn't want to think of it. I still needed to run. The offer of a truck made sense but the need to get away overrode it. The decision was gnawing at me, I needed time and space to think, so I stood up quickly, thanked him for the drink and walked out. He didn't follow.

I wandered a bit, my first time unguarded in this town, lost in thought. It was a good offer. In the time I'd been here no one had passed the road, not that there was much traffic anywhere since the world ended. From all I'd heard, I was the first in a long time. I'd been spotted from miles off, and they were prepared. They had power, food, safety. A truck when the snow melted.

I thought of Marley.

The last time I'd seen her had been at the airport. She was grumpy as all hell at having to get up at six in the morning to drive me there. Hungover, of course; we'd been out the night before. I was only leaving for a few weeks, but it was an excuse for a session, all the gang out on the town, finishing up in Coppers at two or three in the morning.

It was going to be a great adventure. I was so excited. My first time in the US. A chance to see the best in robotic engineering, maybe snag a job for when I finished my degree. Only the best students got that opportunity, and I'd worked my arse off for it. Even Daddy said he was proud of me. You could have knocked me over with a weak fart when he said that.

We sat in Bewley's on hard plastic chairs by the gate. Sipping tea.

"Get the last cup in at the gate," my aunt Peg had warned me. "All the tea is shite over there."

She'd been in Disneyland once and she knew.

"I'll be back in six weeks," I told Marley.

"You'll miss Pride," she said.

"I never liked it too much anyway," I lied, it would have been my first once since I came out. I was terrified of it and excited all at once, but this opportunity was more important. It could make my, no, our, future. "This a great opportunity. It could make my career. It will be good for us. For our future."

"I know, I know," she muttered. "I need an aspirin."

I didn't have a hangover, even though we'd not crawled home until an hour or two before the alarm went off. The whole gang was out on the lash, not a care in the world. That was back when the world was wide open, and nothing could ever go wrong. Back when we didn't care about anything. Who was it said, "We were young, and knew that we could never die"? How right they were.

"I have to work in a few hours," she yawned. "I should really get some sleep."

She stood up and kissed me.

"Be safe," she told me. "No meeting up with strange Americans."

"I won't," I promised.

Then I walked through the gate and was gone.

That was it, the last time I saw her. We'd known each other just seven short months and lived together for six of those. We were in love; I was smitten.

I didn't always know I was gay. Marley told me that she knew from when she was five or six. Growing up in the middle of very Catholic nowhere, I just knew I wasn't into boys. I remember Tommy O'Connell called me a dyke when I didn't want to go to the cinema with him in second year. At the time, I wasn't into in girls either.

While the rest of my class discussed boys almost non-stop, I didn't see the attraction. Even in college, when I'd started at DCU and there was the LGBTQ society, I didn't join. I was starting to think I might be, but hadn't enough interest. I figured that someday I'd just meet the right person, the one who worked for me. I expected thoughts to just bloom.

That all ended in a café off St. Stephens Green.

Chapter 16

I'd been at The Book Cellar in Temple Bar looking for a second-hand copy of one of our predictably very expensive textbooks. Modern Systems Analysis and Design by Joseph Valacich. A hundred and twenty fucking euro in the bookstore on campus. I remember that. Eighty on Amazon but someone told me they had used copies here for thirty quid.

I hadn't found it and was walking to the bus when it started to piss rain. Absolutely lashing down. I ran for a café, to wait it out. Then, of course, the Catholic guilt kicked in and I felt I had to buy something. I bought the cheapest thing I could, some not so great coffee in a chipped blue mug and sat in the window to wait out the rain.

Something in a reflection caught my eye, and I turned and saw her. Walking down a wrought iron spiral staircase beside the counter, she wore a long loose white summer dress, completely wrong for the time of year, but she wore it with a confidence, like it was the middle of summer on a Greek island. The white was in contrast with her dark skin. A half dozen bracelets on one hand—beads, leather, and a brightly coloured friendship bracelet like I made when I was six or seven—caught my eye. A fine silver chain hung around her neck with a flat silver disk.

Still today, I can remember that one image. Etched forever in my mind, the place I'd run to when it all fell apart. In the four years since, that memory has kept me going.

I was staring; I couldn't help it. She didn't move, she flowed. She owned the place. Carrying a stack of plates in one hand and three mugs in the other, she moved like they weren't there. They were just a blurred background to a movie star walking a carpet, a model on a catwalk, completely at ease and not caring who was watching, immune to the camera flashes and my gawping stare. An angel descending to a dingy café. Not the waitress clearing tables.

She saw me and smiled.

I looked away. I probably blushed. I'm sure I did. A minute later she came over with two mugs of coffee and gave me one, moving away my barely touched one. Her hand brushed mine as she did so, sending a thrill that was unknown to me down my spine.

"Refill on the house," she said and sat beside me.

The place was empty enough; myself and two old biddies who were huddled at a table over a pot of tea were the only customers. All just avoiding the rain.

"I'm Marley," she said.

"Haley. Thanks for the coffee."

"No problem." She smiled, and it lit up the room. In that instant, I was on that Greek island with her.

The world stopped for the first time. Everything I ever thought would probably happen someday, slowly or over time, just crashed together, arriving in a huge dogpile on my head. We talked for ages, long after it stopped raining. Even through the lunch hour when she should have been working and the guy at the till was shouting for her every time she sat down. We moved to a bar later, and then she asked me to come back to her place.

For a moment, I was stunned. Was this going where I thought it was? I was suddenly lost.

"I should get back," I remember I told her. Something about an assignment due.

"Well, call me," she told me, putting her number in my phone. And then she kissed me.

It was the third kiss of my life, and the first one that counted. Tommy O'Connell, who called me a dyke, tried to get me drunk before shoving his tongue down my throat when I was fifteen. That didn't count. His breath was stale cigarettes, and his teeth ground against my gums as he tried to grope my ass.

Some guy, Brian something, drunk in my first week in college was better. Flashy smile, lots of charm. Then he tried to unhook my bra under my t-shirt while we queued for drinks. I left him standing there in the student's union bar and never saw him again. I don't think he went to DCU.

Marley, though... She knew exactly what she was doing. I never did get that assignment finished.

Chapter 17

Here I was, stuck thousands of miles away, with a chance to be safe. What would Marley do? I was sure she would come for me. No matter what. So I would do the same.

I turned and walked with direction. Back to where I'd hidden the drugs. I took another dozen Keflex and a pack of aspirin, then hid the rest further away, covering them fully and went back.

"I still have to go," I said when I walked into the same kitchen where I'd eaten all my meals.

Erik, Jon, and Claire were sitting there.

I handed over the pills. Dozens of them.

"Take these. You need them more than I do. I know what we're doing is dangerous, but I need that gas, so I hope this makes up for it."

Claire had tears in her eyes. What she now held in her hand was worth more than a fortune. It could save her kid, a kid I had never met.

I went out for a walk, going nowhere, anywhere. I just needed to be alone. I was sitting on top of a hill when Jon found me later.

Jon sat beside me and handed over the bottle of whiskey. His rotgut in the strange bottle, not the Jack. I took a drink. He looked like he'd had more than a few already.

"That's a lot of drugs you had," he said. "Have you got any more?"

I said nothing.

"Not that it matters, they're yours. But thank you. It's tough watching the kids die."

He took another swig.

"I'll get you the gas. As much as you want. For more though, you can have anything you want."

"I just want some gas and some food," I told him.

"I just want a cigarette," he said. "Always do when I drink. You'd think a few years would have stopped the cravings."

"You think they'd keep you alive like your granny?" I asked.

He laughed at that. I realised I liked this guy. He was straight up, somehow safe, and like everyone else, a whole lot broken.

"You know, back before this all went to shit, I used to be content. Or so I thought," he said, staring off at the town below us. "I was married. Had a wife and a daughter. Olivia. She'd be twenty now. She was a bit like you, stubborn as a mule. They didn't make it, though. Tracy got cancer and died five years ago. Never saw the Fall. A blessing in a way."

He paused, staring off to space before he continued.

"Me and Olivia, we ran for it when Denver fell. She got sick on the way. Died in Moses Lake. There was a doc there, but he couldn't do much for her. Radiation got her."

I said nothing. I wanted to say something, anything, but there's nothing I could say. I'd heard this story before. Everyone had lost everything.

I half moved to pat him on the shoulder, but my hand stopped and handed him back the bottle instead. He took a drink.

"You should never outlive your kids, Haley. There's a natural order to things, and that's one of the things you should never do. I should have quit when she died, but I guess I was too stubborn to. Tracy always said that 'Liv got it from me."

He handed me the bottle. I took a drink and waited.

"It near broke me. I guess it did break me. I started drinking. I'd always drank a bit much but there and then, I drank as an end. There were still places to be looted, so I'd find a bottle or two and disappear, wake up in a ditch covered in my own vomit. One time I found a full case of wine. Was gone for a week. Never been so sick in my life."

"What made you stop?" I asked.

"What makes you think I stopped?" He laughed as he took the bottle from me. "I just slowed down," he said with a sigh. "I guess winter got to me. It got colder and colder, and the snow came in and there was nowhere to go to loot. There wasn't a drop of booze in the town, and we were running low on food and running low on fuel and there wasn't any room for a town drunk. We needed hunters and builders and doctors and workers. Not drunks, too wasted or hungover most of the time to be of any use. Eric and Claire took me in, got me through the worst of it. They saw something in me. Claire wanted a school in this new world. Maybe she was just collecting teachers.

"I tried to be useful. I worked fixing things. Nothing like you, but I could do a bit. Set up a sand filter to clean the water. Helped folks insulate their places. Chopped wood, dug ditches. Without the booze to help, I'd work till I collapsed, hoping for sleep."

He raised his glass and stared off into the murky liquid. "I guess I also watched a lot of people die. When spring came at least half the ones who started there were gone. It near broke me watching the kids. Digging the graves. The smaller they were, the harder they were to dig. I remember one...it was real bad. The kid was so small, maybe two or three, and we had to pry her body from her mom's arms. The mom was young too, eighteen, nineteen. Not a scrap on her, she'd given all her food to the kid, and it still wasn't enough."

I sipped at my drink while he collected his thoughts. I knew what was coming. We'd all lived that first year, seen what the end of times could do to a human.

"I knew then I'd have to dig another soon. You could tell when they gave up. We tried, you know? Well, Claire tried, to get her to stay warm, to eat something. But that girl knew it; you shouldn't outlast your kids. I buried her a week later.

"When we could go out again and look for food, I still looked for booze. But not as bad. I had a goal in life. Sometime between digging all those small holes, I realized I needed to do something. Piss or get off the pot as they say. Follow that girl's lead and give up or get off my ass and keep the kids alive. And that's what I've been trying to do ever since."

I'd heard the story before. I'd lived the story before. It still hit me every time, the collective grief of everyone that was left. All of us who'd lost everyone and everything. The aching loss of seven billion deaths didn't recede with time. Time did not heal all wounds. The loss just hid and then came jumping out, like now, a gut punch.

I said nothing. There was nothing I could say. No one had ever found the right thing to say at a funeral for ninety nine percent of the planet.

"Anyway, that's why you can have whatever you want. I don't want to watch any more kids die. So, we'll give you all the gas you can carry. You can take a truck. I'm serious. Load your bike in the back if you want. We'll get you a hundred, two hundred gallons. More than enough to drive all the way to the east coast. Less worry about the weather, too. Leave tomorrow; I'll manage to fix the other truck eventually. We'll still owe you. Hell, I'll drive you there. Leave us a chance, and I'll drive you to Florida. Two of us, it will be safer. I'll take a gun. You can have a gun. Whatever you want."

He was sincere. His face pleading. It was a real offer.

My mind was already flying along the road. Not just to Marley but an escape from here and now and his awful grief. I fled to facts. Pros, cons. It made sense. The offer of a truck was already tempting; it would be the only way to take enough fuel and not worry about the snow. With two of us, it would be easier. Jon was resourceful and would be a huge help. But could I take him away from this community?

The journey was always going to be extremely difficult, but with Jon and a truck and a gun and so much fuel, it was more possible. Almost possible. A truck was harder to hide, though. The bike could go off road, small and easily hidden. A truck had less options. Some off road but not the narrow gaps a bike could squeeze through. But it was a better chance to make it. Worth the trade.

I was still thinking when Jon pointed to the north.

"Clouds are building. Looks like there could be a storm coming," he said. "We should get back."

The sky was dark in that direction, huge black clouds looming. I noticed how cold it suddenly was. We started walking. Then we ran. The storm came from everywhere, all around us, clouds building on every horizon and converging.

The wind picked up, gusts from east, from west, from north and south, pushing us off balance and whipping debris towards us. We hit the edge of town as the rain started, the wind driven drops pelting us. We made it to the UPS truck as it turned to hail. I went to run inside, but Jon pulled me on. The hail was stinging, the ice pellets growing bigger and bigger, leaving marks as they attacked.

We ran for the basement I'd been in the first night and Jon shoved me inside and slammed the door behind us. The rattle of hail sounded like a tommy gun outside. I caught my breath.

A single dim bulb lit the room and the few people huddled there. I saw Jake and Addy rummaging in the boxes at the back. Eric and Claire sat on my bed with a young guy they introduced as Charles, their eldest son.

We sat on the steps and I noticed that there was a solar panel resting against the wall that hadn't been there before.

"We've seen these storms before." Jon had seen me looking. "When they come, everyone gets underground and waits them out. We move the animals if we can, or if not then we hope they find shelter. We move the panels indoors or drop them under cover. There's an old Chevy out there with a tree fallen on it. Not going to move in this or any storm. There should be two panels under it. We'll probably need to re-run the wiring, but the panels should be okay. Everyone has a place to shelter and wait it out."

"I've seen storms," I said, "but never this fast. And it came from everywhere at once."

"There's freak weather here," Jake said coming over. "Same thing that kept the worst of the radiation away gives us all the weather all at once. It will die down in a few hours. At least we have some light. For that we thank you Haley."

"Where's everyone else?" I asked. "I mean, where are all the shelters?"

"All over. There's a basement or two around. Eric and Claire's other kids are probably in the one at the end of the street. We made some other shelters, dugouts to hide in. Propped up stone walls for cattle to shelter behind. Chickens will be in a half-buried Volkswagen. The Hanson's are over by the lake; there's a concrete shed there. Dieter and Erika are still away. Everyone has a place to go."

"Where are Dieter and Erika?" I hadn't heard of them before.

"Away," said Eric before anyone else could answer.

A crash from outside interrupted us.

"What was that?" I asked.

"Just the wind blowing something. There'll be a mess in the morning," said Eric. "The wind gets pretty strong in these storms."

I was worried for my bike. More and more, a truck made sense. If I was caught out in a storm like this on my bike, I'd be screwed. I'd seen the storms, hidden out for a few of them. Out in the open you were as good as dead. I'd seen it all.

Chapter 18

Seven weeks after the Fall

That was back then when we still counted time as if to name and number it would give it a start and, we told ourselves, an end.

The fires had started in a town. Anyone who was left lit campfires. No more microwaves, no gas stoves. Fires started all the time; no one knew what they were doing. One had grown and was covering the horizon. There were no fire crews to put it out.

We were on the side of a mountain, a picturesque plateau with a small stream falling off the edge and bubbling down the slope. A postcard perfect campsite where we watched the world burn around us. Zeke knew a place in the mountains, further in where we might be safer. An old military base. Law and order. We were headed there, now just five of us left, but the forests around us burned, blocking our paths, smoke darkening the sky.

Zeke, the doctor and leader among us, had us all wearing wet rags around our mouths. The area we were in was clear, the closest trees a few hundred yards away. Wait it out, we thought. The fire will pass us. Nothing to burn. We have water, we'll be good.

Mark told us he had a cousin who had once worked on wildfires in California. "We need to clear the brush," he told us.

There was none near us. We were engineers though, engineers through and through. This was a problem we could solve. We had a stream, a flat area, and a surrounding inferno. Ideas were floated; dig channels, build a mini moat around us. We were arguing over the specifics.

"We should dig it out," Benny was saying.

"With what?" Mark scoffed. "We have nothing to dig with. We can redirect the water with a dam. Build a whole lagoon here."

Lee interrupted us and pointed to the clouds. "You're wasting your time," he said. "It's probably going to rain."

It was definitely going to rain. No probably about it. Heavy dark clouds were building. Quickly, we started arguing about the shelter. All we did was argue. I think we wanted to hold on to what we knew, like what we'd learned in our universities would save us.

We had a tent which we started to unpack as around us it got quickly colder. Then the rain came. It came in buckets, in gallon drums, in fire trucks. All of us packed in the tent and the rain flattened it against us. It got colder, and colder.

As the temperature dropped, the rain turned to hail. The tent was getting destroyed, the flimsy fabric no protection against the onslaught. We gave up and ran for it, racing for the trees as quickly as we could. The fires were down to patches, a bright fight between the bellows of the wind driving the flames madly and the river of rain pushing them back. The trees were swaying, bending, dancing. Twigs and leaves were flying everywhere. The wind was howling and gusting, pushing us on, shoving us down. We were soaked and freezing, getting hammered by the hail.

"Get in further," someone shouted. Benny, I think. "We need shelter."

We were getting in where the trees grew closer and there was more undergrowth. The wind eased, and we were sheltered from the worst of the hail. It still fell, but with its speed broken by the canopy above, it was just chunks of ice falling, not flung. The cold was getting worse, though. We needed solid shelter, we needed warmth, a fire.

A huge crack and a longer groan echoed, and we saw a tree fall in slow motion. I think I shouted. Or someone did. Lost in the noise of the storm. It fell, and Lee was gone. One moment huddling with us, the next crushed under a massive branch. The rest of us got scrapes and bruises; Lee got a crushed skull.

There was nothing we could do. We didn't even try. A single glance, a glance that would haunt my dreams for months, could tell us that he was gone. We just ran and ran, until we found a road and then we ran along it, ignoring the storm and trying to outrun the trees.

We came to a house and ran for it. The door was locked, and no one answered our fierce pounding, so we broke a window and went in. We were bruised, bleeding, small cuts from fleeing blindly among the trees. Once we stopped, sheltered from the wind and rain, we were all freezing. There was no electricity. There was a fireplace, but it looked like it hadn't been used in years, and there was no fuel. Mark saw a barbeque outside, blown over on its side, and ran out to drag it in.

There was still propane and then we had heat. With no thoughts for modesty, we stripped and covered ourselves in what we could find, blankets and towels. I remember looking around. When the world fell, we had been seven, and now we were four.

Chapter 19

Back in the basement, we were wrapping ourselves in blankets, ready to wait it out. The storm raged but we were well protected. Outside occasional crashes prophesised more of a mess.

I picked a corner and dropped. I was exhausted. I wasn't expecting to get the sleep I wanted. My mind was drifting, and it was hard to concentrate.

I kept coming back to Jon's offer. A truck. Company on the drive. Protection, a gun. Much safer in a storm. Enough gas to get to the east coast. We could take his Geiger counter. The whole east coast was a mess from what I'd heard. So many cities there had been a prime target. So many nuclear reactors to just give up and spew uranium or plutonium or whatever they used all over the place.

I wanted my map. I wanted to know where the cities were. Where I was. A route. The shortest route to the ocean. The safest way.

Addy dropped down beside me. "What are you thinking about?" she asked.

"Nothing," I said.

"You're still leaving," she said, her tone accusing.

"Yes, as soon as I can. Before the snow comes."

"Take me with you tomorrow," she said.

"No, it's too dangerous."

"Everything is dangerous."

"Some other time."

"You'll be gone some other time."

I had no answer.

We sat in the silence of the storm a while.

"Tell me about Ireland," asked Addy. "What's it like?"

I was thrown a moment.

"Well it's kinda like here I guess," I said. "A lot of farms. I grew up on one. Ireland is small; I guess you could walk across the whole country in a few days. It rains all the time. All the fecking time."

"Did it get hit?" she asked.

"I don't know," I said. "I hope not. There's nothing there to hit. It's not a target for anyone."

"Do you think your family will still be there?"

"I don't know."

I hadn't thought about it. I didn't want to think about it. Home to me was Marley, not the farm in Monaghan that smelled of disappointment. The neighbours might disapprove. It was nothing overt, but it was always there.

The one time I'd taken Marley home, she'd thought that everyone was lovely. If you knew them though, it was all there, in the glances, the half looks and odd silences. The unasked questions. Would there be grandkids? What would people say at mass? Never spoken but understood.

A world of hurt that had been hidden for a long time was waiting under a scab to be picked at. When you're fighting to survive it's hard to think of anything else, but here, safe from a storm, I saw an actual path out. A real and realistic path home. In Maslow's hierarchy of needs I'd moved beyond the Physiological and the Safety for the first time in a long time, and everything else was there waiting for me. I couldn't put it aside as impossible. I was going there.

Home. Would Monaghan still be there? Would Kavanagh's stony grey soil still stand in drumlins? Would the chapel pews still smell of Pledge, elbow grease and guilt? Would I be good enough, and could I ever fit in?

It was Maya Angelou who said, "You can never go home again, but the truth is you can never leave home, so it's all right." I didn't think she was right. I think I left on Aer Lingus flight EI 143 and the end of the world blew me and home too far apart. But maybe the dry black bread and sugarless tea of a four-year penance could charm back the luxuries of a lost childhood.

I wanted to cry. I wanted to run out of there, but I was trapped in a basement.

A small hand took mine.

"I'm sure they're okay," Addy said.

I didn't know about them; I knew I wasn't.

Chapter 20

"You got everything you need?" asked Eric a third time.

"Sure," I answered for the third time.

The storm had died as quickly as it had come, and we'd found that it had done little damage, so we were good to go. We'd come to an agreement in the night. We'd get the gas, then me and Jon would leave the following day. I'd leave behind enough pills to pay for the truck, a gun, food, and enough gas to get me to Florida. Jon would drive back after leaving me there. I didn't tell them, but I'd still have half of my stash of pills left.

We were taking the truck I'd fixed, me and Jon. Addy was watching from a door, glaring at us. She'd begged and pleaded but we still weren't letting her come. The back had a selection of tools and rope. I held the Geiger counter, and Jon was driving.

"Ready?" Jon asked.

I checked the Geiger counter. Barely clicking.

"Ready," I said. "Let's go."

We drove off, up a track and across the hills. It started to rain. We hit another road, muddy and unused, and we kept going. In the background, the counter clicked a little faster. Still low. The rain was starting to turn to snow.

On we went, on where the road was mostly gone and we had to go slowly, picking a path through the mud and the potholes.

"Why did you have to run?" I asked, to make conversation. "When you left Moses Lake. What happened?"

Jon swung wide to avoid a hole. More of a crater, really.

"There was no room for us there anymore," he said. "I guess the Patron decided who was useful and who wasn't. We weren't really in his territory then, but everyone could see how it was going. The guys with the guns were his. The leaders in the town talked of joining up, safety in numbers. The common good."

"I remember," I said. "New Seattle was just settled, and we'd survived the first winter. The Kings tried to attack, and the Patron collected all the guns. A defence force, he called it. Talked of gathering more towns. Of course, then we'd given up our guns and he was in charge. The common enemy were the Kings."

"Yeah," said Jon. "We had few guns to start with, but we had given them all up to be rotated among a guard. The Kings, they kept picking us off. Like you, we formed a guard and at first, we were all part of it. And then we weren't. Suddenly it was just the same group of people, and they all wanted to join up with the Patron. Then the rest of us needed to be useful. Working, cutting timber, gathering food, trying to plant crops. Less and less food for us though, and more and more work. Then it got worse and the guys with the guns started to work less and make up more rules. People were beaten, shot even, for not doing enough work. We were at the bottom of the food chain and a lot of us decided to leave. We took two guns and a lot of food and stole some trucks. That's why we had to run. They wanted all that back."

"What happened?" I asked. The story was all too familiar. We'd traded our guns for safety. Someone told me that Benjamin Franklin had a comment on it—those who would trade their liberty for safety deserve neither. I don't think Franklin had any idea what the end of the world was like.

"We lost them. Eric had this idea of almost draining their tanks before we left. We only left enough gas in all the other trucks to get them a few miles. By the time they noticed, we were four or five miles from town, and they were out of gas. They'd just jumped in and chased, and now they were stopping. When they got out, they'd have found the spare cans they had were all empty. We guessed they'd have a long walk back. Then the damn Kings came."

The truck lurched as a dip appeared from nowhere.

"Out of nowhere," he continued. "We were maybe thirty miles away and suddenly there's shots and five or six guys on Harleys come roaring up and shooting. We kept running and shooting back with the few rounds we had. We were running and fighting for two days before we lost them. More would come, and we'd run or fight. There's an advantage in having a large truck against a Harley. They get too close, and we'd just run them off the road. Of course, you have to get close, and they had more bullets than us. Anyway, we lost them when the radiation got bad."

There was a clang in the back as we hit a crater of a pothole, but he drove out and everything looked okay when we got out and checked.

"So, what about you?" he asked as we got back in. "How do you know the Patron?"

Chapter 21

We'd been hiding out in a cabin in the absolute middle of nowhere for half a week. Just me and Zeke. We'd buried Benny two days earlier in the soft earth out back. We were stuck in shock and grief and shame, when a gang in camouflage gear chased us out. They were carrying big guns and moving like a trained unit. Just rolled up in a pickup, guns at the ready, and moved in. I'd been out, looking for firewood, and saw it all. They arrived, kicked Zeke out, and took over. Just like that.

I met him a half mile down the rough logging track.

"Where now?" I asked.

He shrugged. "East, I guess. There's nothing left west, and we need to get out of the mountains. Winter comes and there'll be six feet of snow."

I'd never seen six feet of snow before, but I'd seen the road signs that Benny had told me were on tall poles because snow would bury normal ones.

"You sure?" I asked. He shrugged again and we started walking.

I wanted my stuff. The backpack I'd been filling for the last two months was at that hidden cabin, but there was no telling what could happen if I went back there. All I had now was a knife in my pocket and the clothes I was wearing.

We walked, getting hungry. We stuck to the back roads, the small trails. Every house we passed we searched for food, clothes, anything of use. A bicycle. We had found two before, but they were back at the cabin. All the ones here were long gone. Gas had run out and we were at the tail end of the streams of refugees who had picked every house clean of anything of use.

By night, we each had a bundle of the stuff no one had looted. I had found heavy curtains in one house that would be blankets. Zeke had found a knife in a drawer. Just a small one, a dinner knife, but better than nothing. For the first time I'd looted a body, an old guy in a Honda who had a heavy coat. I was sure the blood would wash out.

"Should we just stop here?" I asked at one house.

"No, keep going. We need to get over the mountains before the snow comes," he told me. "It's getting colder already. There'll be more places further on. We'll need food, we can't stop. We could be a week or more here."

We kept going. It was past the end of summer; the days were warm, but the nights would be cold. Everywhere had been looted. Cars and trucks littered the roads as we walked by, out of gas and dumped where they stopped. Houses had broken windows, all cleaned out. Signs of campfires in the kitchens. Furniture smashed for firewood. The ones not built for the storms were damaged, rooves caved in, siding ripped from walls. We kept moving, dragging empty stomachs on tired legs.

When the sun was on the horizon, we stopped. What had once been a grand house with a great view was now empty. Large windows, now broken, looked over a valley. The house had six huge bedrooms, each trashed and ripped of anything of use, and a massive dream kitchen with two stoves, two dishwashers, and a table to seat twenty. It was a mess, the marble countertops covered in a thin layer of dust, drawers ripped out and emptied on the floor. A propane barbeque was out back, but the tank of gas was missing. Still, the house was shelter. An illusion of safety.

"We should stop here," I told Zeke when we finished searching. "Get some sleep, go on in the morning."

"Yeah, the fireplace looks like it works. I'll get some wood," he said.

I started pulling what furniture was left to form a wall around the fireplace, and Zeke started breaking things for wood. We got a fire lit and sat down, huddled in old curtains, hungry.

Zeke leaned in close, and I shifted away.

"Just trying to get warm, Hales. Don't be so full of yourself."

A noise outside stopped a fight before it could start.

We were both silent instantly. We could hear footsteps on gravel, a low murmur of voices.

We didn't need to talk. We got up quickly, grabbed our stuff, and ran. We hightailed it to the kitchen; I'm no dumb blonde in a horror movie getting trapped upstairs. I cracked open the back door, an escape route for us if needed.

We watched through the dining room as two men came in the front door, guns raised. We'd need the escape.

"We should run," I breathed to Zeke.

"Wait," he whispered, straining to see them from his crouching position.

"Fire's still lit, they're probably still here," one of the men said. He was tall and stringy, with a mop of dark hair.

"Let's check," the second guy, a stocky balding guy with bad skin, said.

They came towards the kitchen. I got ready to run, but Zeke put his hand on my shoulder. "Wait," he hissed, and then he called out, "Alfred?"

The balding guy paused, swung around with the gun.

"Who's there?" he called, the gun sweeping the counter we crouched behind.

"It's me, Zeke," he answered.

"Doc? It's you? Hey, Bob, it's the doc. You on your own Zeke?"

"Yeah. Well, there's just Haley with me," he said, standing up.

"Come on out. Hey good to see you, good to see you, we could use a doc. Hey Bob, bring in Kathy, bring her in. We got a doc now, it'll all be okay." He lowered the gun, and I watched as he and Zeke did some complicated bro-shake.

"Come on out, Haley," Zeke called to me. "This is Alfred, an old friend. Dodgiest man in Belltown and all-round good guy, come on out."

I stood, still ready to run for the back door as Bob came back with a woman in her thirties, blonde dishevelled hair and a limp. Kathy, I assumed. "Zeke here's a doctor, he'll fix you right up," Bob was telling her.

"Caught my leg on some wire running from the marines back there," she told us as Bob helped her to lie down in front of the fire. "Tried to clean it but…"

"We saw them this morning," said Zeke. "Maybe the same guys. Here, let me take a look. Haley, can you get us more light?"

I poked at the fire and threw some more wood on it to build it up. It was all I could do.

In the flickering firelight, Zeke used the scissors on my pocketknife to cut open her jeans. The gash up her leg was red and angry. I'd seen this kind of infection; it hadn't ended well for Benny. While Zeke cleaned it with what he could, Alfred told us some of his story.

"We were down in Portland when it happened, doing some business, just on our way out. We heard it on the radio, and then the bombs landed. We were far enough away. When the tsunami hit, we were on high ground, luckily enough. It was close, though. If the waves had been another ten feet higher, we might have been swimming. We just hightailed it out of there. Swung right and headed as high up as we could until we ran out of gas.

"We found the military. They set up a camp in the high ground; it was like they were ready for something like this. Hundreds and then thousands of people crammed into tents and eating these cardboard things they called MREs. Tasted like shit. More and more people coming in every day, but they weren't set up for the numbers. They had enough tents for five hundred, I think, and they started turning people away when it got past two thousand. Started rationing the meals. Threating to shoot anyone that looted or broke curfew.

He sighed heavily.

"Then everyone started getting sick. Massive diarrhoea and puking. Just shitting water and shitting everywhere. They didn't make it to a toilet, not that those fucking porta-potties were much use. They only had seven for all of us. Then they dug trenches and told us to go there, but everyone was getting sick. Someone said it was the water and someone said it was the food."

"Cholera," said Zeke, looking up from his work. "That many people, not enough clean water. Rice water diarrhoea, nausea."

"Yeah, Doc, cholera," said Alfred. "That's what the army doc said, too. Anyway me and Bob, we weren't doing too bad. We had a deal with a sergeant for some of my product. We got bottled water, but when it was running out, we decided to get the hell out of there. Been hiding out and running ever since, trying to keep going.

"A few days ago, we were trying to get a car that we found to start when this bunch of Marines came roaring up in a pair of black trucks. Well, they were just going to take our gas and everything, they wanted to take Kathy, too. I guess they gave up on their refugee camps. We just ran for it and they started to chase us in the trucks, but we got off the road and into the trees and they gave up. We were crossing an old wire fence when Kathy caught her leg. Bob tried to bandage it, but he's no doc."

"Nope, never was a doctor," said Bob. He extended his hand to me and I shook it. It was rough and calloused from years of hard work. "Bob Peterson, and this is my girlfriend Kathy that Zeke is fixing up."

Zeke looked up. "We need to get her some drugs," he said. "We'll need some antibiotics.

"Thought so," said Alfred, reaching into a backpack. "Got these but not sure which ones or how much. Was going to try them soon if it didn't clear up."

He pulled out a large Ziplock bag. Inside were several smaller baggies. I saw pills, grass, and a white power that could have been coke or speed or possibly anything.

"I knew I could count on you Fred. You always had the best stuff," said Zeke, rifling through the bag. He pulled out some prescription bottles and checked the labels. "Doxycycline," he said, opening one. "Perfect. Here, take two of these tonight and two in the morning. We'll look again then."

He gave the bottle to Kathy, and Alfred reached for the bag.

"Mind if I?" said Zeke, pausing in the act of handing it back.

"Sure Doc, go for it."

Zeke took a pill from another bottle; I didn't see what type. He went to close the bag, but then took another pill and put it in his pocket before handing the bag back to Alfred. Then he lay back with a contented smile and the rest of us sat around the fire.

"You got any food?" Bob asked.

"Nothing," I answered. "We had some, but the guys this morning got it all."

Bob looked at Alfred for approval first. "Oh yeah, we got some. Let's get that stuff cookin'. We got a pair of rabbits earlier. Not a lot but we got enough to share. Gotta feed the doc."

I was left to the cooking. I didn't mind. Two fat rabbits for five people wasn't a lot, but it was food.

We left in the morning as a group. Safety in numbers. Zeke was blinking against the bright light of day and muttering to himself. We walked on east, following Alfred who always seemed like he had a plan.

He said there had been a town. Or a crossroads at least. Two days later we'd made it there, the five of us. A small cluster of houses on the east side of the Cascades. They were built of heavy stone and huge logs, made for the winter, for the nearby skiing. Big, expensive cabins for the Microsoft and Amazon millionaires to escape it all.

The buildings had survived the storms, but not the exodus from Seattle. The few who had survived the blast and the waves fled. Most had taken the I90 to the south. We were a little way off it, on the back roads, but enough people had come through that there was fighting and looting, and two of the houses were burned to the ground.

The locals had organized, and a barricade of sorts greeted us when we arrived. A burned-out shell of a school bus blocked the road. The houses ahead were silent. Boarded up windows, signs of fire, but no signs of people. Enough signs of security, of safety, though.

"Let's be careful here," Alfred said, as a guy appeared on top of the bus, a large gun in his hands. "We're not here to steal anything," Alfred called to him. "Just passing through. We can trade if you want."

Alfred and Bob kept their guns raised. Then two more appeared at each side of the bus.

"No need for anyone to get hurt here," Alfred shouted, his rifle pointing at the first guy.

"No need."

I spun to the voice behind us. Two more guys with guns pointed.

"You just drop your guns and get on out of here," he continued.

He was young, a teenager. He should still be in school.

Bob and Alfred were spinning, guns pointing.

"We're not giving up our guns. We're just passing through, getting down out of the mountains. No one needs to get hurt," Alfred said. "Let's just be reasonable."

"Or we just shoot you and take your guns," the kid said.

"Let's talk. We can trade," said Alfred. "You can shoot, yeah, you'll get two guns but what use is that? We'll take a few of you, too."

Bob and Alfred were further apart now, guns swinging. I was looking for an exit. To one side it looked like I could dodge behind a rusting panel van and hope there was a path to the trees.

"We'll get more than guns. You said you have trade, so we'll get that too." The kid was smirking now. I was ready to run, to leap for the van.

"Not so much. We got a doctor. You need that?" Alfred asked.

"Do I look like I need a fuckin' doctor?" the kid asked.

He raised his gun, and Alfred raised his. Bob sidestepped away, pointing his gun behind us.

"Put it down," came a shout from the bus. "Josh, let them in."

The kid paused.

"Josh, let them in now," the guy on top of the bus shouted, his tone leaving no room for argument.

The kid lowered his gun. Alfred turned his back on him, lowering his gun like he was unconcerned.

"You need a doctor?" he asked.

"You're a doctor?"

"Fuck no," said Alfred. "But one of us is. How about we all lower our guns and come in and talk about it? You need a doc, we need some food and some transport."

"Josh, bring 'em in," the guy called.

The kid led us in. We had to get on the bus and climb between the rows of seats and out the back door to get into the town.

"Good setup," Bob hissed. "Have to go single file, slowly. They can pick us off."

"Yeah, well, there's no other way out," said Alfred.

Zeke was unconcerned. I guessed he was high again. He'd been talking to Alfred this morning, whispering in the corner, as we readied to leave the abandoned house we'd stayed in. They'd come to some agreement, made some plan. He didn't tell me what it was, but it didn't matter, my choices seemed to be limited to sticking with them or dying.

We were led to the first house. It was built of huge logs, long and low with a high-pitched roof. The guy from the roof of the bus was waiting for us along with four others. Everyone had guns, but they were lowered. We went in.

The house was full of people, maybe twenty-five in there. We were led to a back bedroom where beds had been crammed in and six people were lying, groaning. The place stank. Pus and bile and puke.

"You're a doctor?" the guy from the bus asked me.

"Him," I nodded at Zeke.

"Do your work, Doc," said Alfred.

Zeke was looking around like he wanted to run, wanted to object. Alfred leaned in, a hand in his coat pocket, gesturing and whispered something. Zeke looked at the pocket, thought a moment, and nodded.

"I'll need some things," he said. "Water, clean water. Hot water." He pulled a ratty bandanna from a pocket and wrapped it around his mouth. "We'll need some space. Haley, come help," he ordered. "Everyone else, leave."

Everyone else left. I searched my pockets, but having nothing to tie around my mouth, I started to pull my t-shirt up around my mouth.

"Don't bother," he told me. "It's not contagious. Just the smell."

"What's wrong with them?" I asked.

"Not sure, but dysentery I would guess," he said and rattled symptoms off from memory. "Contaminated food or water causes it; it's not spread by coughing. Nausea, vomiting, dehydration, cramps, pain. It's a form of food poisoning."

"So, what do we do?" I asked.

"I'll check them," he said. "You clean them up, get them clean sheets if you can find some, get them drinking. Check the water; make sure it's clean. That's about it. We'll give the worst cases some pain killers, some antacids if we can find them. Also wash your hands a lot. I don't have gloves so see if you can find me some."

I left the bedroom. Alfred was in the hall talking to the guy from the bus. The kid, Josh, was standing by, glaring.

What is it?" the guy asked.

"Dysentery, he thinks," I said. "We need that water. Also, clean sheets and some gloves. Two pairs."

"I'll get it, James," a man with a gun said.

"Anything else?" the leader, James, asked.

"We need to make sure the water is clean, I guess. Where do you get it from?"

"The town supply still works. The reservoir is still full."

"Are there any other sources?" I asked.

"River a half mile away. We could use that. You think it's the water?"

"Most likely," said Zeke coming up behind me. "Definitely dysentery."

Someone came back with two-gallon jugs of water. I opened one and sniffed. No smell, but I could see small particles floating in it. I pointed them out to Zeke.

"We'll need to boil it all before they can drink it," he said.

"All of it?" asked James. "You mean for the whole community?"

"Everything," said Zeke.

"Should do as he says," said Alfred. "Doc knows what he's talking about."

"Ok, we can try I guess," James agreed.

"Do more than try," said Alfred, before Zeke could answer. "If you don't this will spread. You'll lose half your people."

It was three months since the Fall when I arrived at what would be my home, at what would become New Seattle. And in the first few minutes, Alfred was making deals, becoming the leader. Becoming the Patron.

Chapter 22

Present

Jon pulled over the truck. "Check the counter," he said. "We're here. It's just over the rise."

The Geiger counter was picking up, clicking away in the background.

"That's not too bad at all," he said and put his foot on the gas, driving past a forlorn and faded sign welcoming us to Elko, Nevada.

Elko was still a town, a lot of concrete, most of the buildings still standing. They had broken windows and collapsed rooves but walls of brick and stone. I even recognized a building that could only have been a McDonalds. No sign was left or needed; the shape was the same in a thousand other places.

Jon pulled up at a gas station. The awning had fallen but there was a pump still standing. Rusted and dented but still there. It proclaimed that regular was $8.87 a gallon. I remembered the complaints in Seattle. Would the oil crisis end? Or would Iran keep going? I remembered how cheap that was; in Ireland it had been almost four euro a litre, more like seventeen dollars a gallon. Now it was free. A five-fingered discount.

I got out and started to take off the cover off the pump. It didn't take long; we'd brought all the tools we needed. Underneath, I found the pump and the motor that ran it. I levered off the belt and hooked up the tire iron to the pump. We then hooked the hose to a barrel and started turning the pump by hand. It was slow and it was hard work. Rust had set in; the pump hadn't seen a drop of oil since the Fall and hadn't been turned since the last time Jon was here.

Jon took over, and I checked the gas. It was dirty but not as bad as it could be. We'd need to clean it, but that was a job for another day.

I went to search the ruin. A can of WD-40 would be just the find to make this job so much easier. I found nothing, so I took my turn cranking again.

Maybe an hour later, we finished with the big drums. Two hundred and twenty gallons. I started on the smaller cans, filling everything we had. Another hundred and twenty gallons. We topped up the truck, and then took off our pump.

Jon looked at the Geiger counter. It was ticking quietly.

"We're still good," he said. "We have time to hit the school. I try a different place each time I come, see if there's anything useful. First aid kit would be nice. Propane tanks would be great. If nothing else, a few more bulbs that work."

We drove up to the road to a long grey building with all the windows broken. Some of the rooms had fire damage. We went in and found the science lab. Jon found a half full propane tank and filled a box with glassware, tubes and flasks that he wanted. I found nothing but two old relatively undamaged textbooks. I took those. Another brick in the wall for Claire's school.

"Anywhere else?" I asked as we piled it all into the back of the truck.

"There was a Wal-Mart nearby," said Jon. "Radiation is so low, we could try it. It's been pretty well emptied, though. I've been before, but with the air so clear today we could go again."

He looked to me for confirmation, and I nodded.

The place had been cleaned out and then some. The doors were smashed, and all the food emptied. A few things were left, toppled shelves and a deflated football, empty gun racks. We dug around the shelves in the pharmacy area, but it had been picked clean. I found a pile of clothes in the storeroom, protected from the worst under a fallen shelf. Jeans that nearly fit and two new t-shirts. A luxury.

I piled some more clothes into a cart to drag out. There wasn't much, no heavy coats like we'd need, but I did find a Radiohead t-shirt that would fit Addy. Time to replace the Clash.

Jon had found some books, useless to looters except for burning, and piled them into the truck, too.

"We should go," he said. "We've been here too long."

I nodded.

"It's going to be dark in a few hours and we want to be back before that," he said.

There was nothing else to do; we'd gotten all we came for and more. We drove off, slowly now, the truck straining under the extra load. Jon drove carefully, and when we were an hour out, the Geiger counter ticking dropped off.

We drove in silence for a while. Most of the way. Jon was steady at the wheel, concentrating on the road, getting us home safe. There was something about the way he did it, like this was his place in life.

"Are you content?" I blurted. "I mean, yesterday, you said you thought you were content, before all of this. But are you now?"

He thought about it before answering, "Yes, I think I am. You know before this I was happy. I loved my family, I had a decent job – not great but okay A nice house. Everything I wanted. I lost it all, but I got something I didn't have before. Purpose. Not that I wouldn't give it all up in an instant to go back. But now I have a place in life. You know?"

I nodded. "I guess I do. I've been lost since the Fall but then...well, since I decided to go home, there's something. A goal. A reason. Not just trying to survive."

He nodded.

My thoughts had crossed the ocean to Marley. I was ready to move on, to take as much gas as I could and find her.

Chapter 23

The rain was clearing up and the sun was setting behind us as we turned towards the last hill and into the orange glow. Jon was about to speak, but as we cleared the trees, we could see sparks, shooting high against a dark sky to the east. Clouds of smoke were lit by the orange sky.

Jon hit the gas, sending the truck sliding on the mud track, the wheels throwing up showers of dirt. "Slow down," I screamed at him as we started a slide off the road.

"The fire," he screamed back. "We have to get there!" But still he slowed, a little.

We drove on, and as we crested the last rise, we could see the town below in flames. Outside of the ring of fire, we saw unfamiliar vehicles. Trucks, bikes, people milling about. The Kings.

Jon slammed the brakes.

"We have to get out of here," I was screaming, but he was already reversing. The wheels found grip in a spray of dirt, and we went back.

"Did they see us?" I almost whispered, as if they might hear her over the roar of the engine.

We'd been silhouetted against the setting sun. We had no lights on, but we'd have been hard to miss.

Jon swung the truck around and went careening back down the track we'd taken. He kept glancing at the mirror while I turned in my seat, trying to catch anyone on our tail. A half mile on, he swung into the trees. We couldn't go that fast; the truck was overloaded; the barrels were wobbling in the back. We needed to hide. He switched off the engine and we waited. Barely daring to breathe.

Nothing happened.

"What was it?" I asked.

"The Kings," he said. "You see all those bikes, who else would it be? The town's on fire, they like to burn things. We have to go back. We have to help."

"We can't." I was shaking. We both knew what was going to happen there.

"I have to," he said. "You shouldn't. Go, run and hide. I'll go back."

I wanted to. I wanted nothing more than to run.

I couldn't though. There'd been a jeep down there that I thought I recognised. A battered, red Suzuki Vitara that I'd fixed a shock on a lifetime ago for the Patron.

Zeke. The Kings. I didn't know what was worse.

"Wait," I said. "I'm coming with you."

I couldn't leave them. Not after all they'd done for me. It was me that Zeke was after, and the people down there didn't deserve this. I didn't know how they could be there together, the Kings and Zeke. Were they fighting each other in the street? Or had the Kings taken Zeke's ride? I somehow knew they hadn't.

"We'll leave the truck. No way they will miss it. I don't know how they missed it the first time. Go back on foot."

Jon was rummaging in the back and came back with the tire iron. I still had my knife.

"Let's go," he said.

We wanted to stick to the trees, but we ran half in the open, trusting the quickly falling dark to hide us. There was still no one coming looking for us. We got to the top of the hill and threw ourselves to the ground. The town was on fire. There were two obvious groups. One group had guns and weapons, and the other group didn't. The group without the guns sat in a circle, surrounded and cowed.

I bit off a scream as I watched a huge man savagely backhand Claire, knocking her to the ground. Jon jerked as he stopped himself from jumping up.

"We have to do something," he hissed at me. "We can't just leave them. The Kings, you know what they do."

There was desperation in his whisper. What could we do? We were unarmed and there were just two of us. And I did know what the Kings did. The stories about them had us locking our doors at night.

"Some are missing," I said. "Maybe they got away; I don't see Addy for one."

Jon looked again and I could almost hear him counting.

"I make twenty-six," he told me. "With me and you here, there should still be another seven down there."

"We should look for them. There's strength in numbers," I said. "In all of your hiding places, are there any guns?"

"They're all down there," he answered.

Down the hill, they were still searching through the rubble. Then I saw someone I recognized.

Zeke walked into the circle of firelight, holding a small silver packer. The Keflex I'd given Claire earlier. I didn't need to hear him to know what he was shouting at them now. He was looking for me.

Erik was shaking his head. I guessed he was saying that I'd long gone. Or that they'd gotten them somewhere else. A tough behind him reversed a rifle and hit him with the butt end in the kidneys. He folded over and fell to his knees.

"Let's go," I told Jon.

I didn't want to watch. I couldn't watch. I needed to run.

"Where?" he asked, like he thought I had a plan.

"Your place," I said, inspiration striking. "We need a diversion, so anyone who's able to can run."

He nodded, suddenly understanding, and we crawled back and then ran for it. He led the way; this was his home field, and he knew his way in the dark. I followed, tripping and stumbling. We got to his shed, and he started pulling out what we needed. Empty bottles. He emptied a large bottle of what he told me was about eighty percent alcohol and we split it, half filling five smaller bottles.

Meanwhile I tore the sheet from his bed and shredded it with my knife.

"What now?" he asked. "We can't just throw these. Our people are there."

"We need to distract them, and we need to give everyone a chance to run," I said. "Their bikes are all over, and the bikes are their best option to follow anyone on foot. Target them. It should give us the distraction we need. I hope everyone knows where to run and hide. Maybe they can lose the Kings in the dark."

He nodded and we set out. We crept on but didn't get far. A group of two Kings in their leathers and two others, one of whom I recognized vaguely from New Seattle, were at Jon's overturned van workshop. They'd found my bike.

"That's Zeke's," Ron, I think that was his name, said.

His friend, a guy with a bad mullet cheered. "The bitch can't be far."

"Spread out and find her," Ron ordered, and to my surprise the Kings did just that.

Why were the Kings taking orders from Ron? I wondered. I couldn't believe they would work together.

"You keep an eye on them," he told mullet. "I'll take this back to Zeke."

"We need to stop them," I whispered. "Or get past them. I think the bike will distract them a little."

"Who's Zeke?" asked Jon.

I thought a moment. How could I explain this? That it was all my fault. That I'd brought this on them.

"He's the one I'm running from," I said. "No time now, I'll tell you everything later."

He looked at me for a moment, questions in his eyes, but nodded. We moved along the trees as they spread out to come for us. They had one old oil lamp between them for light.

"We can't get past them," said Jon. "We need to stop them. Stay here and when they get anywhere close, make some noise and run."

He turned without saying anything else and moved away. It didn't take them long. They approached the trees. Mullet was in the centre, maybe twenty yards to my left, and one of the Kings was dead ahead. Another twenty yards on, stumbling in the dark, was the other King. I let them get a little closer, and then I broke and ran right. A shout rang out, and I looked over my shoulder. As they turned to give chase, I saw Jon jump up behind the last guy and whack him with the tire iron. He collapsed and the others didn't notice as they gave chase.

I ran back to the trees and the two others followed. I tripped, over a root or something and fell, hitting my head hard enough to stun me for a moment. And then they were there. I tried to turn, to stand, to get my knife. Mullet reached me first, a grin on his face, the King on his heels.

"You're so fucked now," he told me.

"Grab her," he told the big guy behind him.

He moved towards me, and then there was a crash of glass as Jon threw the tire iron and smashed the lamp. Oil spilled everywhere; Mullet screamed as the oil splashed on him and went up in flames. In the chaos, I jumped forward from a crawl and rammed my knife into the knee of my other attacker, who fell with a scream.

Jon helped me up, then picked up the tire iron and pulled out my knife from the guy's knee.

"We have to run," he said, handing me the knife.

Mullet was still screaming as he rolled around on the ground, trying to fight the flames. The King was trying to stand. I kicked at him, and he lashed out, grabbing my foot. Jon smashed the tire iron on his arm, and he let go with a yelp.

We ran for it, scooping up our Molotov cocktails at the edge of the trees. We came up behind the ruin I'd slept in the first night and slowed, creeping around the side for a view of the road. Ron was holding my bike and Zeke was screaming at everyone huddled together.

"Where is she? If no one talks…" he yelled, pointing a gun at a woman on the ground. She was tied side by side with another man. Both were bleeding and bruised. They were both blonde and in their twenties I would guess. The man was big, even sitting on the ground, hunched and bleeding, I could see he was tall and muscled. He'd stand out. She was small beside his huge form, almost unremarkable. I didn't know either of them; I'd never seen them before anywhere.

"We got to do it now," whispered Jon, as he took out an old Zippo. "You go left," he told me. "Get those two bikes. I'll run right and get that truck. As soon as you drop them, run back. If you head up the hill, there's a large tree at the top. That's where a lookout would be. If anyone ran, there should be someone there. Otherwise just run and hide."

I nodded.

"Haley," he added, pulling all five bottles together to light them all at once. "Good luck."

They all lit and quickly. I was afraid of them blowing up in my hand and covering me in flames like Mullet. I ran for it.

There were two bikes on the road and one guy standing watch. He saw me but moved too slowly. The first bottle was already in the air and broke in front of him, a wall of flame as he shouted. The second went right by him and hit the side of a bike, covering it in flames.

He yelled and I ran, glancing behind me. Jon had hit the SUV square on, and I saw him throw another towards Zeke, but it missed. He was yelling at everyone to run and as he went to throw the last one, a single shot rang out. Jon looked down, surprise on his face, and then folded to the road. The bottle of grain alcohol fell on top of him, flames whooshing up, and there was screaming. I ran around a corner and out of sight.

I almost stopped, but I didn't. I ran like a coward into the night. Away from that last image of Jon falling, the flames swishing around him. All I could hear were the screams as I ducked under the low branch and around the overturned van and ran for the trees. I swung left, away from where I'd last seen Mullet rolling on the ground and powered up the hill. Behind me screams, shouting, and then the crack of bullets.

Chapter 24

I glanced back. Silhouetted by the flames I could see people running, Kings, the people who'd sheltered me, maybe Zeke. I didn't know who was a friend or who was danger. They ran in all directions and some I hoped would be safe. Behind me everything was on fire.

I dodged between trees and came to the top of the hill, a clearing, and right at the top a large tree. Bare now in the Autumn, I saw no one and nothing there.

"Over here," a voice called. Addy. "This way."

I ran on, down the hill and she was there, on her own.

"Where's everyone else?" I demanded, out of breath and bent over with a stitch in my side.

"They're all back there," she said. "Come on, we have to run."

She took my hand and led me off. I didn't have the breath to argue so we ran on into the dark while behind us the sounds of the chase faded. A motor started and came in our direction before it veered away. Addy led on and we came to a lake a mile, maybe two from the town.

"We need to stop a moment," I told her, trying to breathe.

"Not much further," she said, pulling me on.

"Where are we going?" I demanded.

"Not far," was the only answer, as we ran on into the night.

She led me around the lake, over a gravel shoreline which would leave no trail, and then to a boat. It wasn't much of a boat, just a very old rowboat with an old plastic milk jug with the bottom cut off to use as a bucket.

"In here," she told me.

I didn't think it would float, but I did as I was told, and she pushed it out and jumped in. There were oars, and we took one each. We were both panting as we pulled on the oars. I saw in the half-light where we were going. It wasn't a huge lake, but it was big enough to hold a small island with a few scrubby trees.

We weren't halfway across when Addy had to give me her oar to bail the water from the bottom of the boat. She'd just started when we saw the light of a truck on the hill. I stopped, almost dropping an oar as the headlights turned in our direction. We were sitting ducks, nowhere to go. I dropped down in the dirty water at the bottom of the boat with Addy. The boat was a dark colour, but we had only hope left.

We were peering out over the edge as the truck swung towards us, past us, and back again. Around me I could feel the water getting deeper, crawling up my legs as the boat slowly filled. I reached for the milk jug, carefully scooping water as if they might hear me, dropping it over the side behind me, away from the light.

The truck came closer, and Addy gasped. I could see a figure running in the headlights. They weaved and disappeared, and the truck turned, catching them again. A shot echoed across the lake, but we saw the headlights catch the runner again as they veered towards some trees.

"Quickly," I hissed at Addy.

I shoved the jug into her hands and as she bailed furiously, I grabbed the oars and hauled for all I was worth, all the while watching the hill, watching the scene play out. The figure in the headlights, jumping out of the beam, caught back in as the truck turned.

I could barely make it out, but I saw them stumble and a second or two later the sound of another shot reached us. As the shot echoed, the boat hit bottom and we scrambled out in knee deep water to pull it up behind cover. In the distance, I heard the engine of the truck stop, a door slam, and a laugh.

I turned my head away. I hadn't been able to make out who had been running. I didn't want to know. The truck turned away and drove off becoming a silhouette against the light from the burning town.

The island was small, maybe twenty yards long and thirty wide with a few trees in the middle and some scrubby reeds patching the shore. We pulled the boat between the trees, behind the little cover, hid behind it, and watched. The truck turned away, drove off, searching for more prey.

"We're kind of stuck here," I told Addy when the truck moved away from the body.

"No," she said. "It's the only boat on the lake. Unless they want to swim out to check, I think we're good. It's pretty hard to see us here. I hide here sometimes."

"Who do you hide from?" I asked.

"No one. I just like to hide."

I let that go as the truck turned and came closer. It drove on an old road that went halfway around the lake before turning south. I could make out two guys with guns, standing in the back looking out. I could hear them calling out to the driver but couldn't make out the words. They drove on. They wouldn't see us in the dark, not a chance.

A cloud covered the moon so we were hidden and safe for now. With that, the adrenalin surge dropped, and all I knew was how cold and how tired I was. I just wanted to curl up by a fire and sleep. Beside me, Addy had leaned against me, getting close for warmth.

I felt a drop on my hand. And another. Rain. In a moment it was really coming down.

"Quick," I pushed Addy up, "turn over the boat and get under it."

We flipped it quickly and crawled underneath. It didn't help; the rain just flowed along the ground. We had to move a little, adjust it on a slope and wedge it behind some bushes and at an angle on a log. Now the rain flowed by us, but we were already soaked and the ground was mud. We huddled together, under the leaky boat, cold and wet and tired.

We stayed like that until long after the rain had stopped, holding each other close, listening for more trucks. With the morning I woke, shivering and curled up with Addy who had burrowed half into my jacket. She was shaking too, shivering in her sleep. I shook her gently.

"Wake up," I told her. "We have to get warm."

She mumbled and tried to curl up more.

"No, Addy, we need to move." I shook her harder until she sat up.

The rain had stopped, but the sun was only a weak presence behind clouds to the east. I crawled out and stayed low to look around. We were well hidden here, now that I could see in daylight. The scrub looked sparse but there was enough to hide us. I guessed that from the shoreline the boat couldn't be seen. I crawled around so that I could stay low and see in all directions.

The shore looked empty in every direction. Could we risk it? Could we run? There were the ruins of a few houses visible. One almost stood, a solid looking stone cottage, missing some roof tiles. It could be warmer. We needed heat. But when would they give up?

"Are they still looking for us?" Addy asked.

"I don't know. I guess they are, but I can't see them. We need to get warm, and I don't think we can stay here. We can't have a fire; the smoke would be seen for miles."

It had cleared up, and the air was still and cold. In this weather, smoke would go straight up in the air, not a breath of wind. I crawled around again and searched the horizon. We couldn't have a fire, but they certainly would.

I could see a black pall back where the town had once stood. The town of Sanders was still burning. Further west there was a thin wisp of smoke and another, a few miles to the south. They had split up.

"Where can we hide and get warm?" I asked Addy.

She pointed back towards the town.

"Everywhere we hide is over there," she said. "There's shelter on the shore," she pointed at the stone house, "but that's it. There's nowhere in there to hide, just a shed out back you can wait out a storm in. No one comes here. I'm the only one."

"We should go now, while we can," I told her. "Help me with the boat."

We turned it back over and got it in the water. We got in and had just dipped in an oar in the lake when a shot broke the air. We stopped. Frozen.

"Back," I hissed, and we jumped out, Addy tripping and falling in the water as we dragged the boat back. I crawled through the scrub to look. I could see nothing, but I could hear an engine in the distance. When it came into view, I recognized it. The truck I'd fixed, the one we'd taken to fill with gas. They'd found it and all the gas that would take me away was gone.

Addy had crawled up beside me and was hugging close when she sneezed. She was soaked. So was I, my clothes still damp from the night and now after crawling on the wet ground.

"Let's get back," I said.

We turned the boat back over like it had been for the night, our only real shelter against the occasional rain. I made Addy strip and huddle in my jumper and coat, which were somewhat drier. I searched in the lee of trees and under bushes for anything dry to sit on. There was nothing. I laid out her clothes to dry, on damp ground; they wouldn't dry much.

We sat tight together, shivering, bent low under our boat roof. I heard the truck come closer, circle the lake, and then drive off. We waited and sometime later a bike went by, a Harley I guessed by the rumble.

The sun came out a little more and we moved out to sit in the little warmth. We sat together, our backs against a tree trunk, in a small patch of sun, and waited. Addy's sneezing got worse.

We heard another truck and were under the boat before it crossed the hill. Guys got out. We lay, hidden, peering through the scrub. They pushed a little through the reeds at the edge of the lake where someone might have hidden. Searched the house and the ruin. I could hear a loud laugh as someone made a joke, but I couldn't make out the words. Then they drove on.

"We'll wait until dark," I told her. "Then we make a run for it."

I had no idea where we would run to or how. We needed to go, though; Addy was getting sick. I could feel a cold coming on too. This was not a time for the flu.

When our coats had dried enough, we put them back on. The weak sun had us mostly dry. I got the boat ready, hidden as close to the shore as I could. We waited.

In the last of the daylight, I saw smoke, this time further south and more to the west. North was still a cloud of black smoke as the town smouldered. They were still looking.

I wanted to wait for it to be darker, but we needed to move. I had to get Addy dry and warm. Another night in the cold and we could be done for. Addy sneezed again. I had to get her shelter soon.

Chapter 25

We slipped the boat into the water and made for the shore, rowing as hard as we could.

"We should hide it," Addy said as I pushed the boat back into the lake.

"No, leave it. It will sink, or they'll find it. Either way they're looking for us. We don't have time to hide it properly. Come on, run a little, it will warm us up."

We couldn't run much, but we managed a fast walk south a little where I made an effort to leave a trail, walking through the mud and hoping our footprints would last. After a half mile when the ground got firmer, I pulled Addy to the east and then we circled back north.

"That's back home," she hissed and followed it up with a sneeze. "They're there."

"I hope they've already searched there," I said. "They'll probably see our trail and hopefully go off the wrong way. There's no way we can outrun them. We need to get warm. Is there a place we can hide up here?"

She nodded and led me on.

I recognized the place she led me to; it was the shed Jon had made his booze in. I thought it had been well hidden in the trees, but they'd found it. It had been bad when I'd last been here, what felt like an age, but was only two days. Now it was trashed. The booze was gone, the window broken, everything scattered. But it still had the bed, the dirty blankets, and the stench.

I found an old shirt of Jon's and got Addy into it and she huddled under the bed in a blanket while I threw her clothes around the room, spreading them out to dry a little and hoping they blended in with the rest of the mess. It was the best I could do. I then took off my coat and got under the blanket with her, dragging my coat up to cover our heads. We were children, hiding from the bogeyman under the bed. I hoped it was enough.

When I woke up, it was still dark. We were warm again. Addy was a furnace pressed against me. I put a hand on her forehead and thought she might have a fever. I wasn't sure. How did that actually work? If I was cold, wouldn't anyone feel hot?

I felt a little better after sleep and warmth, so I got up carefully, exchanged my coat for pulling a box over to that side of the bed, and left. I skirted the town. There was nothing left. Everything had been burned to ashes. I saw shapes that I couldn't look at spread on the ground, some burned, an arm, a leg, a face. Too many. Very few had made it out.

I forced myself to go on, to see if a basement was still accessible. Choking on my breath, trying not to gag, I found the doors had all been opened. Every place I thought to search had been found and destroyed. There was nothing left.

As I searched, I came across a body I recognized. Claire, face down, the back of her head gone, covering a body. A boy, a teenager, his empty eyes reflecting the stars. Beside her, reaching for them, a charred sleeve could have been Erik.

All my fault. Every last one. I brought their deaths with me.

I ran as fast as I could away from my sins, dry heaving all the way to the east, and groped around in the dark until I found where I'd buried the pills. I grabbed them all and ran back, just as the sky in east started to turn pink.

I shook Addy gently; she was groggy and definitely running a fever. I gave her an aspirin and helped her dress. I took the blanket, rolled it up, and we ran for it. In the distance, I could hear the rumble of an engine. Addy thought there was a place where we could hide, further east. Eric had set it up when they'd first moved to town. They'd planted small crops all over, and each of them had a shelter nearby to hide in, in case anyone came by as they worked, she told me.

We stayed off the road, in the trees where we could, crawling low through ditches and staying low, staying out of sight. I hoped they were all searching further out since they'd been here already. A truck went by the road, and we jumped into a ditch to hide even though we were a hundred yards away and behind trees. We lay in a few inches of muddy water until it passed. Later, a group of bikes went by, the loud Harley engines giving us warning, and we crawled under a bush, covering us in cuts and scrapes.

We crossed open farmland, running bent over or crawling, staying as far from the road as we could. A mile, two, and we heard a motor in the distance. We ran and ran, as far from the road as we could, praying that we were far enough away to not be noticed. The truck went by slowly and drove on.

Addy was coughing and not able to run well, but she led on. By the time we came to a small copse, she was hardly able to stand. I tried to get her to sit, to rest while we had cover from the trees, but she pulled me on, coughing and pointing.

"What is it?" I asked.

She just coughed and pointed as she tried to catch her breath.

A fallen tree. I helped her over, but she didn't sit. She reached down, pulled at a branch, dropped to her knees, and disappeared. An entrance I hadn't seen, even standing right beside it. I followed her in. They'd dug out a small shelter, almost a cave, under the tree. The tree itself was huge and half buried, so it wasn't going to move in a storm. They'd made a roof with an old tarp, a tent dug into a rise, under a tree and piled with dirt. An invisible hideout sheltered from a storm for anyone working out here.

It was perfect. Maybe five miles from the town and off the road.

Inside was larger than I expected when I followed Addy in. You could have five, maybe six people squeeze in there. Plus, it was dry and out of the weather. I had almost dared to hope we'd find someone there, a survivor, but it was empty.

Chapter 26

Addy collapsed in an empty corner. I covered her with the blanket and checked my pills. Her eyes lit up when she saw my whole stash. "Are they all real?" she was disbelieving.

I nodded and gave her two more aspirin and told her to rest. I looked through them; I had nothing I recognized for a cold. Nothing labelled decongestant or even more helpfully labelled, "Take two of these if you have a cold." A fortune in pills and all useless to me. Water, water, everywhere, and not a drop to drink.

Addy fell quickly asleep. Now I had hunger to deal with. We had a place to hide and we had pills, but we needed more. Water, food, the basics. I watched from the entrance for several hours, but nothing came by. In the end, I got under the blanket and slept.

I don't know what woke me. Some noise I couldn't remember, but I woke fully and quickly. One instant asleep and the next wide awake. I almost sprang up but forced myself to stillness and listened. Nothing. I crawled out slowly. Addy mumbled something, but I reached back to put a hand on her shoulder and whispered for her to quiet down.

Nothing was moving. The moon was out, and I could see around, so I crept towards the road. There was a house with broken windows, a missing door, and holes in the roof. Inside, I could see the light of a fire. Parked out front were a truck and a motorcycle.

A chill ran through me when I saw the bike. It was mine; I'd recognize that chipped blue paint anywhere. The dent in the tank from when Zeke dropped it drunk one night. This could be my chance. If we could get that bike and enough of a lead, we could be gone.

I crept in closer, circling around and coming up behind the house, carefully picking each spot before I moved, not daring to make a sound. I found a spot at the side of the house, deep in the shadows of two large trees, where I could see in a window.

"Where's the booze?" a voice asked.

A mutter in response.

"Well go get it," the first voice ordered. He came into view, and I recognized him. Back when I'd first fled, he was the guard on the gate at Brehem.

I heard someone getting up and saw them come out to the truck. This guy was one of the Kings, a heavy leather jacket and a red bandana around a wrist signalling this loyalty. He was short, near my height, and I was never tall. He opened the truck, found two bottles, and went back inside.

I recognised the bottles. Jon's Jack Daniels and one of his home distilled whiskeys, the one in the odd shaped wine bottle.

"You think they'll find her?" Shorty asked after they'd all drank some.

"Hope we find her," someone I couldn't see said. "Zeke's offering good drugs. A fortune."

"Nah, she's long gone," the guard from Brehem said. "Smart one, that. She wasn't back in that town, else they'd have given her up. She'd gone through, only left the bike 'cause she traded up. Zeke said she had a ton of pills to trade. She's long gone."

"Still, a reward would be nice," Shorty argued.

"Oh, shut up," was the response.

Shorty shut up.

I shifted my position, looking for a better view of the room. Shorty sat on a low stool, a cup in his hand. Beside him, on a sofa that was falling apart, sat another King. A big, heavy guy, muscled, long dank hair, and matted beard.

I moved around some more, and I almost missed the fourth guy. He was in the shadows, looking out at the trucks. It was only when he turned to Shorty that I saw him.

"And quit drinking. You've next watch," he said.

Shorty grumbled.

"Quit it. You stand your watch or I'll shoot you myself," Brehem said.

"Okay, okay," said Shorty, and put down his mug.

I watched him pull a hip flask from some pocket and carefully pour the contents of his mug in.

I wondered again why this was happening. Brehem was giving the orders; the Kings were doing what he told them. The Kings killed anyone and everyone. With three of them, the guard from Brehem should be dead. I knew why I was being chased; Zeke wouldn't give up soon. But why were the Kings working with, or working *for*, the Patron's men?

How much of the drugs did Zeke offer them? How long had he been working with them? Did the Patron know? I filed this knowledge away, leverage for the future.

I didn't think I was worth it. The pills were a huge fortune but was that enough? I wasn't sure.

The guy watching at the window moved away to get something, more food maybe, and I took advantage of the moment to slip away. If they were keeping watch, I was much too early.

I checked on Addy. She looked like she was sleeping a little better. I crawled in next to her, out of the cold and covered up to wait. *Just a few hours,* I thought. I'd give them time to get to sleep, then sneak in, disable the truck, take the bike, and roar off. I could double back later for Addy. I shook her awake briefly to tell her to stay where she was, that I'd be back. She mumbled and went back to sleep.

There were so many things that could go wrong with my plan, so few that could go right. I thought out each step and long past midnight, I slipped out again.

The moon was sinking in the sky as I made my way back to the house. The truck and the bike were still there, nothing had moved. I stayed for ten minutes watching from the trees across the road but couldn't see anyone on watch.

Carefully, I slipped across the road and followed my previous path around the back of the house. Peering in the window I saw three bundles on the floor, sleeping. I couldn't see the watcher until I moved around the side of the building and caught him. It was Shorty. He'd pulled his stool near the door and was sitting just inside, wrapped in a blanket. I watched to see if he moved.

After a minute he jerked, as if he'd nodded off and woken with a start. He looked around quickly and then straightened a little. Glancing first at his companions, he pulled the hip flask from a pocket and took a sip before resuming his watch. I waited, and again his head dropped a little. It was still a few hours till dawn; I had time.

Moving slowly, I got closer to the house and crawled, putting the truck between myself and the door. I rolled underneath, under the engine. I tried reaching up to find wires to pull, but couldn't reach any.

I could let air from the tyres, but it would make noise. Would Shorty notice the hissing? I rolled towards the bike and crawled from under the truck.

Nearby some animal screeched, and in the house, Shorty jerked awake and stood up. I saw him lift a shotgun from where it had leaned against a wall and point it outwards. I froze and watched him twisting and turning, pointing the gun. My breathing stopped until I saw the gun was still moving. He hadn't seen me. It passed over me twice as he searched for the noise.

I waited, for an age until he sat back down. This time he sat straighter. I didn't dare move. Lying absolutely, still the cold seeped in faster and I started to shiver. The slight rustle of gravel under me terrified me. Shorty was sitting up straight, his hand on the gun, waiting for another target.

I started to roll ever so slowly, afraid that gravel would crunch loudly or a twig would snap boisterously under me. I made it to the edge of the truck furthest from the door. The bike was right beside me. I'd never get it away, but I knew this bike like the back of my hand. I knew every inch of it. Carefully, I reached up under the fairing, found the right wire by touch and pulled.

Shorty noticed nothing. Peering between the wheels of the bike I saw him take another drink from his flask before I rolled further out and then inched on my hands and knees around the truck and to the side of the house before I stood to a crouch and ran. Behind me, no one gave chase.

Chapter 27

I got back to Addy and tried to rest for what was left of the night. When the dawn came I was back at the road, well hidden in the brush, watching. There was loud grumbling across the road, Brehem coming to the door to stand and piss loudly.

I waited for them to eat and pack up their things. Shorty got to the bike and tried to start it. Nothing happened. In the truck, the others had the motor running, ready to drive off and waiting.

"Go on, get in the truck, come back later," I willed them.

Instead, the big guy jumped out of the truck and started to help him. They kept at it for a good twenty minutes, checking wires and hoses and trying to start it.

Eventually they gave up, but my smile of victory disappeared as I saw they were leaving Shorty behind with the bike. My whole plan was ruined. He stayed with the bike, fiddling with the wires and trying to start it every now and again but got nowhere. They rest could be back any minute. I tried to sneak closer but without the cover of darkness there was too much open ground to cover. I'd be seen before I got within fifty yards and he might have been the smallest of them, but I knew I couldn't take him.

He also had his gun, an old double-barrelled shotgun; sawed short there was no way he would miss. It would stop anyone in their tracks. I gave up and crawled back to check on Addy.

She was still asleep, so I went to find some water and woke her to get her to drink some and take another aspirin. I wished I still had an antibiotic, and probably did in my bag, but I didn't recognize most of the brands. Most were just in blister packs and not boxes.

As soon as she fell back asleep, I left to go look for food. Addy had said that these hideouts were all over, beside the places they hid or worked. When they'd first came to Sanders they'd planted small lots, spread over miles and miles to stay hidden. Here they had planted food, though she said that they'd left it when it didn't grow much. Trying to stick close to the trees, I searched in the clearing. I found what could have been corn, picked clean by birds, and a tree that looked like it once held apples was also clean.

On one side I saw the remains of a straight line in the dirt. I hoped for vegetables, root vegetables that might not have rotted in the ground. Oh, what I wouldn't have given for a spud. I poked and dug with a stick before I found anything, and I came away with what I thought had been turnips, only half-rotted.

I snuck back to check on Shorty. He had given up on the bike and was sitting on the stool in the doorway. He looked bored. I wondered if I could distract him away, but he kept the gun close by and I didn't want to risk it.

Back in our hideout, I cut away the black and rotten parts of turnip with a knife and cut the rest into chunks as small as I could. I woke Addy again and we ate. They were tough to chew, hard and slightly bitter, but it was food and I felt better after it.

Exhausted, I took an aspirin as well and slept through the evening and into the night.

Once more, I woke in the dark. The moon was low in the west. I guessed the sun was little more than an hour away. I crawled out, waited, and listened. Nothing moved. I followed my path to the road and looked out. Shorty and the bike were gone. I had expected it but had held out hope. Another disappointment in a long line of them.

I sighed and went to wake Addy. She was a bit better than the day before.

"We should go while it's still dark," I told her. "We need to keep moving, get as far away from here as we can. Find food."

"What about everyone else?" she asked. "Jon, Erik, Claire...shouldn't we go look for them?"

I realised I never told her that Jon was dead.

"They all ran in different directions when we started the fires," I said. "They're probably all hiding out and running."

She looked at me. A hard stare from a kid that young.

"They're dead, aren't they?" she asked.

I didn't want to answer. Their deaths were my fault. She wouldn't stop staring, that cold, flat stare.

"I think so," I told her. "Maybe some of them made it, but most didn't."

I reached out a hand to her, but she pulled away and then sat up straighter.

"Where will we go, though? We have no truck, no bike? There's nowhere to go." She was all business now, moved on from all the death. The kid had seen too much. I wondered how she locked away that loss, and would it escape and come back to her? My losses were constantly with me, but Addy moved on immediately.

"We need to move anyway," I said. "We need food. The further out we go, the bigger an area for them to search. We'll find transport. I can fix things, remember?"

We moved out, staying as quiet as we could and keeping parallel to the road and far from it. With no other direction to go, we went east. In the end, it was the way I wanted to go anyway.

"Couldn't we go to Elko?" asked Addy. "I mean, if there's gas there. And if it's a town there's cars."

I'd already considered it. I'd run over every option in my head over and over. How long would we be exposed to the radiation in Elko? How bad would it be, and if we had no Geiger counter, how would we know? Walk in, at least a day, a night to rest, and another day to find, fix a car, get gas and get going. Even then, would the car hold radiation? We could we be sitting in it for days and never know as the gamma-ray saturated car microwaved us slowly, like boiling a frog.

"No," I told her. "Let's keep going."

"I'm hungry," Addy complained before we'd gone a mile.

I was hungry too, but I hoped she wouldn't whine the whole day. Then again, I guessed it was a good sign. If she was whining, then she was feeling better.

"Have you been this way before?" I asked her. "Is there any place up ahead we would find food?"

"Eric went this way, when we first got here," she told me. "Said there wasn't anything. The radiation picks up about twenty miles on. Where are we going?"

Back to endless questions, she was feeling better.

"We'll figure that out. For now, we just need to get as far away as possible."

"When will we get food?" she complained. "I'm so hungry."

"Shh. We'll find something. Just stay quiet and keep moving."

Surprisingly, she stopped talking and trudged along.

We stayed off the road, though it remained empty. Nothing moved. The terrain was tough, lots of brush, lots of dips and hollows and small hills. Addy was flagging. I kept looking, but there was nothing that looked like food. No animals moved in the trees, and the trees themselves were bare apart from an occasional scrubby pine.

We hit another road. It led south, and in the dirt and mud coating, there were fresh tracks. We stepped carefully, avoiding the mud patches, and crossed the road.

"Which way?" whispered Addy.

The road to the east had been empty all day; we could go that way.

"South," I decided. There was radiation further east. "Move back off the road."

"There's chemical spills to the south," Addy warned me.

"We'll try to avoid them," I said. "If all the plants are dead or weird then we turn around, okay? If one of us starts to glow, you tell me."

She didn't smile at my joke, just sighed and picked up her feet. We moved back into the brush and continued on. The area was flat, but there were hills in the distance and few trees. Lots of low scrub to hide behind, lots of gullies and washes to drop into. Lots of holes to trip in, thorns to scratch, slowing us at each step. We kept well out of sight and kept on. Still there was no sign of food. We did cross a stream and drank our fill. It looked clean, and it was fast flowing. And we didn't have many other choices.

Later in the day we heard a motor. A large truck from the sound. We hit the ground and crawled into a gully. It passed on, heading the same direction we were. Then a bike went by in the same direction. A Harley, not mine. Another truck, and then another.

They were all going the same way.

"Maybe we should turn back," I said.

Addy said nothing, just dropped down and sat on the ground. One look and I knew she was exhausted. I was, too. We'd been without food for too long, hiking in the cold and wet. We couldn't go on. I sat beside her.

"What now?" she asked. "We can't just keep walking."

"I don't know," I admitted. "We need to find food, shelter for the night. Then we need to get a truck or something and get as far away from here as possible."

I looked around. We'd come closer to a hill where some trees, bare for the winter, covered it. It looked like it would rain again. We were, I guessed, ten or so miles from the town. Automatically I calculated, a search area for our pursuers of three hundred and fourteen square miles. A huge amount, but then all that traffic had just passed us.

"Stay here," I told her. "I'll go look around."

Addy dropped to the ground, huddled in her coat, and I went looking for shelter. I found nothing. A fallen tree would block the wind but offered nothing to stop the rain that was on the way. Nothing to eat. No evergreens, nothing with leafy branches to build a rough shelter from. Nothing to cover us. Nothing. As I turned around to go back, a scream broke the silence.

Addy.

I ran.

Chapter 28

There were two of them, the big one and the little one from the night before. The giant was holding her off the ground in a massive bear hug. Addy was kicking and struggling, scratching and biting. Shorty reached over and slapped her, hard. I saw blood on her mouth.

"Where is she?" they were shouting at her.

I reached for my knife and ran. The guy holding Addy saw me coming and shouted something I didn't hear. My only goal to get to Addy. Full of anger, full of fear.

The huge man dropped Addy, backhanding her as she struggled to balance and knocking her feet right off the ground before she fell. Then they came for me. Shorty raised his gun, a squat two barrels pointed at me.

"Well look who it is," he sneered. "We thought we'd found a prize but then you come along, the jackpot. What are you two lovely ladies doing all the way out here in the middle of nowhere?"

He kept the gun pointed as I slid to a stop.

"Come on over, Haley," he called as I looked around. "You wouldn't want to leave your friend alone, not with Derek here. He likes them young. 'Younger the better,' he says, don't you Derek?"

Derek nodded and laughed.

"Better," he repeated, his eyes lighting up. "Tender meat."

"Come on girl," Shorty said, his smile showing two missing teeth. "Let's get you two ladies somewhere else. You can't be running around in the woods in this weather. You'll get damaged. Can't have damaged goods."

He stood there grinning and turned to point the gun at Addy who was slowly getting her feet.

"Come on, Haley, don't make me shoot the kid," he whined, like I was spoiling his fun when he was being all nice.

I walked over slowly, my knife hanging in its sheath by my side. I slid my hand towards it.

"Don't get any ideas, that little sticker's no match for a barrel of birdshot. Zeke didn't say you had to come back pretty, just alive. Don't need the kid back either; he didn't say nothin' about a kid. Let's just go nice and quiet and nobody gets hurt."

"Yet," added Derek. He laughed at his own joke, like it was the most hilarious thing in the universe.

I was still looking for a way to run. Addy was standing, shaking her head. She was wobbling, blood on her lip. I willed her to run. I'd distract them. The gun swung around again.

"Don't you go running off girl," Shorty snapped. "Derek, get the kid."

Derek spun and in two steps, he reached Addy and punched her again. No warning, nothing. He didn't grab her or jump to block her way, he just decked her. Addy's legs gave way, and she fell.

"Come on, Haley." Shorty was pointing the gun at me again. "Come on, and I won't leave the kid here with Derek."

Derek was laughing again, reaching down to Addy.

I gave up and went to them slowly. I wanted to shout, to threaten, to fight, to stab but I couldn't control my feet as they shuffled slowly forward, and my voice was a faint whine as I tried to bargain. There was no exit. The thoughts and plans that always raced through my head were replaced with a buzz of helpless white noise.

Derek left Addy alone and came over to me. I was focused on the gun when out of nowhere a fist flew; the world spun, and I fell. Rough hands grabbed at me. I tried to fight but something hard, the butt of the shotgun I think, hit my face.

I could taste the blood on my lips. I could feel the weight of Shorty on me. I wanted to scream, to bite, to tear but I couldn't. I could see Derek standing behind Shorty, laughing and blocking my vision. Their sneering faces filled my vision, the rest of the world fell back, and all that existed was them. The leers, the glee, like they'd won. I could hear the words, but they meant nothing.

"Don't have to come back in one piece."

"Have a little fun."

Hands were scrabbling at my jeans, the button grabbed at, the zipper yanked.

"Dyke'll like it. Maybe she'll learn somethin'. Bitch"

My coat was wide open, pushed up, my hands trapped in the sleeves.

"Last bit of fun she'll have in a while."

I heard the sound of my t-shirt ripping as it went over my face.

"Soften her up for Zeke."

I struggled for air as cold and rough hands yanked at my bra, groping and pinching my breasts.

"Wait your turn, Derek."

The t-shirt was tight over my head, caught in my coat, a gag on my mouth. I struggled, and something hit me, hard. My underwear ripped. I struggled for air and the shirt moved so I could breathe. With my head forced to the side, I couldn't look at what they were doing.

Addy was on the ground, just lying there, blood on her chin. Rain came down. Off, far off, between the bare branches, I saw a patch of sunlight.

I could feel him push at me, his dick groping blindly.

A patch of sunlight, a tiny scrap of sky. My mind blanked on everything except that patch of light.

Rough and in me. Pushing. Forcing a way.

The rain was still falling. In a daze, I saw Addy's eyes open. She blinked, her hand going to her mouth, touching the reddening bruise. I heard Shorty panting on top of me, Derek laughing. Then Shorty collapsed with a grunt and jerked himself out. Warmth ran down my thigh.

"Your turn."

More laughing.

I tried to struggle as Derek unzipped. It got me a kick to the side as I tried to twist away. I couldn't look. The patch of blue sky was gone, black clouds back again, and when I looked back at Addy, I saw nothing but absolute hate. A face of rage and disgust and loathing that terrified me. Addy's eyes were black ice as she wobbled. They didn't notice her.

Run, I willed her, struggling again, twisting away to hold their attention.

A boot connected with my head, but I twisted and caught it in my coat, and I pulled a hand free. Shorty half fell as he tripped, and Derek swung at me.

Addy ran.

Not away.

I could see a rock in her hand and in slow motion, she jumped on Shorty's back. She slammed the rock once, twice, before he threw her off. I saw blood on the side of his head. Addy tried to jump back up and he ran at her. Derek was distracted, half on top of me, half ready to get up. I reached for my knife, but it was still too far away. He was fumbling at my hair, trying to get a hold and I saw his knife. At his belt, around his knees, big and heavy. I fought and twisted and reached it.

He fell on me with a look of surprise. He tried to grab at the knife in his side, but I held on tight, ripping it out and cutting his hand before punching it back in. I shoved at him. He tried to hit me, but his strength was gone, and his hand was still tangled in my hair. I pulled out the knife and drove it home again. And again.

I pushed him off me and tried to stand, tripping on my jeans and yanking them up so I could move. Shorty was on Addy; he didn't see me at all as he pummelled her. She was fighting back. His blows meant nothing as she scratched and bit and punched and kicked and kneed and elbowed, hitting him with everything and anything. I tripped as I ran, still trying to get my jeans up. I knocked Shorty off her and then I swung with the knife.

I missed, and then he was on me in full fury, bleeding heavily and fighting for his life. I thought I was going to pass out but then he stopped.

Shorty fell beside me.

I looked up. The tiny patch of blue sky was back, just above Addy, circling her head. She was holding a rock, a dark stain on the white limestone. She dropped down and hit him again and again. I tried to get up, to stop her, but I was frozen. Afraid.

When I could stand again, Shorty was gone, his head a mess of pulped bone and brain. Derek was breathing heavily on the ground, the blood pumping from his side slowly. Layers of leather and layers of fat had protected him enough to last this long. I kicked him to roll him over.

"Where's your truck?" I demanded.

He just looked at me.

"Tell me or I'll cut your fucking dick off and feed it to you."

He smiled, coughed, a last laugh perhaps, and then he died.

I dropped. I just fell, sitting there on the cold wet ground. Addy dropped beside me.

"Thank you," I said, reaching out to hold her closer.

She flinched. She still had the rock in her hand, and I took it from her as gently as I could.

"Thank you," I said again.

Her eyes were blank. Dead. I tried to breathe deeply. I tried to think, but the blow by blow replay in my head attacked me over and over. *Shorty on me.* No, we needed to get away. *Inside me.* We had to get out of there, run. *Hands on me, pulling and tearing.* We needed to go. *The sudden and absolute violence.*

I stood up.

"We need to go," I told Addy. Or told myself.

I pulled her up.

"We need to go," I repeated.

I couldn't stop the thoughts; they attacked me from every side. *My clothes ripping.* I pushed her to walk. Then I stopped and turned back. *Choking on my t-shirt, trying to breathe.* I grabbed the gun and searched Derek's pockets with trembling hands. A set of keys. Shorty had nothing. His shirt would fit me, I noticed. I left it.

"Let's go," I said.

The rain had stopped, and the sky was clearing with late afternoon light. It would be dark soon. We hobbled back the way we'd came, and I could see another track of footprints in the mud; so they'd come another way. I followed it; we were right there. The road I thought we'd stayed well away from curved and passed just twenty feet from where I'd left Addy. She might have run when she heard the sound. They might have spotted her. I couldn't find the words to ask. I couldn't find any words.

Their truck was there, middle of the road. One door open. I pushed Addy in. She was still in shock. My mind was back racing but with no coherent thoughts, just a need to run and run and never stop. I got in on the other side. The keys fit the ignition; it started, and I drove.

Chapter 29

It was miles before I thought of a direction to run. Before I could think of anywhere but away. I kept south. Miles more before I noticed a bag on the small bench seat behind us. Inside I found a large bottle half full of water and food. Bread that looked like Claire had made it. I tore chunks off and gave some to Addy, and we ate.

She seemed to come around, a little maybe.

"Where to?" she asked.

That was the question. All the traffic we'd seen was going one way. If we went back, we'd run into anyone else coming from way. If we went forward, we'd run into wherever they all went. Back into rough hands. *Grabbing and pulling.*

I kicked my thoughts away.

"That way," I pointed forward, my course already set. "We take the first turn east at a crossroads."

We had three quarters of a tank of gas. I hoped we had passed the nuke to the east. We drove on.

***

We'd found the first crossroads a mile on and went east. I was shaking as I drove. Fear of being caught again, shame, disgust, and anger at myself and at the world were driving me. Denial. *My fault.*

"Just keep driving," I repeated over and over and over like it could block out the tune playing in my head. The screaming. The laughing. The grabbing. The absolute and complete helplessness. The crushing guilt.

Rain came and went. I hoped it hid any tracks. Addy sat, staring out the window, saying nothing. There was still blood splattered on her clothes. Her face was a mess of bruises and blood. I wanted to talk to her, but there was nothing to say.

It was slow driving. We went over patches of snow, trails of mud, hard tar roads covered in debris, blocked by burned out cars. *Hands tearing at me.* I pushed away the memory.

Just keep driving.

We turned south at another crossroads and then east again. We drove for hours, taking random turns, always south, always east. The odometer showed we'd gone over two hundred miles.

When the engine spluttered to a stop, it was full dark. I managed to pull it over, off the side of the road and down a gentle slope into a field. I hoped it was out of view. Addy woke up as we jolted over the verge.

"Where are we?" she asked, sitting up and looking around.

"Safe," I replied.

She sat back. That was all that mattered.

I reached back and found the bag of food. We ate more bread. I could have eaten it all, but we needed to ration. We drank more water, too. It was almost empty. I knew I should do something about it, try to refill it somehow in the rain, but I was tired, and everything hurt.

"We should get some sleep," I said.

I knew I couldn't. I couldn't stop thinking. Feeling. Trapping myself in a loop of memory.

I stretched out as much as I could. Addy lay down, falling against me. I stared out in the dark as the attack replayed in vivid detail, over and over and over. Every time I awoke it was with a gasp, not knowing where I was or what was chasing me, just a need to run as far and as fast as possible.

When I finally gave up on sleep, it wasn't because of the weak sunlight but the pains all over demanding attention. It was maybe noon, and all the adrenalin that had driven me this far had disappeared. I was wrecked, limbs heavy and sore, cuts and bruises all over. I was exhausted, but all hope of sleep was gone.

I looked down. Addy was asleep still, her head in my lap. Her face was swollen and dark. Two black eyes, cuts on her lip, a blue bruise covering fully half of her face. Only now did I realise that her nose was broken. It would need to be set. I thought briefly of doing it now, while she slept, rather than wake her first.

I didn't. Instead, I tried not to disturb her and to not hurt myself any further. It hurt to move my arm. I flexed my wrist and made a fist and opened it. Pain flashed up my arm, but I could move it. I tapped my fingers along my rib cage; bruised, but I didn't think there was a break. What did I know? I'm no doctor.

I checked my teeth with my tongue. Another gone, this one on the left. I'd lost a top and bottom on the right already. Toothpaste wasn't a thing anymore and whatever vitamin you needed against gingivitis was something I wasn't getting. I don't know, I never paid much attention in those classes.

I moved, and a stab of pain in my back told me I'd pulled something. In my pocket, I had a lot of pills, and I figured this called for some. I took them out and found some painkillers. I wanted to take two, hell

I wanted to take three. But I broke one in half and took that. Addy would need them more. We would need them to trade.

She shifted and woke up. I could see it all flash through her eyes in an instant. She didn't know where she was; there was fear, a hurried twitching of eye muscles as she looked for an escape, before realising what was going on and then she quit. She just gave up, and her eyes went blank.

I'd seen the blank stares before.

Chapter 30

The Fall

I was the only one from my class to get the trip to Seattle. Two months to intern at Amazon and see the some of the top robotics in the world. Six students from all over were there; Benny was from London and Mark, Amy, Lee and Seth were from different colleges in the US.

Once a week they organized field trips for us, away from work, just to see America. Tours of Seattle, to a National Park, and this last time we went whale watching out of Bellingham. I remember that day. Cold, bright, the choppy motion of the boat. Three hours trying not to throw up and seeing exactly zero whales. Everyone was so happy. It was an adventure.

I'd FaceTimed Marley that morning, but she'd been running out to a gallery. We only talked for a minute. She promised she'd be up early for me to call when I got back.

Everything was perfect. We'd stopped at a bar, celebrating our day off and our bright and shiny futures. It was a craft brewery that our whaling tour guide promised us had the best Scotch Ale in the northwest. Zeke was there, downing beers and entertaining everyone. His dad had been one of the first hires at Amazon and was now filthy rich. Private-plane, mega-yacht filthy rich. He'd dragged Zeke in to lead our tour, I think to dump this group of students on someone else so he could get back to work. Zeke was tall, extremely rich, and charming. Almost finished med school and soon to be a doctor. Life of the party.

I can still see it clearly, him standing by the bar, regaling his audience with some story, beer in hand, while behind him the TV switched from some sport to news. Heads turned, conversations stalled, and Zeke was starting to get pissed that everyone was ignoring the best part of his tale. There was a crash outside, and horns blared. No heads turned; everyone was staring at the TV.

The volume got turned up. There were cries of disbelief echoed by a wail of sirens in the distance. War. *Everyone* was at war. No one said what started it. Russia, Korea, France, China, all at war. Hawaii was gone. How could Hawaii be just gone?

The anchor had a look of panic cracking through the layers of foundation, contouring and powder. They showed clips of places totally destroyed. We heard screaming and running and crashes outside while the TV promised a statement from the president to come.

The feed disappeared; we saw static. The barman slapped the side of the tv and nothing. He found the remote and started hitting buttons. He found another channel.

"...can confirm a nuclear strike in Washington DC..."

Static.

"....New York....may God have..."

We didn't ever find out what God might have. All channels stopped, and we ran for it.

As the bombs flew over our heads, we ran. Zeke knew a cabin, his uncle's, up in the hills. Our driver was from Bellingham and knew the roads. Zeke handed him a fistful of cash and as the I5 jammed up, we were spinning up back lanes and away. We were frantically trying to tune the radio to see what was happening, to get any update. But every station was just an emergency broadcast on repeat.

"Attention. Attention. This is the Emergency Broadcast System. Take shelter immediately. Take shelter immediately. This is not a drill. Repeat, not a drill."

Then it stopped playing at all.

The driver wouldn't take us all the way, he had to get to his family; he kicked us all out a mile or so from Zeke's uncle's place before tearing off. The cabin, an old two-bedroom house, was perched on a mountain with views of the sea.

It was there we watched the world fall.

A huge curtain of smoke was building over the southwest. We didn't want to think about what had happened to Seattle. It nagged at my mind that it wasn't a mushroom cloud, but a black and oily cloud like a spreading thunderstorm. While we watched, there was a change in the air, like your ears were going to pop, and then the ocean dropped in front of us. It came back a huge tsunami, driving inland. We were a mile from the coast, up high on the mountain, but the power of it stunned us even there. The whole plain below us disappeared, almost in slow motion as a blanket of ocean was pulled over it. When it pulled back, just like a magic trick, everything was gone. The scale of the destruction was beyond comprehension. I couldn't grasp at the enormity of it; all those people gone in seconds. Entire cities I'd driven by just hours ago gone. Completely obliterated. My mind refused to accept it.

We tried everything to get the TV to work. When you have six electrical and mechanical engineers in a room, there's a lot you can try. Panic was hovering, waiting for us to fail, but here was a problem we were comfortable with. Zeke hit the whiskey he found in the kitchen, and we six hit the task like an end of semester assignment.

The satellite dish on the gable was still there, but obviously those channels were down. We found wire and foil, and soon we had a huge antenna. All we got was static. The terrestrial channels were gone.

Amy found a radio. A small AM/FM job, single speaker, bright pink plastic that ran on batteries. All she got there was static as she carefully spun the dial. But we were engineers. A screwdriver later, and the radio opened. A bit of wire in the right place and then it was attached to our TV antenna.

After a few minutes of fiddling with wires, we picked up a new emergency broadcast.

It didn't say much. Shelter in place. Your government is taking action. Curfew in effect. Looters will be shot. There will be an update later.

There wasn't.

When the broadcast was repeated the second time, panic moved in and took over. There was nothing more familiar to do, no more puzzles to solve. Just the sinking realization that the world was forever changed. What we knew was gone.

Seth was the first to go. He stood up and started pacing. Then he started talking, louder and louder, and then he was shouting. Refusing to accept it, refusing to believe it. Then he started throwing things and hitting the wall.

We tried to calm him down, but he ran outside. We let him go. This wasn't an engineering problem. Later we found him, just sitting in the dirt, staring at the smoke-filled sky, his face blank. He'd given up.

We looked to Zeke; he was the doctor. But he'd numbed himself with a half bottle of Maclellan and wasn't ready to help.

"Shock," he announced, slurring his words.

With no other remedy available I made Seth tea. It went cold in front of him. Later, he had to be half carried indoors as night fell. In the morning, Amy was gone. We didn't know where she went. We never saw her again.

The next day, we were still trying to tune in the radio We'd hear bits and pieces between the fuzz of static. Not the radio stations, but ordinary people with home equipment. Seattle was gone, completely destroyed. A direct hit, a mushroom cloud if you were close enough. The suburbs were still burning. The Canadian border was closed. Looters were being shot.

Seth was still sitting, staring blankly at the walls.

We saw the first looters that afternoon. Three rednecks with shotguns came and took our food. There wasn't much in the cabin, but they took whatever they found and drove off in their truck. We had no weapons to defend ourselves.

When the second group came – two men, one with a shotgun and the other with some kind of military rifle – there was little to steal. One of them hit Benny with the butt of his gun. Zeke jumped on him, but a shot rang out and then the men ran off.

The shot missed Zeke but took Seth in the leg. Zeke tried but there was nothing he could do. All the while Seth just lay there, his breathing getting shallower and shallower, his eyes blank, lost to the world as the pool of blood grew around him. And then his breathing stopped.

Chapter 31

"Hey Addy, you hungry?" I asked.

I helped her sit up and rummaged around for food. I handed her bread, but she didn't take it. Didn't move. I held water to her lips, but she didn't drink.

I tried to talk to her. I stroked her hand; told her everything would be okay We were safe now. She was staring off to another world. I hoped that other world hurt less than this one.

It took a while, but I managed to get an aspirin in her mouth and get her to drink by tilting her head back and pouring water in her mouth like giving a dog a pill. She coughed a little, and then she drank. She would drink if forced but nothing else.

I checked our stash. We had enough for one more meal. We had a bag of drugs, but I couldn't identify most of them. There were some painkillers, which was what I needed anyway. We needed more water. I was covered in cuts and bruises. So was Addy. I needed to clean them before they got infected. I made sure Addy was warm, and I left.

The truck was in a dip. I checked to be sure it wasn't going to be easily seen from the road. We had some small measure of safety. Some rainwater had pooled in the truck bed, but it was muddy and oily. I hiked up to the road to start to walk.

There was nothing moving. As far as I could see in any direction there was no movement. Not a breath of wind, no rain falling, just gently sloping hills. It didn't take me long, a mile, maybe more, and I found what I was looking for. A small bridge, nothing much, and a large concrete pipe under the road with a stream. The water flowed over gravel as it came down the slope. It looked clean enough. I hoped it was clean enough.

I tasted it. It seemed good.

I filled our bottle and then sat beside the trickle of water and washed my cuts. Every cut and bruise I could find, I cleaned, picking at the crusting scabs. Then I stripped off and sat in the cold trickle, scrubbing every inch of me. Some hard cuts re-opened, any skin not blue with the cold was red from scrubbing. Then I got back into clothes I wanted to burn and hiked back.

Addy hadn't moved. Her eyes were still open, seeing nothing.

I gave her a pain killer and then another and started to wash her face. She winced as I cleaned the blood from her nose, but otherwise didn't move.

"We need to set that," I told her. "It's going to hurt."

No response.

I turned her towards me and felt at her nose with my thumbs. No reaction. I could feel the break. I could feel where I would pop it back in. It was swollen and red, paired with two black eyes.

"On three," I said.

No response.

"One," I said, and pushed.

She screamed, briefly. A trickle of blood from a nostril. I cleaned her as best I could, going back for more water twice. In the afternoon I tried to get her to eat but had to settle for breaking off crumbs of bread and putting them in her mouth. She wouldn't chew but would drink if I tilted her head and poured. I hoped it was enough.

I left her again to go search out where we were. We were at least two hundred miles from Zeke and the Kings. *A one hundred and twenty five thousand, six hundred square mile search area* my brain's autopilot told me. I figured we were safe, but by now, he knew where I was going. There weren't many other directions. South or get snowed in. East away from the wreck of the west coast. East towards home. South away from the radioactive wasteland from Boston to DC to Chicago.

There was still nothing moving. I crossed over the bridge and kept going. A few miles further on there was a crossroads. A bigger, wider road, running north-south had some signs of use. It was quiet and empty now but there were ruts in the dirt.

There was nowhere to hide. There were no trees beside the road to hide in if we followed it. Just miles of gently sloping scrub and grass. We'd be out in the open. I walked on to the nearest rise and looked out.

I could see a car further along the road. It was on its roof, smashed up. It just sat there, upside down, the nearest thing to a sign of civilization for miles. The air was still, but in the distance, clouds were building. It would rain again. Maybe snow. It was cold enough.

I left the road and went to into the scrub. I thought we could stay beyond a rise. Find dips and hollows to hide in. I gave up quickly. What looked like grass and scrub was lots of prickly, stingy brush that caught and scratched. Avoiding them would take forever. Bulling through them got me cut to shit.

I went back to the stream to wash the fresh cuts and then went back to check on Addy.

She was still huddled on the seat, shivering slightly, staring out at nothing. She was cold. I wrapped her coat tighter around her and sat in close, sharing my coat like a blanket. I tried talking but there was no response. Slowly I fed her the rest of the bread, and then I slept.

I was woken by a car. A loud engine booming along the road above us. I scrambled out and up the rise, crawling to stay hidden, and saw it disappear off in the distance, going west. It was an old Beetle, faded orange paint and rust just bouncing along the road. I'd never seen it before. It was going the wrong direction; it was possible it wasn't after us.

I went back to check on Addy. She was awake but once more staring out.

"We have to go," I told her. "We can't just stay here."

She turned her head towards me, but her eyes were somewhere else.

Her face was still a mess. The swelling had gone down a little, but everywhere was black and yellow.

"We have to go," I repeated. "Can you do that? Can you walk with me?"

The slightest hint of a nod. Or maybe that was my imagination wanting it.

I searched the truck fully before we left it. We finished all the food, but I checked for anything else that I might have missed. There was nothing. I had the shotgun with two rounds, a knife for me and a knife for Addy.

We left and walked east. We filled our water, then we hit the cross-roads and turned south. It started to snow, big wet flakes falling gently.

"Come on, Addy," I urged her. "Let's go a little faster. It will warm us up."

She half jogged along behind me. We walked, we jogged, it snowed, we shivered.

Four hours later we stopped to rest. We'd not gone far. Eight, maybe ten miles. A track off the road led to a farm. We'd almost gone past it; it was well back off the road and hidden by trees.

We were shivering in the cold. The snow was starting to stay on the ground, and we needed to rest and get warm.

The old walls, concrete and brick, still stood. Even most of the windows weren't broken. The door still stood, locked, but a few good kicks opened it. We went in, gun ready.

Inside was dusty, but not dusty enough. I knew once we pushed in, out of the snow, that we'd made a mistake. Someone lived here. Addy was shrugging out of her coat.

"Sssh," I warned her. "Someone might be here."

She froze. We didn't move, straining to hear anyone else in the house. We'd made too much noise with the door; they could be waiting, armed and ready to pounce.

We listened, but nothing was moving. Maybe someone passing through, like us. Though the door had been locked, there could be another way in. Or a key.

"Stay here," I whispered, and I went down the hallway and into a kitchen, gun leading the way. Someone had been here. The counter was wiped clean, chairs sat around a table. They weren't here now, though. I checked the bathroom, the bedrooms. Used but not in a day or two I thought. Maybe someone passing through.

I went back to Addy. "Someone's been here, recently," I told her. "They might come back. Check for food, and then let's get out of here."

"I'm cold." It was the first thing she'd said in days.

I wanted to stop, too. We needed the rest.

"We'll stay a little, just a half hour. To get warm again," I told her. "Then we have to go."

We searched the kitchen. The cupboards were empty. I wondered who had been here. I wondered about the family that had lived here. Where had they gone? Why did they leave. Clothes still hung in the closets in the bedrooms, untouched for years. Musty and damp and falling apart.

I found gloves for Addy in a drawer that were still wearable. Too big, but warm.

I wiped dust off a photo frame on the floor. A young smiling couple on a beach. I found another, the same couple, later with a baby. Outside a church. In one of the bedrooms, the walls were a faded pink.

"We should go," I said.

Addy nodded. We went out the back. There was a shed. I had to check; there might be a car, a truck, anything. Even if it wouldn't start, a tank of gas was useful. I could run back for our truck with a gallon. Anything.

There were none.

Only bicycles, covered in years of dirt, wheels flat, and every bit of metal rusted. One had been a man's, a mountain bike. A smaller one, tiny and once pink. I could picture the people from the photos clearly on these rusted bikes. A girl, three or four, flying around the yard, the streamers on the handlebars whipping in the wind as she squealed in delight.

Another was bigger, also pink, not as bright. Two daughters. A man with two daughters had lived here. They were gone. No one had been in this shed in a long time.

"We should take the bikes," I said.

Addy said nothing. She wasn't talking again.

I checked the two bigger ones. The mountain bike had a pump attached to the frame. I pumped the wheels, and they held air. We left, taking another track that led from the shed out through the fields. It was still slow going. The snow was now lying in patches, and we slid and slipped.

"Just a little further," I urged. "We'll find somewhere to warm up."

It was getting to late afternoon. Behind us, our tracks led plainly back to the farm, but I hoped the falling snow would cover them.

We came to another road. A small backroad in the middle of nowhere. We passed other houses, fallen, burned. At dusk, we turned off the road to one that still stood. The door was knocked in, the windows were all broken, the roof caved in at one side. This one showed the years of dust and neglect. Safer.

"Take the bike inside," I told Addy as I tried to stand the door up a little to cover the yawning gap.

In the back, the kitchen was a mess. Overturned chairs and table. Looted a long time ago. I checked the back door. It opened easily; a good exit. The yard behind was ringed with trees but there was a place to run if we needed. The windows here were broken, too and the wind coming in was cutting.

I checked the bedrooms, but there was nothing there to use. In the end, we settled in a bathroom. It had the smallest window; one I could block up.

"I'm cold," said Addy.

There was a fireplace in one of the rooms, but with large broken windows it would be like being outside. She was right though; we needed heat.

"Stay here, try to get warm," I told her and went back to search the kitchen. In the mess I found some pots and pans. I broke a chair to pieces and dragged it all back to the bathroom. I put the pot in the tub and set a fire in it.

The smoke was terrible; the heat was wonderful. I moved the pot closer to the window. The growing wind just blew smoke back in.

I tried to remember Jimmy's fire, the exhaust pipe stove. He had explained it to me, the differences in air pressure, cold air in, warm air out. I went looking and found no pipe. No handy roll of tinfoil left lying around. Nothing I could fashion to a chimney.

In the end, I blocked most of the window and cracked open the door a smidge to get the draught going in the right direction, and we sat in a smoky room and warmed up. When we burned through what we had, I doused the flames and covered the window and door with bundles of rotten blankets from the bedroom. We buried ourselves in a heap of the cleanest ones we could find and slept.

I woke, stiff and sore. The fire had gone out, and it was cold. Very cold, I could see my breath in the little light there was. I stretched a little. My bruises were starting to heal. Beside me Addy slept on, a little whistle escaping her swollen nose. I pushed the pile of covers over her and stood up. The crack in our covers on the window told me it was morning out, and any smoke from a fire would be seen.

I stood, my back cracking as I straightened, and stretched a little and left the room as quietly as I could. Once I hit the kitchen, I saw it.

Everywhere was white. During the night, the snow had come back with a vengeance. I ran to the broken windows to see it piled six, seven, maybe eight inches deep and still coming down. Everywhere was covered. Our tracks were gone, but so was the lane we'd walked down. I ran outside. I knew which way we'd come but in the flat land, it was hard to see what was road and what wasn't.

Winter was here, and we were still too far north. My knees gave way, and I sank to the ground.

We were done for. No food. We could burn the house for heat now; in this snow no one would be by to see. I tried to think. To work the numbers.

"Think Haley," I tried to tell myself. "It's an engineering problem."

I thought I knew where we were, roughly. The Gulf where we were headed was at least six hundred miles, maybe eight. On bicycles, maybe fifty miles a day, twelve to sixteen days. At best. More like twenty or thirty.

Now with snow, we would be trudging; we'd be lucky to manage five miles in a day. With no food, we could last in the house a week before we gave up. Hunger strikers lasted over a month, but we were tired and beaten and already starving. If we left now, we'd be lucky to last the day. We were done for.

"You're an engineer," I told myself over and over.

The bikes were no good. Snow, skis, sled, huskies. All options I knew nothing about. I'd never been on skis in my life. If there was a husky around it was breakfast, not transport. A sled. I could make something, but for what use? To drag stuff with us? To slide down hills? We were past the mountains. There was no downslope we could slide for miles on. The ground was mainly flat, some dips and hollows. Nothing there.

Snowshoes. Looked something like tennis racquets. I had no idea where to begin.

Skis, something flat, poles to push us along. Could we do that? Faster than fighting through the building snow. There was nothing to make them from. There was metal around, a washing machine and tumble dryer sat rusting behind the kitchen, but no tools to take them apart and do anything.

I'd gotten so far and got so many people killed, and now it was over. I'd never see home again. Never see Marley. I'd die here, maybe to be found years later, our two sets of bones rotting in a ruin. Or maybe never.

I screamed into the white void. We were done for.

I trudged back inside. I didn't care anymore.

Addy came in, knife at the ready. "Are you ok?" she asked. "I heard a scream."

"Yeah, it's..." I let it go.

She nodded like she understood.

I built a fire in the fireplace and burned anything I could find. I gathered snow and melted it for water. And more snow. And more. Pots full of snow made half cups of water. I filled our bottles. We sat right up close to the fire, drinking warm water and wishing it were food.

I wanted to say something. I wanted something to say. I needed some answer.

"We'll need to go soon," I said. "It will just get colder."

She nodded.

"There's a barn. We'll check for food." I had little hope.

We checked, but it had mostly fallen in, and there was nothing. Some old machinery rusted to nothing, and a tractor with flat wheels and peeling paint.

Addy grabbed her bike as we left.

"Leave it," I told her. "It will slow us down."

We walked. The snow was deep, and we sank at every step. I went ahead, creating some small path for her to follow. I tried to follow the road which was, perhaps, a little clearer. Maybe the wind swept it a little, but with the wind picking up, there would be drifts.

I could feel the sweat building as we fought our way through them. Then I could feel the sweat freeze and my clothes hardening, crackling with each movement.

At noon we'd gone a mile. Maybe. We passed another ruin. We needed the rest, so we stopped, and while Addy sat and shivered, I searched. Nothing. I gave it twenty more minutes to rest but I knew that if I left it any longer I wouldn't get up.

"We have to keep going, Addy," I tried to rouse her.

She was shivering. Beginning hypothermia. She tried to stand but couldn't.

Heat, we needed heat. The cold was numbing my thoughts. Even with a fire we would die of hunger right here by this crumbling wall with the wind pushing through the broken window and the snow in piles beneath the holes in the roof. We couldn't last much longer, but I wasn't going to end here. Not without a fight.

"Come on, Addy," I begged her. "Just a little further. Another mile. We'll stop, have a fire. There could be food, just around the next bend, come on."

I pulled her to her feet and half carried her along. She stumbled slowly, but it was progress.

We trudged on, hoping we were going in the right direction. The wind was building but it had stopped snowing. All around us was a pristine white sheet, a hospital bed waiting for us to fall on it, with the wind a knife gone through us. Addy fell.

I turned to help her. I fell. I pushed her standing and then clambered up.

"Just a little further."

Everything was getting darker. Ice was building on my lashes, and I could no longer feel my face or my fingers. And then there, among the white...a light. A light shifting and swaying and blinding and flashing.

"Come on, Addy, a house." I pulled her, stumbling. There was a noise of wind, a rumble as we pushed towards the light.

"Come on, Addy." I pulled her. "Come on."

The light went out, blocked by a figure. Tall, towering above me. A huge head against the winter sun. I tried to reach past him. To reach the light, the house, safety. Warmth.

"You okay, Miss?" the dark shadow above me asked.

A hand reached down. I realized I was on my knees; I'd fallen and not known. The head came closer and became a face with a curly red beard and a wide-brimmed black hat. I noticed a heavy black coat over a flash of a white shirt.

"Come on, let's get you inside. You're freezing."

"Addy…" I tried to say.

"What's that? Come on Miss, let's get you in the car,"

"Addy," I managed. "Where is she? We got to find…."

"It's okay, I got her," another voice called, distant in the snow and the roaring of the cold.

The dark shape in front of me became an old VW Beetle. Confusion swamped me. Where was the house. I wanted to cry for the lost warmth and shelter. A door was opened, and I was half lifted, half pushed into the back seat. Addy was pushed in beside me. The door slammed.

The front doors opened, and two men got in. Addy screamed when she opened her eyes, reaching for her knife, fumbling. I could see nothing but terror in her eyes as a large hand swiped the knife away and grabbed at her coat. She tried to squirm away, to grab the knife back but her movements were slow and clumsy. I tried to help her, to fight, but there were hands all over me, too. Pulling at my clothes.

I was back in the woods. All I could see was Shorty and Derek leering at me and I fought as hard as I could, kicking and screaming. I wouldn't give in without a fight. I'd die before I let them hurt me again. Voices were shouting, some of them mine. And then they stopped. I grabbed at my coat to close it but a hand held me back. I fought against it, but my strength was gone. Someone said something about heat.

Addy was beside me, trying to hide behind me, her breath heaving, her body wild and trembling. I tried to help, to shield her, but my body was too heavy, my limbs trapped by exhaustion. I gave up and passed out.

The pain woke me. Not long afterward, I think. We were driving slowly along a snow-covered road, and I was in agony. A million shards of glass pierced me. I wanted to scream, but my breath was gone. A face was in front of me, peering at me.

I realized I was half naked. My coat was gone, my jeans, my boots. My gun. I was in my underwear and a t-shirt. It wasn't my t-shirt. I found my breath, and I screamed.

"You're okay, you're okay, you're okay." The old man in the front seat was holding my hands back from clawing his face off. "Calm down, you're going to be alright."

I wanted to fight. I screamed; it was all I could manage. My body was held tight by the pain and wouldn't move.

"You've got hypothermia," the man was saying. "We had to get you warm. Your clothes, they were all soaked."

I tried to hear him, tried to process what he was saying, but the heat in the car was injecting itself into my frozen limbs, a million tiny syringes prodding me at once. Shooting acid into my veins, burning from the inside out.

"You're okay, Miss. You're okay," he kept saying. "We got to get you warm. We got to get you warm."

Warm. The heat was killing me, the pain all consuming.

"Pull over, Daniel," he told the driver. "Get them the soup."

The car slowed carefully, and the driver got out. He went around the car and opened the back. He took some things from beside the engine and got back in, brushing snow from his feet. He handed me a steel water bottle as he slammed the door behind him.

I dropped it, the metal burning my hands.

The old man caught it before it hit the floor. "It's okay. It's just soup, you have to drink. You need to get warm. Just sip it."

Meanwhile Daniel was turned around, holding another bottle to Addy's lips. She was out of it. I reached for her. Her skin was ice. The thought pierced the fog in my brain. We needed to get warm. That one thought took over, and my ravaged body could only focus on that. That and the pain.

I groped for the soup. A hand helped and handed it to me. I drank slowly, the heat burning my mouth, searing my throat, stabs of agony as my fingers thawed. Then I passed out again.

I woke again later, with less pain, Addy sleeping beside me. She was still cold. An old sleeping bag was thrown over us. The car was hot. In the front seats, Daniel was driving in rolled up shirt sleeves, sweating like crazy. The old man was staring ahead at the road. They heard me move and he jerked around.

"Are you okay?" he asked, voice full of concern.

I nodded.

"You had us worried there for a while. You were lucky we found you two."

Again, Daniel pulled over and ran out to the engine. He came back with more soup. "You should eat." He smiled as he handed it to me. "Guess you're probably hungry."

"Slowly," the old man warned. "Take it slow, just sip."

It was delicious. I hadn't tasted it the first time while it was burning me. I wanted to wolf it down, to demand more, but I forced myself to slow.

The two watched me. I didn't care. I was starving.

"You and your friend look like you had a rough time," the old man said. "Not to worry, you'll be safe now. The Lord sent us to you in your hour of need and we will do His work. My name is Jacob, Jacob

Shetler. This here is Daniel. We're headed back to New Bethlehem and a place where you can warm up and get some healing."

My thoughts stopped. Something was trying to break through. I looked again and saw the clothes. The clean white shirts. The black jackets and vests. The broad brimmed hats. I knew what it was. The new religion. Safety, warmth, food. True. But we could be in more danger than ever before. I needed to warn Addy before she woke up and said the wrong thing.

Chapter 32

Nine months after the Fall.

Spring had been a long time coming. The snows had cleared late, sometime in May, I think. New Seattle had survived the vicious winter, refugees streaming in to replace the hundreds that died that first year, and we were starting to become a community.

I was working on a tractor with Jimmy. We needed to get crops in the ground fast; if we got another early winter, we would starve. Alfred was getting in the way with his suggestions, but even now, everyone was already calling him the Patron. The man who'd led us through the winter, brought a doctor, found the medicine.

He'd take charge of everything, whether he understood it or not.

We didn't mind him being there with his rifle, though. We'd had our first encounter with the new bandits, the Kings a week before. A gang on motorcycles, each with the red token that we would come to recognize, had attacked a group of families a few miles off. The survivors had made it to New Seattle where Alfred promised them safety.

We were out on a plain, just east of town, trying to get the ancient Zetor tractor started when we saw the preacher. He came walking in the road from where the attack had been, black suit, white shirt and broad brimmed hat. He leaned on a long walking stick.

We stopped to watch. Once, I would have waved. Jimmy was holding a hammer, and Alfred was moving to the rifle he'd left propped against a wheel. I grabbed a wrench.

Three on one. We still needed to be careful.

"Blessings," the preacher said as he came near. "May God bless your labours."

"Morning, Reverend," said Alfred.

"Preacher, please. I am no priest, just a wanderer with a message from the Lord," he said. "I passed a terrible scene back there and thought to come and offer comfort."

"Not that we wouldn't question a man of the Lord and all, but where are you coming from, where are you going, and are you armed?" Alfred demanded, his rifle held tight. "Just to be careful is all."

"I am un-armed." The preacher raised his hands to his side, his coat falling open. "A small knife such as is useful, and my staff will keep most animals at bay. I did have an encounter with a particularly troublesome badger last week, but never mind that, it's a story for another day. I come from the east, and I go where the Lord wills it. A messenger from God."

No one laughed at his small joke, but he didn't seem to mind.

"Well, we don't need a preacher here," said Alfred. "We need farmers, doctors, schoolteachers. Someone who can fix this tractor. We're men of the earth, not of any fancy God."

"In a previous life, I was a barista," he said with a smile. "But..."

He paused, a smile, working his crowd.

"My father was a farmer, and I grew up working a Zetor just like this one. The 7745, isn't it? It may be the Lord sent me here to help with more than spreading His word. Perhaps I could help with this in exchange for some food and a chance to talk to your people."

"Well, you say a prayer and see if it starts, and then we'll see."

He peered at the engine and the parts we had on the ground.

"Piston rings?" he asked Jimmy.

Jimmy nodded.

"Common enough on these, I don't suppose you have any spare parts?"

"Nope," Jimmy shook his head.

"Well let's open it up and take a look."

He rolled up his sleeves and set to it. Between himself and Jimmy they stripped the engine in an hour, then cleaned and rebuilt and sealed it back up.

"Start her up," Jimmy told me.

It started first try.

"It won't have all the power, there's no way it will have full compression," the preacher said. "But it should plough your field."

"Well let's go see if we can't get you a meal," said Jimmy, shaking his hand.

Alfred looked pissed but let it pass, and we all went back to New Seattle. Jimmy took the preacher to Dolly to feed him while I went back to continue working on a bike. Later in the evening, when everyone was done for the day, the preacher just set up in the middle of the road and started preaching. He got an audience.

"Technology," he told us. "Technology and the computers and the internet brought this down upon us. When we look back, we can see that it was mankind's obsession with these things that brought about our fall."

There were mutters.

"Now don't get me wrong my friends," he continued. "I am to blame as much as the next man. Before the Fall I spent more time tapping on my phone than talking to my friends. More time looking at porn on the internet than with a girl. I saw the world on YouTube, talked to friends on Facebook, and you know, I couldn't tell you if it was raining when I walked down a street without asking Siri."

There were a few laughs. He continued, more seriously.

"I was there, I was one of you."

"Then..." He paused. "It all ended. Now some say it was Korea attacked first. Some say Russia. Some say us. But their bombs which should have obliterated the planet, didn't. They failed, and yet they spread this gloom and sickness. They left us few upon the earth. Now this may be the Rapture, no one can say it is or it isn't, but for the few of us left it might as well be.

"The power plants and the chemical storage, they all were meant to be secure, but their technology failed and poisoned the earth. I saw this my friends. You saw it." He pointed at Dolly. "Did you see it sister?"She looked embarrassed at being singled out but nodded anyway.

"Of course you did. This good woman here, she was a slave to the technology too. But now she seeks the Lord in her own way. When I was hungry, she gave me food to eat. Just as the Lord commanded. And you, brother, what about you?"

A farmer nodded. Him, too.

"None of it works anymore," he continued. "The older cars, the simple ones, work just fine. But a new one with a computer? No. The phones, the computers, the iPods they're all gone, and I will tell you why, brothers and sisters. I will tell you why."

He waited while we all leaned forward, eager for this news.

"It is because the technology was cursed by God above. I was lost after the Fall. I was wailing and weeping when nothing worked, when our futures seemed to have been stolen by chaos and destruction. De-stroyed by nuclear holocaust, obliterated by tsunamis, hidden under a cloud of nuclear winter. But God came to me in a dream and told me to leave it all behind and spread his word.

"So, I did. I left my home in the ruins of Sacramento and went to seek the Lord. And I met others, wandering in the wilderness. They too had heard his voice. They all knew that the computers were to blame, and that we must leave that evil behind to live as God intended so once more this great country will be an Eden. A paradise on earth. God has promised us this my friends, my brothers, my sisters. Turn your face away from the ways of old, those that led to the fall from grace and the glory in God's wonderous work. We who have lived through his wrath can feel His divine love."

He paused to let his promise of a better future sink in.

"But be careful my friends. There are others who did not hear God's voice. There are others out there who rejected the call from above and listen to another voice. I have seen them, dressed in black and red; the colours of Satan, my friends. The Kings, they may call themselves, but I name them for what they are. Servants of Prince Lucifer. I have seen their work. You have, too. Not three miles from here, I passed their work.

"That led me here. If the ones who fled those evil men came here for refuge, I could see they fled towards God, towards a good and God-fearing community. His voice spoke and commanded me here to tend to his flock. To keep you in the ways of the Lord and to keep you safe. For if you follow the way our Savior has laid out, you too will be saved, and He shall keep you safe."

Everyone was gathered now, all listening intently. I had little time for religion. Growing up, I fell out of mass and rosaries, the wasted time in school on some mystic bullshit. But he spoke simply and clearly. In a world full of darkness and hurt, he offered light and hope.

Here I listened. I wanted to believe in the simple promise though my rational brain snorted dismissively.

As I looked around at all the faces, desperate for hope, I saw a flicker of emotion cross Alfred's face. Rage, I thought, but then it was gone, and he was listening like the rest as if en-raptured.

The preacher finished as the sun set and the cold came in.

Alfred walked up to him. "Thank you, Preacher," he said, looking around. "We have tried to be good people, and we will offer safety to all who flee these gangs. Our little technology is only what will benefit our community. The tractor you helped fix will help feed us this year. The electricity will light our town. I think having you here to minister to our people will help their souls."

He had to have the last word. Our town leader, our Patron.

A few days later, the preacher came to visit our little shop. We made tea, and he chatted about the tractor a short while before he turned to me.

"Haley, you're not married," he said.

I shrugged.

"In these times we must, as the Lord commands, 'Go forth and multiply.'"

"Well, I am quite good at math," I said, turning back to the part for the plough I had been trying to hammer back to shape. *Is he hitting on me?* is what I was thinking.

"There are many young men here. You are young, and time is slipping away. There are plenty of men for this work. Would you not be better suited in a home?"

"No," was my answer.

"The Lord commands us to His work, Haley. We cannot avoid it. To avoid our duties to God is a sin. There are many young men here, suitable for marriage."

"No interest in marriage, Preacher. And I'm sure as hell not ready for kids."

"But that is what brought the world low. We moved away from the family and replaced it with technology. When marriage was no longer a sacred bond between a man and a woman, when contraception took over and we moved to the internet in search of love, not to each other. Divorce, abortion, technology. That is what brought the Fall."

"I'm still not ready for marriage, Preacher," I told him. "And we were taught all that crap in school. Marriage wasn't one man and one woman. It was King Solomon with forty wives. Is that what you want here, forty wives?

"Oh no, you get me wrong," he said. "I have chosen a life of celibacy to do God's work."

"Well, so have I, and right now God wants me to get this plough straightened."

"Think about it, Haley," he said. "It's better to choose than to be driven. God has laid out a path for you to follow. It is, in a way, your destiny. Consider the young men in this community. Look to the future. We need children. We need mothers, not mechanics. Your militant feminism has no place in God's plan. And thank you for the tea."

He left me to stew.

"A little rude maybe, Haley," said Jimmy.

"Fuck him." I was still pissed. I'd heard this crap before.

"Oh yes, he's full of crap, that's true," said Jimmy. "But you need to be careful. Religion always has power. There's a lot of folks listening to him. Watch the Patron, see how he changed to welcome him? Alfred knows which way the wind is blowing. Sometimes the line between church and state can get a little blurred and if you piss him off you may end up in a lot of trouble."

"So I should get married and have lots of babies like a good girl? Is that it?"

"No," he sighed. "Just be careful. Lots of people are scared, and when people get scared, they ask questions and look for someone to blame. Religion offers some answers. Next, we'll get to blame someone else. At the moment, it's those bandits on the road, but if they go, then we'll blame the Jews, the blacks, the Chinese. Whoever's convenient. But there's also blame for anyone not following the rules and right now that could be a young woman who won't get married. Just hold out, don't be rude. Act like you're considering it. Let's wait and see what happens."

Zeke hit on me that evening. It started out nice, but he dropped hints. "The way things are going." "Safer with me." "Join up."

It never happened.

A week went by where the Preacher came by a few times, and I stayed polite. Barely. Everyone gathered to hear him the first Sunday. Afterwards, the Patron stood to thank him. Reminded him of the progress we were making.

"There was progress before the Fall, but it was all false progress," the preacher admonished him. "Do not seek after your technology in the false name of helping people. Seek the way of the Lord."

That night, a kid came running into town. His family had been attacked, five miles from us, where they were working on a farmhouse. A gang with red patches. The Kings. The Patron left with men with guns and asked the preacher to come along to bless the dead. The Patron came back, and so did the men with guns. A fierce fight they told us, but none of them had a scratch. The preacher, though, was gone.

As time went on, we saw more occasional preachers come through. After the first one, the Patron led the Sunday service though, and it emphasized hard work and responsibility to each other. Harsh pun-ishment for transgressors. He invoked God as he judged a guy who killed his wife. As he sentenced a captured King to death. As he had a woman whipped for stealing.

The other preachers that came through didn't last long. They'd leave in the middle of the night. But not before they'd mention sin. The sin of technology and the sin of unmarried young women not doing their part for God and country. One wanted to impregnate me before he left. Didn't even need a wedding.

"God's will," he'd told me, cornering me behind a truck. Jimmy coming in had saved me. "Until next time," he'd promised me, but then he'd disappeared that night.

Chapter 33

Present

N ow I was stuck here, with no escape. The snows had trapped us. We couldn't last a half day without these men. We needed their food, their shelter and warmth. But I didn't know if it was worth it.

"Are you okay, Miss?" Daniel was asking. "Miss?"

I'd been lost in my musings.

"Yes, I am. Sorry. Thank you for the food."

"What's your name child?" asked Jacob.

"Haley."

"You're Irish," he said. "You're a long way from home. And is this your sister?"

I looked at Addy. Once she opened her mouth, they'd know there was no way we could be sisters.

"A cousin," I lied.

"You've been through some rough times."

We were still all bumps and bruises. My clothes were crusted with blood.

"A gang of the Kings," I said. "They ambushed our group a few days ago. They killed everyone we were with; we were lucky to escape."

A kind of truth.

Jacob blessed himself and muttered a short prayer.

"Those evil men are everywhere," he said. "They grow like weeds, and good men need to stand against them. But we have confidence in the Patron. He has driven them from his lands, and unfortunately to ours, but he offers help to drive them to the furthest reaches of the earth."

The Patron. Rock, meet hard place.

"Isn't the Patron further north, near Seattle?" I asked, hoping that the terror and shock were hidden by the bruises and the blood.

"The Patron and his forces now bring security to most of the west coast. We have been to meet with him. Come spring, he will send men to help secure our communities all the way through to Texas. We will send men to bring God's word to his people."

It had always been his plan, to expand past New Seattle to most of Washington and beyond, but now Alfred looked certain to take over all of the US. A sigh left me, taking with it every ounce of hope, draining each and every one of my cells of any thought of a chance of escape.

"Don't cry, you're safe. The Kings won't get you with us. New Bethlehem is safe and secure, protected by the hand of God," said Jacob, perhaps seeing a tear.

Safe, that word again. Like we were safe before. Hidden. I was pissed off with people telling me I'd be safe.

"We should get going, Daniel," said Jacob turning back around. "We should get them back to Martha as soon as possible."

Daniel eased off, and the car broke through the snow. The snow had stopped falling for now, but it was deep enough that even with the chains, it was tough going. We had to stop often to dig out the car. They wouldn't let me help. I really wasn't able to anyway.

Addy woke up during one of these stops. Jacob and Daniel were out with shovels to dig a path. She looked around, fear in her eyes, and then she screamed. The two men came rushing back, but she had passed out again.

It got darker, and Daniel asked if they should stop.

Jacob was peering out into the falling snow. "We really should get them back, as soon as we can," he answered.

"It's getting worse though." Daniel had slowed the car right down as it pushed through the snow. "We're still some hours out at this speed."

"Maybe the old Johnson place?" Jacob suggested.

Daniel nodded.

The old Johnson place was a half collapsed and burned farmhouse with a fallen barn behind it. A newer concrete shed still stood though, a rusting steel door guarding it. They both got out to check it out, Daniel with a gun. When they were satisfied, he gave the gun to Jacob and pulled the door open.

We were well off the road and behind a hill on a narrow track. Inside what was left of the farmhouse was cleaner than I expected. Daniel and Jacob dragged sleeping bags and food from the car and set up in a room with a cast-iron pot-bellied stove ringed by three sofas and a supply of wood. They'd been here before.

"Let's get your friend into bed," said Jacob. Daniel lifted Addy easily and dropped her on an old sofa. He covered her in blankets gently and put the back of his hand to her forehead.

"She's warming up at least," he said.

Jacob brought our clothes in. "Still wet, but we'll hang them by the fire, and it'll be alright," he said.

Daniel started the fire, and I grabbed a blanket.

"Here, sit right up close, Haley," he told me. "You need to stay as warm as you can. As close to the stove as you can for the two of you."

"You sound like a doctor," I told him.

"I spent a year fishing in Alaska. Hypothermia is a big deal, and you learn about it quick. Just stay dry, warm, and get hot food and liquids. You'll be okay. We'll need to check your fingers and toes for frostbite, but I think you're okay. No booze though," he said, wagging a finger.

"Why don't you see if you can get us some of that hot food?" suggested Jacob, dropping heavily down on a sofa beside me with an exhausted sigh. Daniel went off and started on that while Jacob looked me over. It wasn't a leer; it was a trying to figure me out look.

"You've been here before," I said.

"Yes, we've stopped here from time to time," he said. "But for now, why don't you tell me what happened?"

"We were attacked, and we escaped," I said.

"Well, where are you from and where are you going?" he pressed.

"We were looking for Genesis," I told him. "Ten of us. We'd worked a while in Idaho and when the work ran out, we left."

"Genesis is a myth," he told me. "We see occasional people looking but there is no where it could be. I think God may have sent you our way for a reason."

"We had nowhere else," I told him. "We weren't welcome any-where. We heard Genesis was south. Louisiana." I'd decided on my story during the drive; I hoped I could tell Addy in time. It might be the only thing to save me. "My husband went looking, months ago. We were following. Did you see him? Sean?"

"Sean...I don't think so. Daniel?"

"Don't remember a Sean, though we have a few travellers pass through. What does he look like?"

"He's tall," I said. "Six two. Red hair and beard. He stands out, my overgrown leprechaun."

"Nope," said Daniel. "I never saw someone like that. When'd he come through?"

"He left three months ago. He got kicked off the farm we were working and went to look for Genesis."

It was a tired story. There were workers who travelled from farm to town to farm, slaving for food, shelter, a place in life. They were treated badly, but then so were the ones with a place in life. It wasn't an easy world. Some would be in New Seattle for a week or two at harvest before running south for the winter.

"And when you were attacked?" Jacob pressed on.

It didn't matter; I'd sown the seed. I was married, unavailable. I'd seen a flash of disappointment in Daniel's eyes.

"There were ten of us," I continued. "Crops were in, and we were kicked out. Sean had gone south, and he hadn't come back so we followed. We needed to get south of the snow anyway."

"You had transport?" asked Daniel quickly. "Where did you get the gas?"

"Bicycles," I said. "No need for gas. Slower, but we thought we'd get south in two or three weeks. Far enough from the snow anyway. Mary had a map; she said we could make New Orleans in a month. We were going to meet Sean there, you know, after he'd found Genesis, if he didn't come for us first. John had a gun, he could hunt for food. We had a crossbow which was better though, since we didn't have many bullets. We hoped we would be okay We made it this far, you know, four winters already. We could do it again."

I couldn't see if they believed me, but I kept going.

"Then a few days ago it all fell to sh…I mean, it all fell apart. A group on motorbikes came roaring up. We split and went off the road and were running and hiding but there wasn't any cover, and then they just started shooting. Me and Addy got lucky. The direction we ran in, there was a house, but we never made it there. Ran smack into a hole. I near broke a leg falling down. Wasn't deep enough for a well, not sure what it was, but we fell through whatever cover there was and the guys following didn't see it, so they just roared right by. We stayed there until it was dark. When we came out everyone was gone, so we buried our friends and left.

"We ran and we hid, and we hid, and we ran, and then the snow came, and we needed to get south and we were out of food...and then I guess you found us."

"The Lord sent us," said Jacob. "There's one thing you're leaving out though, Haley."

He reached in his pocket and took out a bag. I recognized it immediately. My heart fell. He was holding my best bargaining chip.

"We found these when we were taking off your wet clothes," he said, voice stern and staring directly into my eyes. "That's a lot of pills. A whole lot of pills."

"They're mine," I objected.

He moved them out of my reach.

"Where did you get all of these? These are worth a fortune, would have guaranteed you shelter for the winter in any town. Where did you steal them?"

"I didn't steal them," I said. "We found them."

"Everywhere in the country has been picked clean long ago. There's nowhere left where you could have found them."

"John found them," I said. "Two days before we were attacked. There was another attack. Two huge guys on motorcycles. Came at us around midnight. John shot one, and the other went off. We searched him, thought he might have something we could use. Bullets for our gun, anything. We found these."

Jacob stared at me.

I wished I could cry on demand. Now was the time to have a single tear roll down a cheek. I settled for scrunching up my face.

"That's why they came after us, isn't it?" I managed moist eyes, no tears. I was calculating, awake and aware and in huge danger. Could I grab the pills? No. Could I take them down? Unlikely. I was weak and hurting all over. Jacob maybe, he was old. Daniel, no. Plus, I had no weapons.

"They came looking for their drugs. We just wanted to get away, Ben was sick. We thought...."

I let it slide and hung my head.

I felt a hand on my shoulder.

"I understand," his voice was gentler now. "You tried to survive, as we all do. Don't worry, Haley, you're safe now. God will take care of you. He brought you and these pills to our community. Martha is a fine nurse and will know just how to use them."

Gentle voice my arse. He wasn't giving them back.

"They're mine. My friends died for them," I insisted.

"And the Lord brought you to us to save. No, Haley, we'll find you a space in our community and these drugs will keep us healthy. The Lord brought them to us. It is all part of His divine plan."

I was too weak to argue. I'd bide my time, but they were mine. I'd trade for the food and warmth now, but I was taking the rest.

Daniel brought food, and I ate. I noticed then that Addy was also awake, lying still, staring at us. Daniel brought her food, she jerked away. At a word from Jacob, he left the plate on the floor and backed away. She grabbed it and ate but said nothing.

I slept. I thought I wouldn't; I was sure that anger would keep me awake. Anger at the men in the forest. Anger at these guys taking my stash. Anger at myself. But I was exhausted. I had been frozen and hungry for too long. Now I was fed and warm, and so I drifted away.

Chapter 34

When I woke, I was stiff and sore. Not just stiff, but barely able to move my limbs. They were held down by a blanket that seemed to weigh tons. It took all my effort to swing my legs out and sit up on the sofa. Across from me, Addy was staring.

"Good morning," I said to her.

"Good morning," a voice behind me said. Daniel. He was sitting on a pile of blankets on the ground. "Hungry?" he asked.

I nodded and tried to stand. My knees gave way, and I almost fell.

"Just stay there," he told me, rising to his feet, and a minute later he gave me a hot tin cup, some kind of weak tea, and a slice of toast. He noticed Addy and brought some for her. She didn't move.

"You could be weak, from the cold," he told her. "I'll just help you..."

He reached down to lift her to a sitting position, but she came alive. A scream filled the room and Daniel stood up, three lines of blood welling on his cheek. Fear, anger, and surprise all flashed across his face at once. Jacob came in almost at a run.

I tried to stand, to get between them and Addy, but I only managed a few steps. Jacob beat me there and took Daniel's arm, leading him to a chair.

"Maybe you could help her," he said. "We mean no harm, Haley. Maybe you can tell her. She's young and been through so much."

I fell down beside Addy. She was sitting up, eyes wide, head twitching, and taking short, fast breaths.

"It's okay," I told her and reached for her hand.

She snatched it away.

"It's okay," I repeated. "You're okay now, they're not going to hurt you. You're safe."

She said nothing.

I handed her my toast.

"You should eat something," I told her. "Addy, you should eat. Addy? Addy?"

Her eyes were still darting around. Daniel stood up, and she shrieked.

"I won't hurt you," he said, coming closer.

She screamed, shrinking back on the bed.

Jacob put a hand on his arm and pulled him back. "Maybe get the car ready, Daniel, give her some space," he told him.

Jacob sat by the embers of the fire. Addy tracked him but did nothing.

"I guess you girls got in a lot of trouble with the Kings back there," he said. "I've seen it before. Shock, after an attack. We won't hurt you, you need to know that, but we do need to leave soon. Before the weather gets worse and we're snowed in for the winter. See if you can get her to eat something. Even some hot tea will help."

It was like he was my granny. Tea will fix everything. The universal cure.

I held a mug to her lips, and she sipped, still twitching and watching everything. But it did seem to help. Tea, even this crap, worked. She sipped slowly.

"These men are helping us," I told her, loud enough to be heard. "They found us in the snow. It's going to be alright." I leaned in to help her sit up and got close to her ear, whispering, "Say nothing."

She didn't react.

"Could you give us a minute?" I called over to Jacob.

"Of course, of course. Daniel, why don't we go check the weather?"

The two of them walked out, trying not to look behind them at whatever womanly things were about to happen. I grabbed Addy's clothes and gave them to her.

"Listen," I told her in a low whisper. "We're safe for now, I think. They're religious freaks; they won't hurt us. I've seen them before. Some people just went nuts for religion after the Fall. You've seen them?"

She said nothing, didn't move.

"We just need to be careful. If they talk to you go along with them. Pray with them, whatever, just agree with them. And whatever you do, don't let them know how old you are. Say you're nine or ten. No, say nine. Safer that. Say you were always tall for your age but make sure you say you're nine. Don't ever let them think you're older. Say nothing else, say as little as possible until I figure this out."

She said nothing, just sat there half up in the bed.

"Addy, we need to get going." I said loudly. "We need to go with them to safe place, and you have to get dressed."

Nothing.

I tried again. No response. In the end I helped her into her clothes. She didn't resist, but she didn't help. When I pulled her out of the bed, she stood. When I prodded her, she walked. But she didn't talk. I took her to the fire and gave her some bread. She started to eat.

The door opened, and Jacob and Daniel came back. She screamed. They scurried quickly out, and I held her until she stopped trembling.

"You need to eat, Addy," I told her.

She did.

"We're going to end up going with them, so you need to calm down. Remember, they won't hurt us." And in a whisper. "Just go along with them and their prayers and their god this and god that and remember you're only nine."

She said nothing.

"Do you understand, Addy? This is really important; we need to be careful. We're safe but we need to be careful. We need them. We can't make it in the snow."

She said nothing but turned her head. I wanted to scream at her. This was important. Our safety depended on it.

A slight nod. A question. I followed her eyes. The car outside the door.

"We can't take it," I told her. "They're out there; we wouldn't get past them. It's not a fast car. Daniel has a gun with him. Even if we could, they'd die here in the cold with no way out. We can't do that."

The door opened, and Jacob sidled in. Addy watched him but said nothing.

"Is everything ok?" he asked.

"Yeah," I told him. "She's just very frightened. She's very young."

He nodded. "You will be safe with us young lady, Addy. God sent us to protect you and keep you safe. That's exactly what we'll do. My name is Jacob, and my young friend here is Daniel."

Daniel had snuck in behind him. His face had stopped bleeding, but there were still three red lines where her nails had dug in.

"We're going to have to go soon. It's going to snow some more I think and it's best we get moving. So, we're going to load up the car. In the meantime, I think there's a bit more bread and a cup of tea. You two have had a rough time and some food will help. So, you just eat up and we'll get you snug and warm in the car and get going, OK?"

He smiled, a big friendly, grandfather smile. Addy stared.

"Just go along," I tried to send a telepathic message.

She nodded.

We ate, they packed up the car, and we got in. They piled extra blankets on us and we left.

It took hours. We couldn't go fast in the snow. Even with chains, a Beetle is no car for those conditions. We rode in silence a while, and then Jacob started praying. I tried to join in where I knew the words. We sat in silence again. Daniel got out and topped up the gas from a can.

"How do you have that place back there?" I asked. "Where we were, last night, you knew it. It's very far from your home."

Jacob half turned in his seat.

"We used to live there, some of us. Well, not far off. I grew up not five miles from there and that was old Johnson's place we stayed in. After the Fall, we had to move, and we ended up in New Bethlehem, but when we knew we needed a safe spot on the road, we knew it was there. Hidden from the road, solid and secure."

"Why did you move?" I asked.

"God called me," he said. "We were beset by bandits. Gangs roved through. There was an army base nearby and when the military fell, they formed a well-armed gang. By then the various gangs united as the Kings and they fought. God led me out to New Bethlehem where we could be safe. Five families to start and more have joined."

"How big is New Bethlehem?" I asked. If I was going to escape I needed to know as much as possible. I hoped he took my questions as eagerness.

"Near fourteen hundred people call it home," he said, a proud smile on his face. "More join every week and when spring comes, we will join up with the community at Jerusalem and be over two thousand. With the agreements we signed with the Patron, we will have peace in the region. Scrub the countryside of these bandits, these so-called Kings, for good. So, you see, you are quite safe."

I said nothing. The Kings had been working with Zeke. Searching for me with him. I didn't know how, but I shuddered at the memory. The Patron had united us to fight them off, and Zeke had got them to work for him. How much did he want to find me? Were the drugs I'd taken worth that much?

Jacob mistook my movement for fear.

"Not to worry. Even now, none of the gangs dare attack us. God protects us."

"That and the ten-foot fence," added Daniel.

Jacob silenced him with a look. "Yes, the fence. Our little town is very secure, and you will both be safe there. In the beginning we had some troubles with wild animals. The zoo in Denver spent years unsuccessfully trying to breed two tigers. Now that they've escaped, they've taken to the hills and bred like rabbits. Another sign of where we all went wrong in the Before Times, when we tried to control nature. Now a fence keeps them out and good men with good guns keep the bandits at bay."

I said nothing, and we drove on.

Snow continued to fall, and the car rumbled on, stopping, sliding, and being dug out every now and again. Each time we stopped, I checked all around. Wide open plains of snow, only the occasional tree to break it. Nowhere to run to. My mind was screaming for escape, to get far away as quickly as I could. My body could barely move.

We slipped and we slid on, and then we saw it, rising from the white as we crested a hill. Below us on a wide plateau, there lay the remains of a town. Everything was burned, buildings collapsed, all of it covered in snow.

"There was a prison break, just after the Fall," Jacob explained. "All those criminals broke out and burned down half the town the first night. Everyone was running for their lives. There was no one to save them. A few months later there was a fight with Kings and the rest of the town burned down."

Daniel drove on through the rubble, and I saw our destination.

"Welcome to New Bethlehem," said Daniel. "Formerly Arkansas Valley Correctional."

The fence still stood. A line of solid concrete buildings had lights on. A tall double row fence led us to a gate by a watchtower.

"When everyone in there was in such a rush to get out," said Jacob, "we went in. It was the safest place."

I saw more as we drove closer. Newer buildings, low and squat, built of wood and rough-cut stone. A second fenced off area joining the original. This newer fence was a mix of wire and stone, sheets of galvanized steel, and heavy wooden posts.

"We had to expand." Jacob was watching me as I stared. "More and more people. We've tripled the area fenced in. Expanded the buildings to almost twice the size."

We drove in closer, and I could see glasshouses built from odd shaped windows cobbled together in a brick and stone structure. Shutters all over for the storms. Small wind turbines dotted the roofs, and a dozen cars, trucks, and SUVs were parked inside the fence.

"Why did you take a Beetle in the snow if you have those?" I asked, nodding my head in their direction.

"They were all needed elsewhere," said Jacob, as Daniel slowed to a stop. "The building works. They can't stop. We're growing too quickly."

The gate wheeled open, and we drove in. I saw a man with a gun up in the tower. Another pulling open the gate, and a third was watching. God may have protected them, but they seemed to not trust in faith completely. The gate closed behind us with a clang, bringing a flash of claustrophobia. We were trapped in this too small place.

An older woman came out of the glasshouse, a covered basket in the crook of her arm. She wore a severe black dress, a white apron and a thick black woollen hat. She stood staring, hands on her hips. We came to a stop beside her as the gate closed behind us. Other people were watching, warily staring at us as we got out.

"Jacob. About time you got here, and you brought us guests. They look half starved. Come on ladies, let the men worry about their business. You come with me and we'll get you something to eat."

The woman, it turned out, was Jacob's wife. Once a nurse in Los Angeles, then in the Nebraska, and now here. She told us her story as we ate eggs and toast and drank some of the strange spice tea they had. The story of so many. A normal life, a normal job, and then it all ended and she was left struggling like everyone. Except she found a God, and found him quickly at that. Some needed the hope. The thought that there was a grand plan, that it would all work out. They weren't screwed, they were saved. I nodded and hoped I agreed at the right parts.

They asked, and I stuck to my story. Addy said nothing. She sat and ate, head swivelling all the time, eyes darting around. I tried not to look around as much, but I catalogued the exits – two doors, the windows had bars – and the weapons – dinner knives, forks, hot tea. My chances? Zero.

"There'll be work for you in the kitchens," Martha told us. "We'll find a place for you, after all you've been through. Don't worry, you're safe here."

"I'm a mechanic," I said. "I can fix things, cars, electricity. Before all of this, I was an engineer."

The things I could fix were my means of escape.

"Oh, hush now," she told me. "Leave that kind of thing to the men. You stay here with us. It's warmer in the kitchen. Better food, too."

Safe. Everyone told us we were safe. But they were meeting with the Patron, so we were anything but safe. I needed to escape. I needed to bring Addy with me. We needed to recover first.

Jacob came in later and showed Martha the pills.

"They're mine," I said.

"God sent them to us; we will do what is right with them. You shouldn't concern yourself with these anymore. Martha, can you put these in our dispensary?"

She took them and left the room.

"You can't just take them," I objected.

"You live here, you live by our rules. Here we live by God's rules, and it would behove you to learn your place. A woman's place is in the home. Stay here and rest. We'll find you a good husband."

He said it almost kindly, like he was being nice, helpful.

"I am married," I stuck to my story.

"If your husband didn't come through here, he's dead," Jacob said flatly. "There are wild beasts on the road, the east is destroyed, bandits to the west. Anyone going south needs to go through here. So, if you had a husband, he is dead. Why not tell us the truth?"

"I am telling the truth."

"If you were one of the wandering groups looking for work and went south last winter, you would have come through here. There is no other way. The radiation in every other direction would have killed you. So no, you came from New Seattle is my guess. Running from something. Not the first, and you won't be the last. Don't worry, we'll get you settled here and safe. When the Patron comes in the spring, you'll already be one of us. Quit with the lies, Haley, if that's even your name. You don't need them here. You're a part of God's grand plan, and we will shelter you in His grace."

I was seething. Yes, I was afraid, I was in as much danger here as anywhere else, but more, I was angry. Furious at the dismissal. I was no one to these people but a kitchen worker to knock up and produce more Christian heirs. Those were my damn pills, and I'd made it this far. I was an engineer not a cook, damn it.

I tried not to let my anger show. Deferential—that's what I needed to be. Quiet. Submissive. Ready to run.

Martha came back in.

"Why don't you find these girls a room, Martha, and see if you can find them some work? Get them to prayers tonight."

"I'll get you some clothes," she told me as we walked. "You can wash yours tomorrow. We'll get you work in the kitchen; it's warmer work for you and a little extra food here and there will do you a world of good. You look like famine victims, the pair of you."

She chattered on. In another time and place, she would have been a wonder, the motherly figure to take care of everyone. Now, everything she said and did was all tinged with the religion. The complete abdication of sense, giving up her mind in exchange for rules in a book written to keep the poor down.

Chapter 35

Six months before the Fall

"It's all bullshit," Marley told me on our third date.

We'd ended up back at her place once again. Third date, second date, and the first one. Turned out I was that kind of girl.

She was standing by the fireplace, an ancient, big, cold stone thing. A small two bar electric heater, powered off, sat there in place of a fire. It was cold, but she couldn't afford to use it. One arm was leaning on the mantle for support, another swinging a bottle of wine. With one clean glass, she'd filled it for me and took the bottle instead of trying to wash another. We were both pretty drunk.

"Bullshit. All a bunch of child fuckers trying to keep us down. Did you know that they cut all the good women from the Bible? Emperor fucking Constantine picked the bits he wanted and junked the rest is how we ended up with this crap. Slaves obey your master. Give to Caesar what belongs to Caesar. Women know your place. Solomon had forty wives; did you know that?"

The wine bottle was starting to swing, to punctuate her sentences.

"Forty wives, and what was he? The wisest. Mary Magdalene wrote her own gospels, but they didn't make the cut? Instead, what was she, a slut?"

I nodded and agreed. We'd been in the Big Tree out in Drumcondra. It was a big deal. A group from class went, and I'd introduced my girlfriend. I remember Tommy Mac from Ballyfermot looking at me strange. Mostly, everyone was nice, but most didn't know I was gay. Hell, I still wasn't sure.

We'd left the bar and some old biddy saw us holding hands and screamed that we'd burn in hell. "God will strike ye down yis Jezebels yis," she was screaming. "Sin, sinners. Sin!"

Marley screamed back at her. Tommy Mac ended up getting between them, all red and embarrassed. "She's only an auld wan," he said. "Leave her be, she's only full 'a shite."

Marley had complained the whole way back. I'd been a bit frightened. It had all gone so well so far. Telling friends I had a girlfriend, my first openly gay moment. And then this.

"Fuck them," I said.

It sounded right. Not that I cared. Not that much. I was going to make it in this world. Nothing would hold me back. I was so sure.

Chapter 36

Present

*F*uck *them,* I thought as Martha listed off all the eligible young men.

"Of course, Jacob will find you a good one," she assured me. "A good, solid Christian man."

The room we were led to could have once been an office. It was small and packed with a set of bunk beds. It was also clean and warm and for that I was grateful. Addy sank to a bed.

"Thank you," I said.

"You should rest up," Martha told me. "Prayers are at five, dinner at six. I'll come and get you then."

She closed the door behind her. I waited a minute and tested the handle; it was unlocked. I stuck my head outside carefully. The corridor was empty.

"Are you ok?" I asked Addy in a whisper, kneeling beside her.

She said nothing, but there was a slight nod of her head.

"We need to be very careful. If they're dealing with the Patron, we have to get out of here, but we could be in a lot of trouble if they decide to stop us. They'll want to keep us in our place, but we'll find a way. For now, make sure you tell them you're nine, that's really important. It's way too young for them to marry you off. I hope. You understand?"

A slight nod.

"Just be careful and play along. We'll be okay. Get some food, get warm. I'll find what we need and get us out of here."

She said something. It was barely a whisper and I couldn't make it out the first time.

"Don't leave me," she repeated.

"I won't," I promised. I took her hand. "You saved us back there Addy, you saved me. I won't ever leave you behind. I promise. Just be careful, and I'll get us out of here."

She said nothing. Just sat and stared.

"Get some sleep, Addy," I told her. "We need everything we have for later. Rest while you can."

After spending most of the day in a car sleeping, I was still exhausted. I dragged my ass into the top bunk, covered up with a heavy blanket, and was dead to the world in moments.

***

Seconds later it seemed there was a knock on the door, though out through the shuttered windows, it was almost dark. A girl, maybe fifteen, came in carrying a basket.

"There's prayers in fifteen minutes," she told me, staring at us. "I'm to bring you."

"Thank you," I said, pushing myself out of the bed, groggy with sleep. "Addy, wake up, it's time to go."

The girl just stood there. Staring open mouthed at us.

"What's your name?" I asked her.

"Chloe," she said.

"Just give us a few minutes Chloe, we'll be right out."

She just stood there.

"We'll be right out," I said again.

"I'm supposed to give you clothes," she said, but still didn't move.

"Is that what's in the basket?" I asked. "Did Martha send you with clothes?"

Chloe nodded.

I took the basket from her. The clothes in there were clean, plain dresses. I shrugged. They would have to do.

"Is there a place to wash up?" I asked.

"There's a bathroom in the hall," she said.

"Can you show us?" I asked.

Chloe nodded and we followed her out. When Addy stood up, I realized how much we did need the clean clothes. She looked like she'd been dragged through a ditch, her t-shirt still bloody. I felt a pang as I realized that I'd never given her the Radiohead shirt. Sanders burned to the ground before I got the chance.

"You have to hurry," Chloe called. "Can't miss prayers. No time for showers."

The bathroom was a large thing with old stainless-steel sinks and rows of toilets. Chloe followed us in.

I guessed she had orders and wasn't going to leave us alone, so I stripped quickly and washed what I could in cold water before putting on the dress. It was heavy and uncomfortable, but warm and clean and I immediately felt better in it. A part of me wanted to scream at the clothes, conforming to their ways in just this small way, but the feeling of being warm and clean won out.

When I looked Addy, she had already changed. There was still a spot of blood on her ear. I went to clean it, but she shied away from my touch. I pointed it out and left her to it.

Chloe led us downstairs, to a large hall. It probably once been a gym. Now there were rows of chairs and a small dais. Martha came bustling over to lead us to chairs at the front. I would much rather have hidden in the back, away from all the stares, the pity for our bruises, the curiosity for the strangers, or the chance someone would recognize me.

"We'll need to introduce you," she leaned in close and whispered.

Jacob took to the stage. He started with an Our Father. At least I knew the words. I had to poke Addy in the shoulder.

"Just move your lips," I hissed at her.

She started to and then stopped. She went back to staring, eyes darting all around.

He went on to more prayers, but not the old Catholic versions, so I got lost and went with my own advice, just moving my lips while trying to keep my head down. Beside me, Addy had completely given up and was staring around again, eyes scanning nervously from person to person, looking for danger.

"Now you all know we've been working with the Patron these last months, and I bring good news," he said. "We have agreed to a coalition with the Patron, an agreement to have him send men here to help us with the bandits on the road. We in turn will send men to help minister to his people. We will also open trade between our towns. The highway between here and New Seattle, every mile of it, will be reopened, a safe corridor of communities living under God, free from bandits."

A cheer went up. I shuddered. The Patron wanted power; this was just a move.

"Our community here is growing. New Seattle is growing. We will build communities all along that road. Safe, Christian communities, working together to rebuild. We will make this country great again."

Loud clapping and calls of glee erupted.

"Together we will bring back America. Not the place of Sodom and Gomorrah it was before the Fall, but before that, when it was a good, Christian country founded on freedom and a love of God. With the Patron, we will be safe. We will be free."

Jacob held his hands up to stop the cheering. He looked so happy, so proud of what he was doing. I'd seen this before; they'd give up their guns for safety, and then they'd give up everything else.

"And more, my friends. We have two more joining us. God led us to Haley and Addy on the road and brought them to our community. They were beset by those same bandits we will drive out, but God has saved them for us to give shelter. Come, my daughters, come and be welcomed."

He beckoned us up on stage. I didn't want to move, but knew we had to. Addy didn't move.

"Play along," I hissed in her ear and pushed her firmly.

The people stared at us, eyes still full of suspicion. Our bruises were fading, but we were both still a mess.

"Let us make them welcome," Jacob called, and there was a response of half-hearted clapping and a few calls of, "Welcome."

We took our seats, and he made some other announcements.

"Now for less pleasant business... bring out the prisoner."

A door at the side opened, and two men half dragged a third out. The prisoner had his hands tied and an old-fashioned iron shackle chained his ankles. His face was bloody and bruised. Fresh bruises, I noticed, newer than my own.

"This man came to our town seeking shelter but brought with him the seeds of our destruction. He brought sin and wickedness, the products of Lucifer, to our town of God."

Jacob held up a tangle of wires, broken small circuit board and plastic.

"What have you to say for yourself?" he demanded.

"It's just a phone, just some photos," the prisoner mumbled. He had an accent, French maybe. He looked lost, confused. "It doesn't even work. It's the last photos I have of my family…"

"This is not 'just a phone' or anything like that," Jacob cut him off. "This is the technology that brought about the Fall. This is the work of Satan, and you brought it to our town. This is the greed and the sloth that brought us down. This is the idleness and the straying from God that left us here."

"It's just a phone," the prisoner said again. He was looking around like he wasn't sure what was happening. "Please… the pictures."

"You were found guilty by the Council. You don't even repent now. The Council has sentenced you to two years of labour where you may learn of God's grace and come to follow his path. May God wash away your sins."

The two men dragged away the prisoner, who still looked dazed and lost.

Jacob said a short prayer, one for the man's soul. He offered hope that the prisoner would learn and come to God, and in doing so, repent and join their community. Beside me, Addy was shaking. I put an arm around her.

"It will be okay," I whispered. "It will all be okay."

"Come and help in the kitchen Haley," Martha told me as people stood to leave. "We need to get dinner out." We followed her out of the hall.

The kitchen was large and industrial. There were electric lights and ovens, so the community obviously generated a lot of power. I wondered where it came from. I hadn't seen much, only three small wind turbines. But large refrigerators and freezers lined a wall, and the ovens were hot. They got power from somewhere.

Martha prodded my shoulder, and I shook my head to clear my thoughts. The place was buzzing, full of women bustling about with pots and trays and stacks of plates, circling each other and moving in a complicated dance between the stainless-steel tables and the hot grills. Shouts and calls, orders and queries, it was busy, and I didn't know where to start.

The smell was amazing. Hot food, fresh food. Lots of it. I wanted to attack it, but we did as Martha told us, carrying pots and plates. The narrow corridor from the kitchen to the hall we had been in was full, lines of ants bringing food from the kitchen. I noticed steel frames at each end where I guessed prison bars and gates had stood. In a side corridor there was a prison door still in place but left open.

The chairs in the hall had already been moved and folding tables were set up. We set up on a long row of trestle tables at the wall and went back for more. Heaps of food, the smell driving us crazy, until at last, it was all there. Jacob said grace loudly, and everyone helped themselves.

The food was plentiful. Meat, vegetables, bread. People were all being nice to us. Polite. Curious. Just a tinge of suspicion. We ate at a corner table with Chloe and her husband. He was older, an overweight aging hipster with grey hair and a long beard, sitting close. She said little, and he held the conversation, asking us about where we came from, where we were going. I stuck to our story, a few words in between mouthfuls. It had been a long time, and my stomach protested the amount, but I ate like I wasn't sure of my next meal.

Addy said nothing, ignoring every question asked of her. I explained it as shock, and they politely accepted it. Her face full of bruises backed up my excuse. We had barely finished eating when

Chloe led us out. Time to clean up. We spent an hour washing and drying and cleaning, my arms getting red and itchy from the caustic soap they used. Eventually, Martha sent us to bed.

"You two look done in," she said kindly. "We have an early start tomorrow. I'll have Chloe come for you."

We found our way back to our room and sank to our bunks.

"Addy, are you ok?" I asked.

No answer.

"I know it's not easy, but we need to fit in here. We're going to be safe; we're going to get out of here. But I need you; I need your help. I need you to play along with them. Play their game. Fit in, or pretend to as much as you can. Stay safe and learn everything you can."

No answer.

"We're going to be okay We're going to figure it out, together, and get out." I was trying to assure myself as much as Addy.

I recalled the callous treatment of the prisoner, the obvious beatings, for nothing, a broken iPod. Chloe was young, maybe fourteen, but her husband was fifty if he was a day. I drifted off to a worried sleep where dreams led me back to the woods and I woke often, a scream on my lips. In my nightmares, Addy wasn't there to save me.

Our place, we were told firmly the next morning, was in the kitchen. I welcomed the chance at food, but chafed at the lack of access to cars, to gas, to a way out. My drugs were gone. Over a thousand miles across the continent still to go and nothing to trade. A clock was ticking down with the Patron coming in the spring. Outside, the snow was deepening. We had till spring and that wasn't very long. Plan, I needed to plan.

The first morning, as we cleaned up after breakfast, Martha spotted Addy's knife.

"You don't need that here. Women don't carry knives like that," Martha told her firmly, but Addy held on and ran, scrambling around a table.

"Give me the knife, Addy," Martha said firmly.

Addy didn't.

"Give me the knife, or I'll switch you till you can't sit for a month."

Addy ran, ducked under another woman coming towards her, and darted for the door. I ran after her. She was in the corridor, eyes darting about, looking for an exit.

"Addy," I said. "It's going to be alright. It's going to be okay. Give me the knife."

Her eyes stopped darting around, fixed firmly on me. "No," she said.

"We have to fit in here, we have to try, and you can't be armed. Let's go put the knife in our room."

She held her stare a moment longer and gave in. When we went back to the kitchen, I saw Martha's words were no idle threat. She held a switch and motioned Addy over.

"We don't carry knives here, and we do as our elders say," she said, tapping the switch off her hand.

"She's just a child," I protested. "She's scared, she needed it on the road."

"She needs to learn," Martha snarled. "Spare the rod and spoil the child. Chloe, hold her down."

I jumped between them.

"Don't you touch her," I warned Chloe.

I didn't see it coming but I felt the switch flying, stopped mostly by the heavy dress. I wheeled around and grabbed it as it as she swung again.

I went to punch Martha, but a strong arm grabbed my hand, and I was backhanded to the ground. I saw Addy leap at the man who hit me, and the kitchen broke out in a commotion. I stood up as he threw her off and jumped at him, the women all around us watching, horrified.

"Stop," someone yelled in a tone used to being obeyed.

Daniel walked in.

"What's going on?"

"The girl needs a switching," Martha told him. "She needs to learn to respect her elders. And this one."

She swung to me.

"Proverbs, 20:30, 'Blows and wounds scrub away evil, and beatings purge the inmost being.' They need to learn the ways of the Lord."

"Come with me," Daniel ordered and walked out.

Surrounded by stares, we had no choice but to follow him. I tried to see the exits. To escape.

In the hallway, he leaned in close. "Haley, I know you've been through a lot. Addy, too. But there are rules here, you need to learn to obey. I'll talk to Martha, but you need to be careful."

He gave me a conspiratorial wink. One that said we would talk about it later.

Jacob walked over. "What's going on?" he demanded. "Martha said you struck Anthony."

"They attacked us," I said.

"Martha told the child to hand over her knife. Elders are obeyed in New Bethlehem."

Addy just stared.

"She's just a child, she was frightened. She's been through a lot."

Jacobs gaze softened, slightly. "It's all new to you here. The Lord is forgiving, as are we. Apologize to Martha and Anthony, and I will speak to them. However, next time you disobey, you'll be whipped. Am I understood?"

I nodded. Addy did nothing. I prodded her. She nodded.

"Then let's clear this up."

I apologized, and Addy mumbled. I had no doubt they would keep their word. More and more, we were to learn our place.

That night as we washed up for prayers, I saw Addy's knife. It was in her boot.

Chapter 37

Weeks went by, and we sank into routine. Addy started to talk again. A word here and there but a start. She seemed to feel safe in the kitchen, but if we left, she shut down, looking everywhere. Jumping at every sound.

Work was hard. We were up at five to start breakfast for everyone and spent hours cleaning the kitchen, peeling vegetables, roasting meat. There was lots of food. Here, there were fields all around the town. Chloe told us they were patrolled in the summer, armed men all over. Hunters brought in meat. Cattle were raised, an outbuilding was full of chickens. The glasshouses produced food most of the year. New Bethlehem also traded with smaller communities as far as two hundred miles away. The community was prosperous, the people healthy, the place safe. But I was terrified.

Chloe opened up to us slowly. To Addy more than me. Both of them were quiet and Chloe was naturally shy, but as we worked together all day every day, she came around. When they worked together, they'd exchange a few words and then more and more. Not like normal kids, but more than before.

We got to leave the kitchen after the first week, working with the chickens instead. Once we were trusted to obey, we got to go around the compound, collecting, delivering. All hard work.

We healed. We ate, better than I had in four years, and had a warmer bed to sleep in than either of us had in a long time. Bruises faded, cuts scabbed over and disappeared. A few would leave scars. We kept our heads down and worked hard, acted submissive while we planned our escape. Snow was piling on the ground all around, and to run without a plan would be death.

The compound was large. It took me some weeks to map it all out. The original prison had been six square buildings, connected in a group of four and a group of two, forming a compound around a green area where they joined with a huge L shaped building. Each night I added to my map, using stolen pen and paper that I hid a broken power socket in the wall. Six large square buildings housed row on row of cells. Locks were no longer used; they housed families now, row upon row of bedrooms. We were in what had been the administrative building, which had also housed the canteen and the gym, the kitchens, and the offices.

There were a lot of smaller buildings, all used. A maintenance building and garage, where they fixed the cars and any machinery. I tried to talk to them but was ushered out. No place for a girl. Newly built accommodations stood where there had once been a basketball court. Rough cut stone and bits and pieces salvaged from the nearby town. There were gardens everywhere. In between the buildings, sheltered from the worst of the storms, and in the glass houses, in tiered boxes along the walls.

Around it all was the original prison fence, double rows of chain link, high and strong, topped with razor wire. At the back there was another large area, newly fenced in. More of the stone, more razor wire. Shipping containers provided walls and buildings in one. On top, more fence. I didn't see anywhere the fence was lower than twelve feet.

Outside the fence, there were fields and smaller fences but still topped with razor wire. The only way to get to those fields was through the main gate. Work was going on to add another area to the south; posts were in the ground for another tall fence, and one side of it was already up. New Bethlehem was expanding rapidly.

Jacob didn't question our story again, but he did work on finding me a husband. Daniel came by more often than was needed. He took pains to walk with me, tell me of New Bethlehem, explain their rules to save me again.

I overheard conversation about a wedding in the spring. I wasn't once asked.

I learned better than to argue and to always be deferential to the men. Bruises were not uncommon. Chloe came to the kitchen one morning with a black eye. She muttered some excuse, but everyone knew. Know your place. Stay quiet. Martha made free use of the switch on children in the compound and on a few of the teenage girls. Addy behaved and avoided it.

All the while, we planned.

Chapter 38

It took most of a month before I saw the prisoner again. Every day, four old cooler boxes were filled with food and taken out to the prisoners. One day, I was ordered to take it, and Daniel drove me. It was over a mile away, and the snow was everywhere. A well-worn path was dug in the snow, and we drove along slowly in his Beetle to a quarry where the prisoners worked. In a shed, we set up the food.

They were all ragged and thin, not dressed for the cold. It was meagre rations for them, the better food was for the three guards with the guns.

The prisoners wore shackles, heavy steel ones attached to a belt. The spoils from an empty prison. They couldn't run, just shuffle about. The prisoners wore bruises, too. I asked Daniel about them. What they were doing. He was trying to be nice to me, his future wife, so he took the time to explain, even as a guard sneered at him for wasting his time.

They needed the rocks. This is how they were building their town, extending the walls. Hundreds of new acres were to be planted next year; they'd been clearing them all summer. The fence around the fields would be over five miles long with walls in between, heavy stone among trees to create wind breaks. They expected the town to double in size in a year. They were prosperous.

He was important in the town, he told me. One of the first settlers. Soon to be an Elder on the Council. A good man to marry, in other words.

"A pity there's not more of them," he finished, nodding towards the prisoners. "So much building to be done; we need more stone. They're just not working hard enough."

I nodded like I agreed, but they were working too hard. It was the image of a ragged prisoner of war camp. What I really saw, though, was a way out. Here was a weak spot. An Achilles heel waiting for an arrow from Paris.

There were only three guards, and the prisoners would be on my side, I hoped. Some looked ready to drop dead, they'd surely help me if it helped them escape; I'd found allies. We had taken a car out, a mile of a head-start from the town. All the details flooded my head. I tried to commit them all to memory, to work out a plan later. Layout, distance, who the guards were, the types and number of guns...I needed to find out more. I'd add it all to my map.

When everyone finished eating, I cleared up and Daniel, again being nice, carried the coolers to the car for me.

Weeks went by. Christmas drew closer, and there were big preparations. There would be a celebration which meant more cleaning, cooking, baking. Work continued to be hard, early morning to late night. Cooking and scrubbing, all day.

Daniel came by more. He sat beside me at each meal. Martha started talking about a wedding. I told her I was married. She looked at me like a child.

"If your husband hasn't come through here, he's dead. It's time for you to move on. Your duty to God, to your community, is to find a man and have children while you're young and healthy. Timothy 5:14 tells us 'So I counsel younger widows to marry, to have children.'

Daniel is a good man, young too. A good choice for you. And we will need to find a man for Addy next year. She is getting old enough."

Addy overheard this and glared. She didn't speak again for days.

Later, as we lay in bed, I tried to talk to her.

"You won't have to get married. I'll get us out," I whispered.

No response.

"We'll work it out, trust me."

Nothing.

"Addy, are you listening?

Nothing. I lay a long while, listening, before her breath softened and she slept. I didn't sleep for a long time.

I continued working on my map. I marked where the gas was stored, where there were cars and trucks. Which ones worked well, which were liable to break down. Where the guns were kept. Who was guarding where and when. All preparation for an escape.

I found where my drugs were. An old safe in a locked office beside the room that worked as the hospital. Martha was there most days, along with Michael who had been an EMT and was now the town doctor.

But everywhere I needed to be, I wasn't welcome. I was there for the kitchens, for cleaning, for marrying and delivering healthy babies to the community, good Christian babies. I tried to offer help, to move to a more useful position, and one better for me to escape from. Nothing.

When one of the freezers broke, and I fixed it before the electrician could arrive. He was furious. Not that he wanted to do the work, but that he'd got off his ass to walk this far for nothing. Only Martha's intervention, I was new and didn't know better, is what stopped it from escalating. I didn't point out that the half-assed patch job he'd done on the other fridge would soon break too.

But there were other things I could do. There were lots of women in the compound. The wives and mothers, cooking, cleaning, gardening. Not all were as Christian as Martha. Some just wanted shelter and safety.

Janet had been an ER nurse in Baltimore. Now she cleaned the hospital. More qualified than our EMT or Martha, she wasn't married to an Elder and didn't have nuts, so she mopped floors. She cornered me one evening after prayers. She'd seen the pills.

"Are there any more?" she asked me. "We need more pain killers. Michael holds them tight for people he likes. Sherrie nearly died in labour during the summer; he gave her no pain killers. Yet if one of his friends has a hangover, he can spare them. If you can get me some, he'll never know."

"I don't have any more," I said. "They stole all I had when they found me."

"Pity. They'd be more use elsewhere," she said. "If you can get some, let me know."

"We could just take them back," I said. "If I got mine back, I could share."

I left it hanging.

"There's no way, they're all counted."

"If I could, would you help?"

She said nothing, just walked off and left me there.

Ellie, the head cook, had once been a chef in a top restaurant in New York. Multiple Michelin stars, that kind of place. She ran the kitchen and mostly she was left to it, even Martha didn't try to argue with her. Cooking was a woman's work, and the food was always good. It helped Jacob and the Elders, part of their promise. In return for obedience to their ways, you got safety and good food.

She saw my work on that fridge and when the last patch job broke, she had me fix it quietly. There was a switch that kept tripping and we'd have to go out in the cold to set it back; she'd been told that it couldn't be fixed without a full re-wire. She asked me to look the next time it went. A small piece of rubber wrapped around a stripped wire fixed it.

Ellie was good to me. I helped her with the things the men wouldn't fix. A quiet corner of the kitchen behind shelves was arranged, a place where I could work without being seen. I still chopped and stirred and cleaned but less so. Instead, I fixed things. When I asked to go out to the quarry top to stretch my legs, I became the regular to go there with the lunches. No one else wanted the cold trip, the hungry stares. Most were frightened of the men, seeing hardened criminals not captured slaves.

Daniel usually accompanied me. He seemed to enjoy these drives. He assumed I wanted to marry him, accepted it as right and proper. He'd talk about a life together. Children, security. A Future. You could hear the capital 'F' whenever he said the word. I told him I needed time. I needed to find my Sean. He tried to kiss me once, but I slapped his face and told him I still needed time. He started to lose patience.

Then he'd try to be nice again. That was him, sure that he was getting everything he deserved and if he was just nice to me for a few weeks, I'd want it too. Why wouldn't I? I wished I'd hit the gobshite harder.

I talked to the prisoners. Just chatter, asked their names. The guards told me to stop.

"Won't God forgive them?" I asked Daniel. "I was always taught that God would forgive us our trespasses."

He was still trying to be nice.

"Let her be," he told the guards.

Most of the prisoners wouldn't look at me, but one – the one who'd I'd watched dragged to the stage for a phone – would talk to me. He told me his name was Alain. He was from Bordeaux and had been in the US for three years before the Fall. A builder, working on construction projects in San Francisco.

"I came over illegally. It was getting worse for me," he told me. "All this hate for Mexicans; we were next. I was ready to give up and go home, but then I met a girl, and you know."

He shrugged.

"Where is she?" I asked him.

"She didn't make it."

I wanted to say something. Make a gesture, pat his shoulder, give him a hug. But I couldn't. The guards, Daniel all watching. He knew it too.

The next day I snuck some cake, just a tiny slice, to Alain. He said nothing when he saw it but later as they all ate, I saw him sharing the morsel with the others, staring at me.

Christmas week arrived. Advent and extra prayers. No lights, no Santa, no trees. Just extra service, extra work, and preparation for a feast on Christmas day. A day of prayer and celebration.

"We'll hold the wedding the week after," Jacob told me. "A wedding is a good way to welcome the new year."

I didn't try to object. I'd learned enough now to know there were no choices here. It gave me a definite date.

Addy was improving. She no longer jumped at every noise but was still quiet and avoided people as much as she could. She worked in the kitchen and Ellie took care of her, perhaps seeing she was with me or perhaps just because Ellie was a good person.

Chapter 39

It was December the twenty first. The shortest day of the year. This was the first community I'd met that tracked the time anymore, everyone else guessed at the seasons to try and plant around the shifting climate, but in New Bethlehem they needed to know when Christmas and Easter happened, so I knew the date. I took the lunches to the prisoners as usual. Daniel didn't come. Instead, Matthew, an old and bent Elder drove me out, peering over the steering wheel the whole way. He complained about the cold, complained about the snow, complained about the noise, the young people, the drive, the food. For a one-mile drive, he got in a whole lot of complaining.

I interrupted just enough to ask where Daniel was, and he stopped complaining just enough to tell me he was gone for the week. He'd gone to Springfield, like the cartoon. I knew of the place. I'd been asking everyone about the area. Where the roads led, what communities were close. I tried to act like I was just making conversation, but each night I'd update my map. I wished I had my old maps, my road atlas. I'd traced a line so often in my head, I knew the way, but my line hadn't gone through here.

Springfield, Kansas, I had found out, was a town fifty or so miles away. A small place, less than two hundred people Ellie had told me.

Farmers for the most part, they traded with New Bethlehem. It's where the turkeys for Christmas were coming from.

Even if time wasn't ticking down, this would be my best chance. Matthew was the weakest link. I would need Addy to help me, though. Could we do it? Could I get far enough away before we were missed? We'd have an hour head start at most. It wasn't enough. I needed more. A truck would leave tracks in the snow to follow, and they would follow me.

When we arrived, I made a big show of lugging the lunches out. Matthew just watched. He wouldn't be fit to help, and anyway, it was women's work.

"Could you get someone to help me?" I asked him. "Maybe that guy?"

I pointed at Alain.

Matthew shouted for him to come, and he hobbled over, his feet still manacled together.

If he was surprised at how light the boxes were, he didn't show it.

"Do you want to get out?" I whispered as we bent over to lift a box. He said nothing, but his eyes widened a little. We lifted. A slight nod.

"This week," I said. "I need to get out this week. I'll get you what you need, you take me with you. Every time I come, help me with the boxes."

We set up, and I dished out the food as usual. The guards didn't notice anything. Daniel often helped me with the boxes. Happy wife, happy life.

When they finished lunch, Alain came to help me load up again. No one said anything.

"How?" was all he asked.

"I'll slip you something," I said. "This week, I'll get you something to cut the chains. Will that be enough?"

He thought a moment. "We'd need a gun."

"There's only three guards here," I said. "There's three guns. How many at night?"

"Two," he told me.

"Can't all of you take two?"

He nodded. "They chain us to the beds, but if you can take care of that…" He left it hanging as Matthew hobbled over, complaining again.

I told Addy that night.

"We're getting out of here," I said. "This week."

"How?" was all she asked.

"There's twenty seven prisoners at that quarry; they're going to break out. They're going to help us with a diversion, and we'll go with them. Strength in numbers. Once we're a little away, we split. If anyone is chasing, they'll go after them, and we'll go the other way."

"How will we go in all this snow?" she asked.

"We'll steal a truck. I've been checking them out. There's an old Datsun that's reliable, and I know where they keep the gas. There's an F150 at the quarry they use for hauling the rock. Two trucks for all of us. It's a lot of us for just two trucks, but I think it's all we can get. We need to conserve gas anyway; we won't have that much. We'll need as much distraction as they can create to get as far away from here as possible. Be ready to go."

"Do you trust them?" she asked. "I mean, they're all…"

She left it there, but I knew what she meant. Martha and the other women in the kitchen warned me to be careful each time I went with the lunches. Dangerous, hardened criminals out there. But that wasn't bothering Addy. No, she was worried because they were all men.

"We'll have our knives, and if I can, I'm taking a gun. Once we can get away, we'll be fine. I promise."

It took longer than I wanted. There weren't the tools in the kitchen, but I managed to sneak out a knife.

"We'll need more than that," Alain told me. "That won't cut through these."

The manacles were solid. Stainless steel.

"Can you pick a lock?" I asked.

"No use." He pointed at the shackles.

I looked closer, there was a spot weld over the keyholes.

I swore.

"I'll get something," I told him. "Be ready."

I tried to find an excuse to go by the mechanic shop. I couldn't. When I did get there, to find someone to fix a leak I'd started, there were too many people. I couldn't pocket anything.

I needed another solution. The days were slipping by.

I found Janet after prayers.

"You still want those pills?" I asked her.

"Yes."

"I can get them," I told her. "I just need some help."

"What kind of help?" she asked slowly.

"The combination to the safe. I know you know it. And I need something to help people sleep. Like really sleep."

She thought a moment. "If you steal them, you'll be caught. Sent to the quarry. Or worse."

"I won't be here. I'm not getting married."

"Your husband…I thought he wasn't real?"

"Something like that."

She thought about it for a moment, looking at me and thinking. "If you're caught…"

"I won't be."

"Don't mention me."

"I'll be gone. With some pills. The rest I'll leave for you."

"I'll make a list," she told me. "Come to the hospital wing tomorrow. Say you're sick or something."

"I'll be there," I promised.

The next day after lunch I complained about my stomach and went to the wing. Michael ignored me. Janet made me tea and had me sit on a bed.

"You want my help still?" she asked.

"Yes. I can't stay here. I can't keep Addy here; she's too young for this."

"You have to leave half behind. Sometimes Michael does need them, and I can't give them out. I can't know anything. But I need aspirin, Tylenol, Percocet. There's some Diazepam in there, those are what you asked for. Two of those and you'll sleep all night. Three and nothing will wake you. Four or five and you might never wake up. You understand?"

I nodded.

"You take those and hide my pills here. Under the mattress you're sitting on now. You leave the rest."

I wouldn't. I'd leave her some, but I was taking mine. I was taking enough to trade my way to the coast. To home.

"Seventeen left, fifty-four right, sixteen left."

"I got it," I said. "Seventeen, fifty-four, sixteen."

I'd need to break in twice. Once to steal some Diazepam, another time to take the rest and run.

I finished my tea and went back to work. There was food to prepare before evening prayer. We went into the hall, ready to take our seats at the back as usual, but I felt a hand on my arm.

"Miss me?" Daniel.

"Weren't you meant to be gone all week?" I said, cursing inwardly.

"I missed you, so I came back early," he said. "Let's get a seat."

My plans were crumbling. Everything had depended on Matthew driving me out to the quarry. The fool was old and lazy; I could do what I wanted, and he wouldn't notice. I still had to risk it. I couldn't stay. Daniel was holding my hand, and everything in me wanted to scream.

After dinner he stayed around. He walked me back to my room and tried to kiss me.

I pushed him off. "Wait for the wedding,"

He pushed back.

"Hey, are you coming?" Addy pushed the door open. "I need your help."

"I should go." I disentangled myself from Daniel and pushed in.

"Thank you," I breathed to Addy.

I explained my plan. We waited. And then we waited some more.

Sometime, past midnight, when all else was quiet, I got up.

"Are you sure you don't need me?" she asked. "I could be a lookout. I can help."

"No," I had decided. "If I'm caught, it's best it's just me."

"Less chance of being caught with a lookout," she said.

I shook my head and snuck out the door, closing it softly behind me. All was still. Bright light shone through a window in the hallway, the moon on snow, I hugged the wall as I passed any openings, moving slowly to the stairs.

I stopped to listen. No sound. Wait, was that a creak? A footfall? Someone turning in their bed. I waited. No more sounds.

I crept on. In the dead silence, the first stair creaked like the wail of a banshee in the stillness of the night. I froze. Nothing moved. I moved my feet to the edges and down the rest of the steps. The ground floor was quiet. I slowly moved up the corridor and around a corner.

A light. A sound. I tried to sink into the wall, to become invisible. A voice. I stopped breathing, willing my heart to stop beating so loudly.

"Is that tea ready?" a voice said.

"Put some booze in it," another replied.

"Oh, I'd kill for a coffee."

Guards, in from the cold, in the kitchen where there would be heat and food. I could hear them now, rifling through the shelves, helping themselves. I needed to go right past the kitchen. I could see light through the open door. I slid down the hallway and slowly, ever so slowly, I opened a door to a bathroom and slipped in.

I had to hope no one else came this way. I hid there and waited, the door open, just a crack to listen. I heard them make tea. Then the light went out, and a door slammed. I waited some more.

Then I ran for it, stockings quiet on the cold tile floor.

The hospital wing was quiet, just the low breathing of a single patient, a hunter who had been mauled out in the woods. He was in the bed, a mass of bandages and looked asleep. I tiptoed past him to the office.

Quickly, I opened the safe and rifled through it, trying to put everything back exactly where it had been. There were a lot of drugs in there. Mine had probably doubled the amount. I found the Diazepam at the bottom and broke off eight pills from the blister pack. Two for each of the night guards at the quarry and on the gate. Then I broke off six more just in case. Then I just said fuck it and took the lot of them. Seventeen pills. I put everything else back carefully and closed the safe.

Back up the stairs, ever so quiet, back along the corridor. Slowly.

"Who's there?" a voice demanded. A man. I didn't know who.

I was in the light of a window.

"Haley," I said.

"What are you doing out of bed at this hour?" he demanded, loudly.

"Bathroom," I said.

He grunted something, and I quickly ducked into the bathroom. I waited a few minutes, flushed and washed my hands, then I walked out and past him and to my room. I didn't know him. One of the guards. In the corridors, out of the cold.

"Did you get them?" Addy demanded.

"Ssh," I breathed. "There's someone out there."

I reached into my dress and pulled out the pills.

"Go to sleep Addy," I whispered. "It's going to be a long day."

Chapter 40

T he next day was Christmas Eve. The kitchens were a mad house. Tons of vegetables to be peeled, fruit cakes to be made, turkeys to be readied. It was going to be a feast. I couldn't do much, but there was so much work to do. I did manage to sneak some food to my corner to try to take with us. When lunchtime rolled around, I expected Daniel to be back, but to my delight it was Matthew again. Old and lazy. "He's busy," was all Matthew told me when I asked.

I slipped Alain nine pills.

"Three each to the guards tonight. Just three, there's extra in case there's an extra guard. You think you can do that?"

He nodded.

"They'll sleep through anything. Do what you need to break your chains. Use a chisel; you won't need to worry about the noise. Then come get me. There'll be guards at the gate. I'll try to have them asleep by midnight. Just be careful and come. You'll need the trucks. You have one here, I'll have another. You'll have to push it out the gate so that you won't be heard, and then we get as far and as fast as possible. OK?"

He nodded.

We had to stop talking, and I had to dish out the lunches. When he helped me load back up the car again, he whispered to me, "We'll be ready by midnight. Be ready to go. And Haley, thank you."

We drove back. I hoped he would come for me, not just break out and run. They could. It would make the most sense. Why risk themselves for me? I shut those thoughts away and held out hope in humanity. I still had a lot to do. I needed to get the gate guards to sleep, and I needed to steal the good truck. Plus, get as much gas as I could, steal enough food, and get a gun if I could. I spent the rest of the afternoon in the kitchen. There was never-ending cooking and cleaning. I got a chance to go clean up before prayers.

I tried to sneak in with Addy, so we could hide at the back, but Daniel cornered me and pulled me to a seat beside him. I was concentrating on keeping his hands away, trying to run through the list in my head of what I needed to do, and so I didn't notice the stranger Jacob brought in.

I didn't notice anything as he led prayers, and I responded automatically. My mind was on escape routes, drugging the gate guards and stealing a truck, not listening to him rattle out times for prayers and more prayers in the morning.

"… and we welcome our friend, here from the Patron," he was saying.

A shock went through me. The Patron. Here.

I tried to look without being seen, to duck my head behind the people in front of me. It didn't work. He was staring right at me as he lifted himself from the chair beside Jacob to say something.

Zeke.

He grinned and winked. My heart stopped.

"Thank you, Jacob," he said. "The Patron is happy to extend his friendship to your community. As you know, he welcomes all good

Christians to New Seattle, where we can work together to rebuild this world, not as it was, but back to the good Christian values that made it so great before all of the sin that led to the Fall.

"The Patron offers protection, laws, and government. Medicine and schools. Let us join together and make a county built on God's laws. Together we will drive the scourge of bandits from our homes."

It was a very pretty speech; he'd obviously practiced it. He got rapt attention from everyone else, hanging on his every word. Except from me. My mind was screaming. Could I run? Where could I go?

"But we all have to obey the laws, and I see a criminal hiding among you." His voice changing from open and friendly to righteous anger. "She fled from justice in New Seattle."

He raised his arm, pointing a finger.

"Haley is wanted in New Seattle, she murdered a man and stole from the Patron. He would see her brought to justice. That is what the Patron brings; law and order, safety for the people, punishment for those who would trespass against us."

All eyes turned to look at me. Daniel's hand gripped my own tighter, squeezing so hard it hurt. I tried to pull it free.

"Is this true?" he demanded.

I shook my head. I tried to deny it, but the room was in an uproar. All around me people were talking, staring, pointing. Jacob was calling for order, for quiet.

When it calmed, he asked, "Are you sure? This young lady has been here some time, a part of our community, about to marry one of our own."

"She killed a mechanic in New Seattle, stole a motorcycle and a shipment of pills bound for our hospital. Children died without them."

I saw the realization cross Jacob's eyes. The pills he'd taken, the ones I'd demanded were mine. Now he was wondering if he had stolen from the Patron. His confidence faded, and his face whitened. All around me, whispers grew louder and louder, a thousand faces all staring, jostling to see. My mind raced in circles, getting nowhere. I was surrounded, there were no exits. At least I wasn't beside Addy, she might yet get away.

"Quiet," Jacob called, and then yelled.

A hush fell, all eyes on him to see what he would say. Eyes flicking back to me to watch. My stomach fell. I felt weak.

"We should speak of this in private," he decided, and turned to Zeke. "We will, of course, help our friend the Patron. For now, Haley is going nowhere. We will confine her until we decide. Jonathan, Edward," he called to two guards who sat at the back of the room with their guns beside them. "Please take Haley back to her room. I'll send for her when we're ready."

I was pushed and prodded from my seat. Half lifted as my legs threatened to give way. Daniel was still gripping my hand until I tore it loose in a sudden burst of terror. Then I was pushed back down the aisle between the rows and rows of seats. The staring eyes, the whispers floating around me. I felt the community quickly turn against me. Already preparing my sentence for endangering their plans. Fear was taking over. I could see Addy, near the back, trying to stand. Ellie had a heavy hand on her shoulder, holding her down, whispering urgently in her ear. At least she might be safe. I was facing the end, but she might be safe.

We made it to the corridor. The map I'd made was clear in my head. Exits, there and there; a truck, two hundred feet of a run. There was no key, lost a long time ago, just a switch for on and a push button to start. The gate was locked and guarded, a heavy steel barrier. Heavy enough that even the truck would just bounce off it.

And there was a heavy hand on each of my shoulders, gripping tight and pushing me forward. There was nowhere to run.

Chapter 41

We went back up the stairs and to my bedroom. I was pushed in, and the two guards lounged by the door, hands on their guns. Big guys. There was no way past them, no way out. No escape from my fate.

There was no fight in me.

A few minutes later, Addy came running in, followed by Martha. She motioned to the two guards to move outside as Addy grabbed me in a hug.

"I don't know what to do with you, Haley. How could you kill a man? And steal those drugs? From the Patron who is trying to rebuild our world? You've put our whole community in danger! And Addy; how could you drag a child into this? How could you lie to us like this? We welcomed you, we gave you a home. Daniel was ready to marry you."

She spun to Addy. "You're young but you should know better. You could have told us; we could have helped. We would have sheltered you, but instead you helped her in her lies. May God help you both."

She shook her head and walked out, the door slamming behind her. The guards didn't come back in, and I heard her ordering them to stand there all night if need be.

"What happened after I left?" I demanded.

"Jacob asked Zeke if he was sure, and he said he was, and then they said they would talk in private. Ellie just kept telling me to sit still, to say nothing, but once Jacob and Zeke left, Martha dragged me up here. Said I must have been in on it. Had to be."

I fingered the pills still hidden in my dress. Eight of them.

"Did you really do it?" she asked. "Kill that man, I mean, like Zeke said? It's okay if you did. I mean, like back there…"

"No, Addy. No, I didn't, I promise. I didn't do it. He was my friend. He was old, and Zeke hit him, and he fell. Then I hit Zeke, and I ran. That's it, really. I took the bike, but it was mine; the drugs were just on it. I had to run. Zeke, the Patron…well, I couldn't stay. Without Jimmy, I wasn't safe. No one would believe me over Zeke, the doctor, important to the Patron."

"Oh," was all she said.

"You need to get away from me, Addy. Make sure they know you weren't in New Seattle. They'll be busy with me. You can stay out of sight. Always say you knew nothing of the drugs, that I forced you to come with me. You only ran from the Kings. You were frightened of me. Don't let them accuse you."

"I won't say that," she argued. "Martha already said I'm guilty. She was dragging me up, saying I must have done something. If they lose their pact with the Patron, it would be all my fault, she said."

I grabbed her shoulders and looked in her eyes. "You have to. There's nothing I can do. I'll try to escape on the road, to come back for you, but you have to say you know nothing. It was all my fault, you were frightened."

She looked at me.

"Please, Addy, please just keep yourself safe. I'll tell them," I said. "I'll tell them we met much later. I'll make them see; Jacob will see."

"Martha said I'll be sent back with you. A trial."

"No, it will never happen."

She was shaking now. She knew what was in store. She was too young to know this, but after the Fall, everyone was so much older. My eyes burned with tears.

The pills. Eight of them. Janet's words ringing through my head. *Four or five and you might never wake up.*

A way out, but not enough for two.

I knew what the results would be if I were sent to New Seattle. I knew Zeke. I knew the Patron.

I took out the pills and held them out to Addy. "They might search me," I said. "Keep these safe. If they...I mean, if they."

I didn't know how to say it, but I saw it in her eyes. She knew. She understood so much, had seen so much. Too much. I saw tears, and she stopped shaking as understanding replaced the fear. She took them from me.

"Take them all," I said.

There were tears in her eyes. There were tears in mine.

"But you'll be good, you know. You did nothing. They're all Christian here, and you're just a kid. Just let them blame me. But...you know... just in case, take all of them."

She understood what no kid should understand. I couldn't say anything. This was it. I was caught and now Addy was being dragged into it.

The door opened, and Edward pulled me to my feet.

"Out," he shouted. "The Elders want to talk to you."

Addy stood, too.

"Not her. She had nothing to do with it," I said. "Nothing."

"Not her, just you. They want to talk to you."I was pushed out and back down the stairs and to a room off the main hall. It might have once been an office. Jacob, Michael, Daniel, and two more of the

Elders, Joseph and Eli, were all sitting around a table with Zeke. The remains of dinner still sat on their plates. I hadn't eaten in a while. The food smelled good. Surprising what you notice in times like these.

Edward and Jonathan stood to either side of me, each holding an arm. Jacob waved them away. "Take a seat Haley."

I sat in the single chair left. It was at one side of the table while the others sat in a semi-circle around me, all staring. One of the guards was right behind me. I blinked away my tears.

"Zeke here, sent by the Patron, has told us you are charged with a crime in New Seattle," he started.

"I didn't kill Jimmy," I interrupted. "I'd never kill that man; I loved him. He was like a father to me. Zeke killed him."

"Please don't interrupt," said Jacob, steel in his voice. "We are told you are charged with murder, and with theft. You were obviously in New Seattle, and you know of the murder."

"I didn't do it. It wasn't me."

A heavy slap to the back of the head rattled my teeth. I shook my head to clear it and looked back at Jacob, who was stern, and Zeke who was smirking.

"Don't interrupt," said Jacob. "Speak when spoken to. You will have your chance to defend yourself later." He took a breath and asked, "Did you kill James Madison?"

"No," I said. "Zeke did. He killed him."

Jacob held up a hand to stop me.

"Did you steal a motorcycle belonging to the Patron?" he continued.

There was no denying it. It was my bike. Well, it was the bike I'd found abandoned and brought to New Seattle, but somewhere along the way it had become Zeke's. Become the Patron's.

I said nothing.

"We need not ask about the pills. Zeke, when we found her, she had some small supply with her. A half dozen aspirin and some cold medicine, a handful of antibiotics. I presume that's what is missing?"

I stared at him. He was lying; he'd taken a lot more than that from me. It wouldn't help me to point this out, though, so I held my tongue. Perhaps some leverage later.

"There was a lot more than that Elder Jacob. No doubt she traded some along the way to the unwary who did not know they were stolen."

He was almost smiling as he said this, staring at me. His nose was crooked now. I'd done that. If nothing else, I'd done that. He saw me stare at it, and his grin faded.

"We will, of course, return them to you. I fear our doctor here has used some, but we can replace them," Jacob said.

"I am sure the Patron will be happy to leave them for you," said Zeke. "As a gesture of our new friendship."

"We are grateful." Jacob inclined his head in thanks.

"I will have to take Haley back with me, though," Zeke said.

"I didn't kill him, I didn't," I insisted.

I needed to say it. To protest my innocence, useless as it might have been. I'd been fleeing this charge all this time, and this was my first, possibly my last, chance to shout it out. I didn't kill him.

Another blow to the head almost knocked me from my chair and sent the room spinning.

"Haley you as much as admit you took the bike, and we know you took the drugs. These are enough criminal acts to send you back for trial."

"Trial?" I snorted.

Another blow, but I didn't care. I straightened up in my chair and stared Jacob straight in the eye.

"Like I'll even make it to New Seattle."

"Edward, Jonathan, take her back to her room and keep her there. We will make arrangements to have her go back with you, Zeke."

I was dragged from the room. I screamed my protests, but they fell on scared ears. I was going back with Zeke. I wondered how far I'd make it. I doubted I'd last an hour. He didn't want me back anywhere near New Seattle.

When I did get thrown into my room it was empty. Addy was gone. I wanted to cry. I was all alone and going to die. I wanted to believe in a God so I could pray. A way out. Hope for Addy. But this was the end of the world. If a god had existed he'd succumbed to Armageddon like the rest of us. Hope was for the before-times, not now. Not after the Fall.

I sat for a while until Ellie came up. I heard her arguing with the guards outside before they let her in to give me some food. She patted my shoulder, a friendly gesture, before setting the plate.

"Where's Addy?" I begged for information. I needed to know she was safe.

"She's in the kitchen, I'll keep her with me. Out of sight out of mind."

"Please keep her safe."

"I'll try," she said, patting my arm as she left.

Night drew on before there was another person at the door. Daniel. I heard him arguing with the guards before he shoved his way in.

"How could you do this to me?" he snarled, pacing the small room. "To us? I thought we had something, Haley. How could you do this? We were going to be married."

Did he love me? Was there a chance here, someone I could have on my side?

"I didn't do it. I didn't kill anyone. Zeke killed him, and I knew I'd be in trouble, so I ran. That's it. I took the bike, but it was my bike anyway, and I ran. Zeke had just left all the drugs on it; I didn't know they were there when I left. Please, Daniel, you have to believe me. I didn't kill Jimmy."

He stopped pacing and looked me straight in the eyes. Like he was trying to see if there was any truth in them. I saw only anger in his.

"Who cares about that?" he asked. "You're a dyke. A filthy fucking lesbian. Zeke told us. A girlfriend back at home. Don't you know what the bible says? You deserve all that's coming. 20:13, You have committed an abomination and will surely be put to death. Your blood will be upon you."

He almost spat the last words.

I could see it in him. The disappointment. He wasn't on my side. Four years ago, he'd have been yanking at his cock staring at Pornhub's latest girl on girl. Now, he could never hope to marry me, a dyke, a sinner, an outcast in the community. Not getting everything he was sure he deserved, the obedient Christian wife, he was pissed. He was in the right, and everything was all my fault.

"Fucking dyke," he repeated.

"I'm sorry. I just wanted to pass through, to go home," I told him. "We were just going south. I didn't want to hurt you."

"But you didn't. You stayed. You lied. To me."

"What could I say?" My fear was changing to anger. I'd had enough of his bullshit. They'd trapped me here. "What could I tell you? What could I do that wouldn't land me chained in a quarry? I was just going through. Just going home."

"Home to your whore, is that it? There's no place in this world for the likes of you, Haley. You'll pay for your sins in New Seattle."

He raised his hand, and I thought for a moment he'd hit me, but the door opened.

"Could you give us a moment please, Daniel?" It was Jacob. The words were polite, but it was a definite order.

Daniel grunted and left, staring daggers. Jacob sat beside me on the bed.

"You'll be leaving with Zeke in two days, Haley. Zeke will stay to celebrate Christmas with us. Until then, you will stay here and see no one."

"I didn't do it."

"That doesn't matter. You were accused, and therefore you will stand trial. There needs to be justice; there needs to be a trial. If you are, as you say, innocent, I'm sure that will come out. Although you've as much as admitted to stealing the motorcycle, and I'm sure of where you got the pills, so I don't think you will be found innocent. Your trial will be in New Seattle where I'm sure it will be fair."

"Zeke will never let me make it that far."

"The Patron is a powerful friend; you will go with Zeke."

"He'll kill me before we're even out of sight," I almost spat at him. The weak fool.

"I will personally be meeting with the Patron in spring. I will ask about your trial then. Zeke knows this. We will expect you to make it to trial. He won't do anything to jeopardize our new agreement with the Patron, we can be sure of that. This new world will have justice."

"I didn't kill anyone."

"But you did steal a motorcycle. You did take those drugs. For those you will go back to New Seattle."

"To die."

"Not to die, unless you are found guilty of the murder."

"You will just let me be killed, just like that? And you call yourself a man of God?"

"Zeke told us of your ways. Your lust for women. You lied to us; you have no husband. Do not seek God's protection. Your kind, with your liberal ways and technology-driven greed, led to the Fall of the world. No, go seek the Patron's mercy, because you will find none here."

There was disgust in his voice. I was nothing but a sinner, and he was glad to see me go. Anger surged through my terror. I had no hope of escaping and still, some old man was judging me. Controlling me. Invoking some God or morals or shit to tell me I was evil.

"You lied, too. A few aspirin? That's all you took from me?"

He said nothing but stood to leave and paused at the door.

"Zeke said you fled New Seattle alone. I thought it best to leave it like that. Addy can stay in our community; God charges us to look after the children. It would be best if you didn't mention her."

I stared at him. It was all there in the look we exchanged. We had an understanding. Addy would be safe – well, their version of safe – here in New Bethlehem if I played along with them. Otherwise, we both knew what could happen. I seethed.

I bowed my head. I'd lost. I wanted to plan revenge on them, but I saw little hope of escape. I'd plan anyway.

He closed the door, carefully but firmly, behind him. The click of the key in the lock rang like a gallows' drop. I ran to the door and put an ear to it. I could make out the words, "stay here," and, "no one is to enter."

A few minutes later the door opened, and a bucket was thrown in and then slammed again.

I checked the window. I was at the back of the building and the ground dropped away. From the ledge it was at least a twenty-foot drop. I checked the beds, worked the math. The sheets ripped to strips and tied together, subtract a few feet to tie it to the bed and over the ledge, I'd get at least fifteen feet. A short drop to soft snow. I just had to wait. Beyond the snow was the high, razor wire-topped fence. And guards with guns. A bullet in the back was not the worst option I was facing.

The window was solid, new before the Fall, an aluminium frame and double or triple glazed. I had no hope of breaking the glass. The pane that opened was much too small to get out; not a ground floor window, no building codes that demanded an emergency exit. I'd have to remove the glass. I didn't have much time; I expected Alain at midnight. My best hope lay with the prisoners creating a diversion big enough.

I scrabbled at the small plastic plugs on the frame. My nails were always bitten short, but I got them out quickly. Three to a side, I'd need to remove at least three sides to pull out the glass. It was large, so it would be heavy. I'd drop it. I thought about it, pillows on the floor and let it drop, quietly I hoped.

Under the plugs were screws holding in the plastic stay. Philips head. It would've been the work of a minute to remove every last one if I had a screwdriver. I tried to get a grip, tried to slide the butt of a fingernail underneath. Nothing.

I heard a noise and spun. The door was opening. I jumped away from the window.

Edward came in and walked to the window where I stood.

"Thinking of jumping, huh?"

He rapped the glass, hard, with the butt of his gun.

"All new windows just before the Fall, triple glazed. Won't break. Even if it did, you'd break your leg in the fall. It's a long way down, girly. Long, long way. I guess the guys outside will come pick you up, maybe even before you freeze with two broken legs. Or you can just stay quiet, so we don't have to come in and beat your filthy dyke ass. Your choice."

He stared at me, waiting for an answer. When none came, he flicked the light switch by the door.

"Lights out. Keep quiet or we come in and teach you a lesson."

He walked out and the door locked behind him. I couldn't believe it. He hadn't noticed the plastic plugs, the exposed screws. Or did he just not care, sure of the fall, of the men outside with guns? Or maybe was he just waiting, looking for an excuse for violence.

"Eat first, Haley," I told myself. "Eat while you can, gather your strength."

I ate everything and drank the tea while I considered the screws. There had to be a way to get them out. The spoon that came with Ellie's stew was too big. I searched all my pockets; my old clothes were back. The metal buttons on my jeans were too big to get in there, the latch on my belt too small to catch. Addy's clothes. The smaller zipper on her coat pocket fit. Almost.

I pulled it off, gripping with my teeth and ripping the pocket until the slider came loose. It was too small. It fit in the screw head, but I couldn't get enough grip to turn it. Back to the coat and the other side pocket. This time, I ripped the coat. Stabbing at it with the spoon, the only tool I had, I ripped the fabric and the zipper right off.

I tried it, with the fabric balled up enough to create grip. I loosened a screw. And then another. I worked slowly, stopping at every sound, ready to jump to the bed, carefully feeling for each screw, quietly trying to turn them.

I guessed the time at around ten. They went to bed early here; most of the community would already be in their beds. Another hour at most and everyone but the guards at the gate, and my two would be asleep. The two at my door would be tired, I hoped. At eleven, I should go.

I'd removed all of the screws, the window just sitting now in place, not held in. An hour to get take the pane out, jump, find Addy and hide to wait for a distraction from the quarry.

I tried to rest. Eat when you can and rest when you can. I'd learned that early on, running and hiding.

I couldn't sleep. I could hear soft mumbling from outside the door as my captors talked. I heard the footsteps in the hallway as one of them went off and came back two minutes later. All the other noises in the building settled down and even outside my door it got quieter.

I gave up trying to rest and stood by the window. The moon was still bright outside, reflecting off the snow. I could see the clear yard which would make it easier for me, but I was going to stand out. *Stick to the shadows Haley*, I told myself.

I counted off time in my head, heard the men at the door settling in. Outside, someone walked by every now and again. There was a view of the gate tower from where I was. If they were looking this way…

I found my old jeans in the closet and put them on under the black dress; it would be cold out. I took the sheets from the bed and tried to tear them as quietly as possible. Without a knife to start the cut, they were near impossible to shred. I bit at them, pulling as much as I could but they wouldn't tear. I tied everything I could together and around the bed post. At the window there was about five feet left hanging out. Even fully extended I'd still fall another ten feet to the snow.

I waited. Would Alain even come for me? Would I be stuck here while all the prisoners at the quarry escaped? Either way, I had to try. Time ticked by.

I put my ear to the door and heard nothing. They were still out there, though; I knew they hadn't left. I checked the window. No one outside. I put down the pillows on the floor and tried to pull at the window. I couldn't get a grip. Nothing.

There was a shout from outside. A light went on in the tower and headlights flashed on the road. And then a gunshot. This was it, my only chance, forget the noise. I kicked and I pushed, and the pane of glass rocked and wobbled and twisted, and as I grabbed at it, it slid right out landing in the snow with a smack.

I threw my rope outside as I heard a key in the door. I jumped, grabbing at the hanging blankets.

Chapter 42

I didn't land on soft snow. My grab at the sheets slowed my fall but I landed on the glass which even now didn't break, leaving me what I was sure would be some spectacular bruises. A shout rang out above my head, but I was off running, ducking around behind the building, and moving as fast as I could. The truck and the gas I wanted were in the other direction but there was no sneaking off.

More noise started as more people woke up. I kept running. Behind me, I heard shots. At me? At the truck speeding towards the gates? I didn't know. I ducked into a doorway and into the first room there. It was a storage area; there'd be no people.

I tried to think. Addy was back the other way; how could I get there? My only chance now was for as much confusion as possible.

I peered out the door. I hoped Addy was with Ellie, two buildings across, ground floor. Back of the building. There were people outside, lights coming on. The guard tower by the gate was on fire. I didn't know how it had happened. More shots rang out.

I crouched, ready to run. I had to go now, while everyone was distracted by the fire. Get across, get Addy.

Headlights swung in my direction, and I ducked further in. I could see in their light that not everyone was distracted; there were some coming my way. I felt my way carefully back into the room, searching for a place to hide.

I was in a storage room, shelves of clothes, sheets, yarn and thread surrounding me. I'd been here before and knew there was a desk in the far corner. I moved forward in the dark until I found a sharp corner with my hip. A desk lamp. I grabbed it and smashed it, giving me a broken bulb and some wires. Making sure the lamp was still plugged in, I pulled a pile of clothes from a shelf and shoved the wires in through whatever was on top, crossing them.

A spark. Bigger than I expected thanks to unreliable electricity and bad wiring.

I heard shouts from outside as breakers broke and lights went out, and inside I was rewarded with a tiny flame. I fed it quickly with paper from the desk more dry cloth. Then I ran for the door, and out into the darkness.

I ducked around a corner as two hulking men came at a trot. My guards were chasing me. I heard a shout; they'd seen the fire. I ducked into the next building to let them pass and looked towards the main building. To where Addy would be. There were too many people and not enough of a distraction. I needed something bigger.

I ran across the snow, ducking behind a long, low glasshouse and around the back towards the mechanic's shop. The mechanics were all gone. If I was to get a car, this was the place. The three that sat outside I knew would never start. There was one inside, up on bricks, with two wheels missing.

I heard a noise behind me, and ran inside to hide. Watching out the door, I backed into something. A propane heater. I lit it quickly and grabbed an oily rag, making a small fire in a corner. Then I turned the heater flame off, put the gas on full, and ran.

I could hear a truck coming my way. There were shouts of fire, but the men I saw were running to the first one.

I legged it around a corner and was ready to run for it. With everyone distracted, I'd run across the yard, get behind the building, get Addy, and get out. She should be on the ground floor. I needed to hurry. The prisoners from the quarry would be leaving. I needed a truck and to get gone while the gate guards were still distracted.

I moved around the building, quickly, staying low ready to run. I didn't get far.

"Hey!"

I spun and ran for it. Edward, one of my guards, was running towards me, gun raised.

I turned the other direction and ran away.

"Stop," he yelled from behind me.

I looked over my shoulder to see him stop and aim. That was when the propane reached the fire and the building beside him blew up, the wave of hot air knocking me to the ground.

I picked myself up. Edward was on the ground behind me. He was trying to push himself up, dazed, blood pouring from a cut on his head. I checked the distance. The wall was too far. I wouldn't make it.

I ran at him and jumped. He saw me coming and tried to raise an arm, but I landed, both feet against his elbow, and even above the ruckus around us I heard it crack as I lost my balance and fell.

I wasn't sure if he screamed. I didn't care. I pushed myself up and kicked, as hard as I could, like his face was a ball and I was O'Gara going for a conversion. He moved it just a bit, but I still connected. His hand scrabbled and grabbed my ankle, pulling me down. As I fell, my second foot slammed out, straight into his nose, and he let go. I jumped up again, grabbed for his gun, and ran for the wall.

It should have been awkward, climbing, tired, sore, and carrying a rifle, but I swear I just ran straight up it like one of those kids doing parkour. One hand for grip on the rough stone and I vaulted over, dropping to the snow below and running for the trees, a half mile in the distance. Not halfway across the open field, the lights of a truck picked me up. I tried to avoid them, but they kept coming.

Unrelenting, they bore down on me, so I turned and raised the gun. The truck slowed. I aimed, ready to shoot the first person to get out. I wasn't giving up without a fight.

"Wanna ride?" yelled Alain.

My body sagged with relief, and I hauled myself inside, squeezing in the packed cab, just then realizing how cold I was. Alain grinned as he hit the gas. The back of the truck slid a little but the weight of the men in the back gave it just enough grip and it sped off over the snow. Behind us, New Bethlehem smoked as the community rushed to put out the flames. No one chased us. Yet.

We didn't get far, an hour maybe, before we ran out of gas. We were in the middle of nowhere, a vast empty plain. We knew that we were on the road and headed in a mainly eastern direction. That was all we knew as the engine coughed a few times and spluttered to a stop.

"This is as far as we go," Alain said.

Already men were jumping out from the back of the truck and heading off in every direction in groups of two or three. None on the road, just away through deep snow.

"Do you want to stick with us?" Alain asked. "Me and Tom here, we got a gun. You got a gun. Safety in numbers."

I didn't need to think about it. I'd already had an hour driving to think it through. I wasn't going to rely on anyone else. No more promises of safety. Besides, I was going back. For Addy. I'd promised.

"No," I said. "But you owe me."

He looked at me. "We have nothing. You already have a gun. You got us out of there, and we do owe you, but we've got nothing."

"I need a coat," I said.

He shrugged off his heavy coat. I recognized it; he'd taken it from one of his jailers. Underneath, he wore the clothes the rest of the prisoners had.

"Stay warm, Haley." And with that, he opened the door and was off running.

I'd been watching as we drove. It wasn't all empty plain; there had been low hills, remains of buildings. I just needed to hide out and wait.

The snow was deep, so I got out and followed the tracks of the tires back a while. The hard-packed snow there was easier to walk in, and I hoped left less of a trail. A trail I hoped they'd just follow to the truck. A mile back there was shelter. A ruin, an old clapboard house that was now a snow-covered mound of rubble. I found a place out of the wind and covered up to sleep.

The gun in my hand offered some comfort as I lay cold and exhausted, wrapped in the heavy coat in the dark. I tried to catch some sleep, but I didn't get any. A truck came roaring on the road. Two men in it, guns visible in their silhouettes.

Then an SUV, again packed, people and guns. I watched them go by.

There were shots in the distance. In the east, the sun was a pink smear on the horizon when a truck slowly pulled up. Two men got out, both with guns. I wondered if they could see the tracks where I left the road, or if they just checking everywhere.

They walked up to the ruin. I recognized one of them as soon as he came near. Daniel. The other guy I didn't know.

"Think we'll find them all?" the tall guy was asking.

"They can't get far in this snow," Daniel replied. "See the tracks here? There's one of them came this way."

"Hey," he yelled towards the ruin. "Come out, hands up, and we won't shoot you. Three of your friends are already dead. Six more are going back to the quarry. Extra five years each. It's a better option that than dying in the cold. Come on out."

I didn't move.

"If we come in to get you, we shoot," he said. "You come on out now."

I still didn't move. They came closer. The house had collapsed forward, and the roof had fallen in almost one piece, a long tunnel of shelter half buried in snow. I was in the centre of what had been an attic. Hidden in the darkness, sheltered from the cold, but they'd see tracks where I came in. I moved to the other side, slowly, quietly.

"Don't make us shoot you," Daniel shouted.

I made it to the other side. There was nowhere to run, just a wide-open field of snow. I crouched down, hidden in the rubble, and waited. I could see through a crack to the other side where I'd stumbled in a few hours before, where they'd come.

"I'll go around the other side," I heard Daniel say. "Make sure he doesn't run for it."

I heard the boots crunching on snow, one going each side of the attic. He was coming right up to me. I waited, holding my rifle tight, my finger off the trigger. I still didn't want to kill them.

I heard a shout, saw a rifle poke in, and I swung, hard and low, pushing off my feet and putting everything I had behind it. My rifle speared right underneath the barrel coming in and connected solidly with a shin. Scrambling forward and spinning to my back, I yanked my weapon up as hard as I could. He screamed as I connected with his nuts, and I saw Daniel try to back away, shocked to see me, shocked at the attack and helpless with the pain spreading to consume him.

I pointed my gun and screamed, "Drop it!"

He was still doubled over, so I swung with the butt of the gun and all my anger. It connected with his head, and he fell. I kicked at his hand, stomping down and smashing at his fingers, before kicking his gun away.

At the other side of the ruin, the tall guy was still straightening up as I pointed the gun.

"Drop it," I yelled again.

He swung to aim, and I jerked on my trigger, missing him completely, but he froze and slowly put his hands out wide. He dropped his gun.

"Don't shoot me," he pleaded. "I've got a wife and kids. I didn't want to be here. Please don't shoot."

"Shoot the bitch," Daniel wheezed from the ground. I kicked at him, but he rolled away in time. I stooped to pick up his gun, keeping mine pointed at the other guy.

"Back away from it," I yelled, walking around the rubble.

The tall man, hands still in the air, moved away from his gun. I picked it up.

"Keys in the truck?"

He nodded.

"Go help Daniel," I said, and I backed away slowly towards the truck.

In the rear-view mirror, I saw him running to help Daniel. I swung the truck around and headed back towards New Bethlehem. I wanted to go there. I wanted to drive in and shoot every bullet I had, drive through the burned gates, take Addy and run. I went a mile before I turned south at the next road and sped on.

Chapter 43

I was away, for now, but I had to go back, for Addy. I had a truck and three guns but not a damn hope in hell. I wanted to just leave, to head east, to go home to Marley and forget all this ever happened. But I couldn't leave Addy there. My only friend left. Not after what she'd done for me. Not with all I owed her.

"Get far enough away, Haley," I told myself. "She's safe for now. Get back in the spring; you can't do anything in this snow."

I passed a town. Canaan, I guessed, just a small group of houses surrounded by a wire fence. Though in the middle that town was a Christmas tree. It couldn't be anything else, a fir tree covered in anything that might sparkle. Old hubcaps, bits of mirror, some coloured cloth in rough bows. I saw it through the fence, but I wasn't waiting for the gate to open to drive through. I went off the road, hoping there was no obstacle hidden in the snow, speeding on and around.

As I drove on, the sparkles in the mirror reminded me that it was Christmas.

Merry Christmas, Haley, I told myself.

The gas tank was half full. I drove for about three hours. Well into the day and far enough that I passed a few communities. Small places, ten or twenty houses, behind high fences and strong walls. No one came out. No one was following.

When the truck ran on fumes, I kept going. When it ran out of fumes, I let it roll to a stop. I didn't touch the brakes, just let it coast, getting as much distance as I could out of it. I searched the truck. I'd already found water, two bottles of it. I searched the back and found a tire iron and a spare tire. Nothing of use. The glovebox still held the old paperwork; no one had ever cleaned it out.

I had three guns – a hunting rifle, a shotgun, and a revolver. I had three rounds for the rifle. The other two were empty. I left them in the truck and started walking.

I walked all day. I walked through the evening, and when it got dark, I kept going. Slowly, lifting one foot out of the snow, then the other. The moon was still full enough to light my way, so I kept going.

The night was clear, and I knew where to find the north star, so I kept going south. Exhaustion had fled and I went on, one foot after the other. I watched the Plough rise, and it was well in the sky, midnight I guessed, by the time I started to look for shelter. I turned at the next side road I came to, and an hour on, I found a deserted house. The windows were broken, the roof missing most shingles, but the brick walls stood.

In a corner, under the most shingles, I dug around until I found what I needed. Dry wood under the rubble. I lit the registration papers from the truck and started a fire. I didn't care who saw it anymore. The cold just hit me all at once. I'd stopped trudging through snow, and it was brutal. The fire lit well, though. I had collapsed rafters around me to feed it and actual dry ground in my corner. I was warm, right up beside the fire. And I had a gun. I made sure it was ready, the safety off. Then I slept.

Sitting in the cold, my back against a brick wall, a fire cracking beside me, in a coat that wasn't warm enough for this weather, I had one of the best night's sleeps in years. Maybe my best in America. I slept soundly and woke slowly from a dream.

We'd been out at the Grave Diggers pub in Phibsboro. We'd been together just three months and sharing a flat in Glasnevin for two weeks. It had been a warm and sunny afternoon and we'd spent the afternoon sipping beer on the green outside the pub, talking life and our future. Our world, together. Walking home, hand in hand, no old farts shouting at us, the world was smiling, and I was in love. More than anything, I was sure of that. Walking home, Marley's hand in mine, everything in the world was right.

I woke with a smile on my lips, the memory hazy for so long, clear and fresh and full of the same hope that we'd had that day. There was a future; I was going to make it. The sun was a warm, narrow path of light sneaking in the hole I'd crawled into. All was going to be right with the world.

The fire was still glowing, a few embers among the black coals. My little corner was still warm. I added another piece of wood to the fire, poking up the embers and causing sparks, more for the look of it than for heat. I'd need to leave soon, but here and now, I was comfortable and content.

A small tongue of flame made its way along the board before I stood and left my shelter. The sun sparkled on the snow. Even all alone, I hid crouched behind a wall to pee, then stood up to the glorious day. Ready for the world.

I didn't hear anything. I felt an itch, then a warm pain, and then a sharp stabbing pain. My shoulder was on fire and I tried to move my hand, but it wasn't going where I wanted. I couldn't lift my arm properly. I looked down at all the blood and the pain exploded in my mind as my knees buckled and I fell.

The pristine white snow, glistening gold in the sun, had a scattering of red droplets all over as I fell. As the snow blackened and the sun went out, I saw figures in the distance. And then I was gone.

Chapter 44

Voices. I heard voices as I drifted in and out of reality, unsure of what was in my head or not. It didn't matter. Marley was there. And Zeke. Arguing about something. Medication. Something I didn't understand.

Marley. I'd made it. Somehow, I'd done it all. I'd made it home. I tried to reach out, but my hand wouldn't move. I tried to call but my mouth was dry and so swollen I couldn't use it.

Addy's voice. I couldn't remember; did I save her? Had she been in trouble? What was she doing here? And Zeke. Why was he in Ireland? Or was Marley here? Had she come for me?

I drifted off. In my dreams, Marley was trying to tell me something. Something important. Something urgent but I was tired. So tried.

"Let me sleep," I told her.

I wanted to burrow further into the duvet, but my body wouldn't move. It didn't matter; I was back asleep. I knew somewhere that if I rose from my deep slumber, cold and pain waited for me, so I stayed under and slept. Marley was in my dreams again.

We were running, running down Glasnevin Ave, hand in hand and laughing and then we weren't laughing. We were running and running and screaming and trying to get away and suddenly all sleep was ripped from me as pain shot through my every cell.

"You're awake."

Zeke.

I blinked, trying to figure out where I was. The room swam out of focus. The walls shimmered and slid. A pain exploded in my face. Someone had hit me.

"Wake up, Haley, time to go." Zeke's voice again, I couldn't see him.

"Leave her alone," another voice, a woman, said. Familiar but I couldn't place it.

"Time to go, Haley," Zeke's voice continued. "Wake up."

Something poked at my shoulder, and I screamed. Pain took over my body. There was another scream, yelling for him to stop.

All the world came into focus, and I was in a bed, in the hospital room back in New Bethlehem. Zeke was prodding my shoulder where a white bandage was stained with blood. Addy was screaming, being held back by Daniel. Janet was yelling at Daniel to stop. Michael was standing watching, twisting his hands, hopping from foot to foot.

"I'm awake," I growled.

"Good. We're leaving. We're going back to New Seattle. Me and you." He smiled as he paused. "And your little friend here."

His grin was evil. How could I ever have believed his charm and that smile? My mind was still drifting; it was hard to focus on anything. Pain stabbed, and my vision blurred.

"She can't leave, she needs rest," Janet was saying. "You shot for her for God's sake."

"Quit woman, don't bring the Lord's name into this," said Michael, pushing her for the door.

He turned around, paused, hopping from foot to foot and twisting his hands and like he was trying to decide.

"I could give her a pain killer," he said.

"No need," said Zeke. "Save them for your community, the Lord's work." He paused. "Though I may take your Percocet, just in case she does need them on the road."

I was too weak to argue, too weak to move. Edward, my old jailer came to the room and carried me to the truck downstairs. Zeke twisted Addy's hand roughly behind her back to shove her forward. Daniel was waiting at the door. He spat on the ground beside me.

"A moment," said Jacob, stopping Zeke and pulling Edward aside. He leaned in to speak quietly.

"Thank you for not killing Daniel. Roman told me what you did out there. You had the guns; you could have killed them and left no trail, but you didn't. I've told Zeke that I will ask the Patron about you. That you not making it back would be frowned on for any agreement. You'll get a fair trial. I will pray for you."

He motioned Edward on. From the look on his face, he really believed it. He would really pray for me. The fool. The stubborn sureness of old white men who ended the world and were still sure they were right. I still couldn't talk.

I was dumped in the back of the truck, a seatbelt wrapped around me. Another man I didn't recognize tied my wrists tightly together, pulling at my shoulder as he did. My hands were through the seatbelt; I couldn't run. Addy was pushed in on the other side, then he got in to drive and Zeke rode shotgun.

As we left, I saw the damage. Half the buildings were gone, more damage than I had caused. Two trucks blocked a missing gap in the fence. A guard tower by the gate was gone, charred struts showed where it had once stood. The community stood and watched, hate and anger writ across their faces at the one who destroyed their town. Disgust at the criminal going to face justice. The gate opened, and we rolled out.

Chapter 45

In the front seat, Zeke was fiddling with a blister pack and finally got a pill out to swallow. *The Percocet*, I thought. He sat back and sighed. While he was waiting on the hit to kick in, I tried to calm my breathing, to think. Evaluate.

The truck was a good one. Decent condition. The 55-gallon drum in the back likely held gas. Snow chains and all-wheel drive. Perfect for the conditions. Perfect to get back to New Seattle. The driver was concentrating on the road ahead, still covered in snow, but he glanced in the mirror regularly. It wasn't pointed at the rear window, instead down to me and Addy.

I was waiting for us to get out of sight, over the next rise. Ready for the inevitable bullet. I could hope it would be quick. I hoped Addy survived.

We drove on, maybe thirty miles an hour, the snow chains crunching out a path. Behind us, New Bethlehem disappeared into the white hills. There was nothing around, no cover to run to. A vast empty sheet of white.

"Thinking of escape, Haley?" Zeke was watching me now, his eyes bright, pupils tiny. "That was always you. Thinking your way out. No problem you can't solve. A regular Miss MacGyver. Of course, you've got to think what will happen if you do run."

He pulled a pistol and pointed it back, but not at me. He was grinning.

"I'll shoot your friend's kneecap out at the first sign of you running. You think you'll be able to carry a cripple? Second time I think you're thinking of running, I'll shoot her second kneecap out. That's how they did it in Belfast, wasn't it? You know what that would do? Yeah, you might get away but your friend here? Well, we'll have to take it out on her. She wouldn't like that, would you, sweetie?"

He turned around in his seat to lean in and push the gun under Addy's chin, lifting it up until she met his eyes.

"Tell Haley not to run," he said.

"Don't run," she said, calmly.

"I won't."

I knew there and then I wouldn't. He would shoot her, the bastard. I just needed to get her free. I'd never make it home to Marley but maybe that was always a pipe dream. The Kings were right; it was Revelations, the world had ended, and we were just waiting it out.

We could go now. I couldn't make it, but Addy could live. I just needed to give her a chance to run. And I needed her to take it.

The truck drove slowly on. The bullet I waited for never came. I dozed; I couldn't help it. My body was done. We passed a small community. Two men with guns recognized Zeke and waved us through. I noticed they were working on the fences as we drove past, building them stronger, higher.

Three, maybe four hours after we'd left, they pulled over. We were in the middle of nowhere, a small crossroads with no buildings, just low hills in the distance. Nowhere to run. No trees to hide behind, nowhere a truck couldn't follow at speed.

In the front, Zeke and the driver, whose name I learned was Robbie, shared some food. New Bethlehem had supplied them well. We were left with none. Still, I was alive. It was possible that they were bringing me to New Seattle, for some reason. I didn't care way; it gave me time to plan, time to free Addy.

"I need to pee," I said.

"Hold it or piss yourself, I don't care," said Zeke.

Addy lifted her head. "It will smell," she said and then went back to silence.

Zeke nodded at Robbie who opened the door and came back to untie me. Zeke turned around and pointed his pistol at Addy.

"Go ahead, Haley, but don't go too far." He grinned.

I got out. Not five feet from the truck, Robbie growled, "Far enough. I'm not running after ya."

I peed. There was blood in my urine. Never a good sign. They watched, and then Robbie tied my hands again. Same way, arms stuck in the seatbelt.

"We'll need food," I said.

"You can eat tonight," growled Zeke. "Now shut up."

The truck drove on. It was getting late. Later afternoon and in the middle of winter, the sun was gone.

"Where are we?" Zeke asked. "Where's the next town?"

"Few hours," grunted Robbie. "More in this."

It had started to snow again.

"Find somewhere."

We came across the ruins of a rest stop. Middle of nowhere, pull over when you're tired, Government issue solid concrete buildings. Robbie pulled the truck a few car lengths from the door and stopped so that the headlights shone in. Then he got out with a gun.

A minute later, he was back.

"Clear inside. It'll do," he told Zeke and then came around to untie me from the seatbelt. He tied my hands back together and pushed me inside. He shoved me to the ground beside a broken urinal. Addy was dropped beside me, before being tied tightly to me.

"How can we eat?" I asked.

"Tomorrow," he said. "Shut up or I'll shoot you in the other shoulder."

Zeke came in. "Place is a kip," he said. "I should sleep in the truck."

"I'll start a fire," said Robbie. "It'll be warmer in here."

He went back and grabbed wood from the truck and two bedrolls. In a minute, he had a fire lit in a corner and placed the bedrolls nearby. We were left to the cold concrete floor.

Zeke was busy getting comfortable, sitting near the fire. I watched as he popped another Percocet. Robbie saw it too, and I saw him shake his head just slightly as he added fuel to the fire. There was a look on his face. Disgust maybe. Was there something here I could use?

"What happened back there?" I whispered to Addy.

"The prisoners got loose like you said they would," she told me. Her tone was flat. "They burned a few buildings. They were always evil men—Jacob told us. Something like that. Later we found out you'd gone missing. Zeke was furious. He demanded everyone drop everything to look for you.

"When Daniel came back, he said you'd tried to kill him. Took his gun and his truck. Zeke went nuts. He was stopping everyone, asking them everything you'd ever said, and someone told him about me. He was screaming at me, had me locked up, and someone came back and said they'd seen your tracks, so they went off. Then they came back and said you'd been shot when you tried to shoot Zeke. Now we're here."

I tried to take it in.

"Why didn't you come for me?" she asked, her eyes flickering towards me. "You left me."

"Oh Addy, I didn't. I couldn't," I started. "I was coming for you as soon as I got out of the room. I set a fire in the storeroom to distract them, blew up the toolshed—"

"That was you," she interrupted.

"Yes, but they still came for me. I couldn't get to you. Ellie's room was too far. I tried. I was going to come back. After I got away. I was going to hide a bit and them come for you."

"I wasn't with Ellie," she said. "Martha kept me with her. She said she knew I was involved, and she'd see justice."

"The bitch," I growled. "I was coming for you, Addy. You saved me, and I owe you. More, we're family now. I'll always come for you."

"Shut it over there," Zeke snarled at us. "Or no food for another day."

He had his head in his hands, covering his eyes. I watched him fumble in his pocket, take out the pills, and then put them back again. He grunted and shifted around, trying to get comfortable while Robbie set about getting food.

We shut up. I gave Addy a wan smile. She half-smiled back and touched my hand for a moment. Zeke glared at us again and she took it back.

I tried to plan my way out. I made a mental inventory. Tapping my ribs hurt; one could be broken or just bruised. The dressing on my shoulder needed to be changed. My head hurt, and one eye was still swollen. If there was a mirror, I was sure I'd find a mess in my reflection. My legs were okay, just cramped from sitting all day, so I slowly flexed and released all the muscles, trying to keep them limber. I'd need to run. Tonight, if not tomorrow.

Slowly flexing my fingers, I found my hands were bound tight. No way I could move them, wriggle them out. I'd need help to get them loose. There was a door, the way we'd come in, and high windows too small to climb out. Besides that, there were the stainless-steel sinks, a line of three urinals, and the broken partition walls hiding the toilets. Robbie was breaking those down for extra firewood.

I watched Zeke, and I could see the drugs take hold. He straightened up, loosened up, and quit acting like everything hurt. The grin came back.

He came over, casually gnawing on a turkey leg and stood over me, staring down.

"We've got to work on your story, Haley," he said. "For everyone back home, you know? How you killed Jimmy. How you attacked me from behind with a wrench and stole the drugs. To feed your addiction maybe. You knew they were there; they're what you were after."

I said nothing, still concentrating on a way to get out. I couldn't really believe him anyway. I didn't know what he was planning but I was sure he didn't want me back in New Seattle to tell my side.

"You won't get away," he said, watching me. "You do, and I'll shoot your friend in the knees and sell her to the first King I meet. They'd like her. Remember the story, Haley. Just go back to New Seattle and own up to it. Anything else and little Addy here...well, you wouldn't like it. Remember the story and she can go do whatever it is little shits like her do."

I still said nothing, but I couldn't figure his angle. Once I was back, once I screamed the truth, yes, I'd still die. But it would be easier for him, easier for the Patron, if I never made it.

"Hey, boss," called Robbie. "Someone's out there."

Zeke moved to the door.

"Light on the far hill, see, over there," I could hear Robbie say. "No town there. The Kings maybe?"

"Ted's crew shouldn't be out there," said Zeke. "He's got them in Canaan tonight. Make sure they know how good the Patron's protection will be."

"Who's Ted?" I blurted out.

"Ted? You know who Ted is," Zeke sneered.

I thought it through. Everyone knew Ted; there was only one. One who Zeke would expect me to know. Who had a 'crew.' Ted, the King of the Kings. The one who had banded together all the small gangs.

It all came together in an instant of pure clarity. I wanted to cry for being so stupid to have missed it. They weren't suddenly working together; they'd always been together. Small communities, independent and armed, had buckled under attacks and came into the fold. New Bethlehem didn't go to New Seattle until there'd been attacks. I'd heard the stories. In the kitchens we had lived on gossip and the stories of the atrocities committed by the Kings had left us shivering.

I remembered the Kings who had attacked us when we went to check the cliff for hydro. They'd been after me. After Jimmy. We were dead then anyway. The Patron had wanted us gone. Jimmy had argued too much, and the Patron had other guys who could fix a truck. I'd always thought that we were safe, but others could change a tyre. Alfred had no inkling of the difference between changing a wheel and rebuilding an engine.

I seethed, but there was still no hope of escape, no chance to run. No doubt that he would hurt Addy. There was only one way out. I'd have to kill Zeke and Robbie. I wondered if I could kill them in cold blood. Otherwise, we'd arrive in New Seattle to die. He didn't want us back for any trial; the Patron wanted me for some other reason, and Zeke was just covering his ass. Revenge for the broken nose was just a bonus. I had to start planning. There were still some days driving.

"Should I go check?" asked Robbie from outside, breaking my chain of thought.

Zeke thought about it. "No, let's wait. See if you can hide the truck. Keep the lights off but make sure we can get out quickly if we need to. This place is pretty secure. We'll stand watch."

I heard the truck drive off and Zeke stood by the door, gun in hand, until Robbie came back in a few minutes later.

"It's behind the other building," he said. "Some trees there so it's hard to see, but it's ready to go when we need it."

"Good," said Zeke. "We'll need to keep a watch tonight."Robbie nodded.

"What about us? You can't just leave us tied here. What if they come?" I demanded.

"Hope they don't," said Zeke. "Now shut up and let me sleep or I'll use you two for entertainment."

"You were in it together. You and Alfred, the Kings, all of you," I accused him. I couldn't hold it in, my anger boiling over.

"Took you this long to figure out? You're not so smart, Haley." He started laughing.

"How long have you been doing this?"

"Really, Haley, you have to ask that?"

I tried to think, to remember running to New Seattle when we first met Alfred. It had all been crazy, a mad scramble to stay alive. The first attacks from the Kings terrified everyone, but they came later. Months later, when people started to question Alfred. It hit me.

"He's been in it from the beginning," I realized. "When no one would listen to him about building an army to defend us, suddenly there was an attack, and we all gave in."

Zeke howled with laughter.

"Of course, they didn't want to do it. Alfred's a genius; he knows what people want. All that fighting, looting, trying to stay alive. Human nature, though. They'd argue over the best way to do everything, fight each other for food. Petty squabbles. If he gave them a common enemy, though..."

"We'd all just come running," I finished for him, disgusted with myself for not seeing it then.

"'Give 'em all a place to run to and the right bogeyman to run from, and they'll be eating out of your hand," he told me. "You always need an enemy. Someone to blame. Jews, blacks, you gays. Whoever. And he was right. Ted's Kings sent them all running to the one guy offering protection. Ted got to do what he wanted, Alfred got to lead everyone. A win-win.

"You knew this?" I asked Robbie, who was standing by the door.

He looked at me like I was an idiot.

"What did you get out of it?" I asked Zeke.

"Drugs," he shrugged. "Lots and lots of drugs. I was pretty addicted there for a while. And power, Haley. The power I deserved. I was the only doctor in town. I could do whatever the hell I wanted, and no one would ever complain. No one dared. No one should ever have anyway. Who are they to complain?" He spat his disgust at all the people, everyone he felt was below him. "Between us, we offered safety. Alfred fought the bandits, and I fixed people. We got what we deserved. This was our life, then someone starts a war and steals it from us? Well, we took it right back. And you all just let us."

"And then I took your drugs," I said, satisfied that I'd stopped him in some small way.

"You think anyone gave a fuck about the shitty little bag of drugs you took? Are you really that stupid, Haley? You thought anyone gave a fuck? We have warehouses of that shit. The first thing after the Fall, everyone's running and fighting and the military's taking over. Alfred knew there'd be looting, everyone running to empty every store in every mall in the country. But he knew the where the warehouses were, and he emptied them while the sheep focused on the small stuff. They were stealing a few aspirin; Alfred was taking hundreds of crates."

Zeke had been with me then. Trying to find a few aspirin. Even for years afterward, people died for want of those drugs. We'd buried kids. Babies who needed a fucking Tylenol, and they were holding out. My fury burned white hot. I knew then I would feel no remorse slitting his throat while he slept.

"Then why?" I asked. Before I killed him, as I was sure I would, I needed to know. "Why all this? Just to chase me across a fucking continent, Zeke? I just wanted to go home."

He thought about it.

"The Patron couldn't have you running off with Jimmy dead," he said slowly. "Someone has to pay. There's got to be justice. If he's not dispensing justice, then someone else is, and he's the one in charge. So, I told him I'd come get you. Anyway, it was personal. I wasn't letting you get away."

He touched his nose where I'd broken it.

I was trying to see an exit. My hands were still bound.

"You let them try to kill me," I said. "The Kings, tried to kill me and Jimmy back in the woods."

"They tried to kill Jimmy, you idiot," he said. "You just got in the way. Why did you insist on going? Just Jimmy. He was too popular, too many people looked up to him. He suspected too much and needed to disappear. You? No, you were meant to be mine, Haley. Remember that night? Remember?"

I remembered.

***

Six weeks after the Fall

We'd been running for weeks. Zeke and Benny and me. It was just the three of us left. We were holed up in a tiny cabin, way up in the mountains. We'd gotten a gun, a small rifle; a twenty-two Zeke had called it. Mark had died in the fight for it.

We kept going, into the mountains, where we got lost running from a bunch of hillbillies with more guns than sense, and ended up on a tiny path, barely a pair of wheel ruts in the grass. A half-mile up, we'd found the cabin. Old and unused in a year or more, but solid. Stone and heavy wood. A broken window from a storm but it was in the middle of nowhere and unlikely to be seen. We could safely light a fire at night, as long as it was gone by dawn to have no smoke.

The motherlode was in a press at the back. Cans of food, beans and peas and meatballs and spaghetti. Then the preserved stuff – pickled eggs, canned peaches, jams and jellies. If you could preserve it in a mason jar it was there. Not a lot, but enough for us for a few weeks maybe.

Food. Warmth. Shelter. We'd made it.

Benny was sick, though. He'd been cut in the fight. Nothing life threatening, not like he lost an arm or anything. Just a long scratch down his left arm, deep enough in places that he lost a lot of blood until Zeke got it wrapped up tightly. But it stank. In just three days it had festered, and he had a fever. He was pale and sweating and sleeping and crying, and Zeke said we needed antibiotics.

We tried.

Really, we tried. We searched that place. One day, we left and jogged the six miles to where the nearest town had been. Everything was gone, looted clean. The next nearest place was in the other direction.

Another fifteen miles. We went back to the cabin to check on Benny, but already we were too late. He was gone.

We buried him in the yard. The ground was rocky, and we couldn't dig very deep, but we covered him as gently as we could. Zeke found a bottle of whiskey, and we sat and drank our toasts, and then we drank our sorrows, and I cried, and we drank some more, and we were all alone. Just the two of us left in the world. The only person I knew who was alive, truly knew, was there beside me.

Alcohol numbed my pain, my mind closed down. Marley was so far away, and I could never get there, and the world had fallen.

I woke up with a hangover. A head splitting, eyes throbbing, heart pounding with fear hangover and a hate of myself that would stay with me to my last day. I didn't know how it had happened. I was never a drinker. I wasn't passed out, but I still let it happen. Zeke woke with a hangover and a smile on his face.

***

"Remember, Haley?" he was saying. "Just the two of us. You were so alive that night; we were so alive. Even as the world fell apart. You could have had that. Alfred said I could keep you once we got rid of Jimmy. But then you had to go off with him and try to get yourself killed. Act like I wasn't good enough for you. Like you're all that. Like you're something fucking special."

His voice softened. "What do you say, Hales? How about another go, for old time's sake?"

"I wouldn't touch you, ever," I told him.

His eyes flashed, and he towered over me.

"That's not what you said back there, when Benny died. 'Oh, so lonely.' I was okay then, wasn't I?" he demanded, anger rising in his voice. "Like you have a choice in any of this. You never get it. When we're done, you'll be begging for me. You think you're going back for a trial? No, you're going back as an example. No one steals from the Patron. No one runs away from me. Especially not some little fucking dyke like you, Haley. So maybe be nice to me and it won't hurt as much. Or maybe your friend would like to be nice to me."

He leered at Addy.

"Hey boss," Robbie called from the door. "Car coming in."

Zeke whirled, grabbed his gun from the corner.

"Get ready," he said. "How many?"

Chapter 46

"Just one, I think," said Robbie, pulling the heavy door closed. He lay down on the ground to peer underneath it, gun pointed through the six-inch gap.

"Truck, no one in the back. Two people, I think," he reported.

The truck pulled up outside. I could see the light from the head-lights coming under the door. I could hear the engine, and I heard it stop. No one moved. Robbie lay on the floor, gun pointed out. Zeke stood beside the door, back to the heavy concrete wall, gun ready.

Nothing. We waited.

A door slammed.

"You see anything?" Zeke hissed.

"Nope. Wait, one got out. Behind the truck. I don't have a shot."

"Zeke, you in there Zeke?" a loud call from outside.

Zeke's face split into a grin in the firelight. "Open the door. It's Ted's guys," he told Robbie.

Robbie pulled himself to his feet and opened the door.

"Ripper?" called Zeke.

"Yeah, Doc. You're not going to do anything stupid, are you?"

"Come on in," called Zeke.

Another door slammed, and we waited in the flickering firelight until two men came in. The first was a huge hulk of a man, seven feet tall and dressed in heavy black leather. A dirty red bandana sat on his head and snake tattoos peeked out at his wrists.

The second man was smaller, older, dressed neatly in black save for a red sleeveless jacket. Wisps of hair stuck up around his ears. Old, kindly, and he looked familiar.

"Ted," Zeke said, shaking his hand warmly. "I didn't know you were here. I thought you'd be in Canaan."

"We've enough men to cover that place, and when we saw the light, I figured it was you. We thought you'd have some food, and of course with the rumour that you had captured your elusive Haley, I had to come. We had to meet the girl who gave you so much trouble, Zeke. Imagine, a girl, taking so long to be found."

"Of course, of course, no problem. Come on in, sit by the fire," Zeke said, poorly hiding a scowl. "Robbie, see what we have. And get the wine, there's a bottle in there somewhere."

"Introductions Zeke" said Ted, nodding at us. "Manners first."

Zeke jerked a thumb at me. "This is Haley. Killed a man and stole from the Patron."

"Alfred never did take that well," said Ted. "A thief never likes to be stolen from."

"And the kid's her accomplice she picked up somewhere, caused no end of trouble in New Bethlehem."

Ted nodded. He came over and hunkered down beside us.

"Zeke has certainly gone to a lot of effort to find you, Haley. You're infamous all over the country. What did you steal?" he asked.

"Nothing. Zeke lost it is all," I said.

"I bet he did," Ted laughed. "I bet he did. Hey, are you hungry?"

I nodded. Addy nodded, too. He smiled, for all the world a kindly old man. But I'd seen what the Kings left behind. He was dangerous. Very dangerous.

"Robbie, bring these ladies some food," Ted called.

Zeke made a noise as if to argue but stopped.

"Ripper?" Ted nodded towards us.

The giant came over, pulling a huge knife from a sheath at his side. More of a sword or a machete than a knife He was terrifying up close. A scar ran the length of his face. I screamed, or would have if I had breath but just a rasp came out. He just bent over and cut the rope between my hands, and then did the same for Addy.

"Eat," he said, pointing at the plates Robbie set on the ground before us.

We didn't need to be told again. Eat while you can, sleep while you can. The food was good. Robbie had been getting it for Ted, not us. Ted leaned against a wall and watched.

"You know who I am?" he asked me, swirling the wine in his tin cup.

"Ted," I answered. "Leader of the Kings. Gangs who rape and pillage. Working for Alfred. I should have seen it."

He smiled at me. "No one does, my dear. Don't beat yourself up about it. And rape and pillage...well, my boys have some fun, but it's the end of the world after all. There is no right or wrong anymore. Whatever God left on this earth, He left for us. As for Alfred...no one ever takes us for brothers."

My mouth must have fallen open because he paused. No one knew that. With those words, he sealed my fate. I'd never make it out alive to tell anyone.

"You didn't know? Oh yes, we're brothers. These days I have some-what of a bad rep, and he's the saviour. Before, it was all different. Back then, he was a small-time dealer, a petty thief, conman and all-round rascal where I was a priest, respected in the church."

He smiled, waiting, watching the effect of his words.

"You were a priest?" I had never heard that, but it fit. Change the red jacket for a white collar and Father Ted was right there in front of me.

I needed to learn all I could, keep them talking, keep them from killing me while I worked out an escape. All four of them stood between us and the door. I wondered if I could give Addy enough of a head start. I hoped she'd take it. Ripper was huge, slow I hoped, but he had that knife. There would only be one chance. It would need to be perfect, one tiny slip and we were dead.

"Yes, things are a little different now. I was a priest. A good one, too. Not one of those pedos that make the news. The quiet ones that visit the sick and help the elderly and bury the dead when there's no one else to show up. That was me."

"What happened? You just give up?"

"Ah, you'd like the whole story. Keep us talking. I like how you think."

He said all this with a smile, toying with me like he was an indulgent grandad.

"Why not, indeed, why not? It's not like we're going anywhere. Ripper, build up the fire. Robbie, get these ladies some wine."

Zeke choked on that. Robbie poured two mugs and handed them to us. Addy looked at me, and I shook my head just slightly. She lowered her mug.

"Oh no, drink ladies, please. It's going to be a long night."

There was a hint of steel in his voice. I took a sip. I know little about wine but enough to know that this was a good one. Not the rough two euro bottles we'd find on sale in Aldi.

Addy sipped at hers. I hoped she wouldn't drink any more. I knew alcohol could numb the pain, and with a little more she'd start to feel the effects and might welcome the release. I needed her to be ready to run. But I needn't have worried.

She spat it out. "It's gone off."

Ted threw his head back and laughed. "Ah young lady. Addy, is it?"

I noticed he knew her name when Zeke hadn't mentioned it. He knew everything already. He was just playing us all. I wondered if Zeke knew that.

"Not ready for wine?" He held up the bottle, peering at the label. "A 2013 Selby Cabernet? You know how few of these bottles are left in the world? Never mind, never mind. Ripper, see if you can find anything for the lady."

Ripper prodded Robbie who went out to the truck. Three between us and the door. I stretched slightly, trying to make it natural.

He just grinned at me. Zeke was looking pissed.

"Well, Haley, where do I start? I was in Oregon; a little place called Salem to be precise. Small town, small church. And then the world ended. There I was, myself and a dozen or so parishioners, all old and all alone with nowhere else to go. The news was coming in faster than I could pray, and then there were shouts and then screaming. You know what it was like; it was like that everywhere.

"Two days later we're still there, setting up a shelter, an emergency place for anyone coming through, trying to collect food, blankets, preparing for the worst as refugees streamed through. Then the army came through, and already they'd given up and were looting. They told us that the coast was lost. The war was lost. We didn't even know who we were at war with. They didn't either, but it was a war anyways and we had definitely lost. Everyone was sure of that."

He waved his cup and Ripper topped it up. Despite his huge frame, he could move with the grace of a waiter at some five-star restaurant for celebrities and politicians.

Robbie came back in with milk for Addy. She didn't drink that either. From Robbie's face, he had probably spat in it. Four between us and the door once again.

"When the army left," Ted continued, "a group came through. Bikers. The bad kind, not the Sunday rider kind. Nearly everything we'd collected was gone, stolen. Everyone ran. There I was, locked in the vestry with a handful of the elderly, hiding, and they came right in, started smashing things, laughing, having fun. A fire started. All that old wood polished weekly by the ladies aux just went right up."

He was a natural story teller, brought us right in. I guessed he had been a good priest.

"You know, all of my life I'd worked in that church. My friends came in to be baptized as babies and went out in coffins. I thought I'd built a community. And suddenly it was nothing and then it was burning. I lost it, Haley, I think that's the best way to say it. I lost it, there and then. So, I picked up a monstrance. You know what that is?"

I nodded. I'd been Catholic for too long to not know it.

"Heavy and spiky, full of our Lord's body in the form of the Eucharist," he explained for Addy. "Well, I swung it with the power of man and the weight of God's righteous anger. I took a man's jaw off. I couldn't believe it. Blood and teeth all over the floor. All my life, all my good works gone in that. You know what his friends did? You know what they did?"

He paused. I shook my head.

"They laughed. Right then and there I saw something, Haley, something I'd waited a lifetime to see. I saw the face of God. God as He truly is. I saw His message clearly for the first time in my life. I saw the path He had laid out for me. His message at the end of the world."

I wanted to look away, but his face shone with a zeal, and it was hypnotizing. A true belief I'd not seen in such a long time.

"And He truly doesn't give one fuck about us. Not one single solitary fuck. He sits in his heavens and does not give any fucks whatsoever. So, I told them that, and they laughed. I saw a toy, lying on the ground, thrown down as they wrecked my church. One from the donation pile. A small bear with a red jacket. And I held it up. I told them that they'd be as well off following that bear as any other God. And they laughed more. Someone gave me a drink, and they laughed more. Another tried to take the drink, and I knocked him out."

He said it all so calmly. Just knocked him out. He could have been saying that he heard the man's confession.

"So, they got me a red jacket and they followed me. I told them about God and how he didn't give a shit, and they said they could follow a God like that. Not a new God, but an old one. Fire and brimstone and fuck anyone else. The rapture had come and we were left behind, but in these end times, we are Kings. Even God won't stop us. If He even has the power left to do so as we are sure he does not have the inclination. Our God simply does not care what we do."

"And now you work for Alfred?" I asked.

I wanted him talking. Zeke was at the wine too, but Robbie and Ripper weren't. If they talked enough, drank enough, if I could live just long enough...

"I have assisted him in some small ways here and there," Ted admitted. "Just a nudge here, a small massacre there. He was always wrong about one thing, though. We are Kings. We herd the sheep where they need to be. We follow only our God and that is all."

"But you work for him?"

"A mistake that is easy to make," he said, and waved a hand to Ripper who moved to the door. "All too easy to make, all too easy. One Alfred made himself."

Silence.

Chapter 47

"What mistake?" Zeke asked. He was smiling. The fool. "I don't understand."

Ripper moved like a snake striking, hard to even follow, impossible to believe for such a large man in the heavy coat and leathers. Robbie fell, the knife right through him, the handle poking from his chest and the tip making a blunt clang as it hit the floor with his back.

Zeke froze, just for a moment, before he reached for his gun. Too late. A massive fist moved, there was a wet thud, and the gun was on the ground. Ripper took him in a bear hug. Zeke was struggling, trying to fight him off, but it was David and Goliath if David had no sling.

"Don't," said Ted, and Ripper dropped Zeke to the ground, coughing and spluttering.

Ted stood and walked over to Zeke.

"I think you broke a rib, Ripper," he said and casually kicked Zeke who screamed. "Yes, definitely broken. Take the guns, Ripper."

He smiled down at Zeke.

"I never liked you, Zeke," Ted said. "You were always a selfish bastard with a taste for pain. I've no doubt these ladies know just what it is you do. What you've probably done to them. Please tell Alfred that the Kings bow to no one. He'll double the tribute, or we'll burn New Seattle to the ground."

I stared, Zeke on the ground, Ted standing over him, a smile on his face like he was wishing Zeke a pleasant day.

"Ladies," he said to us, tipping an imaginary hat. "Good luck, but please don't kill him. I do need my messenger."

"Why?" I asked. I had to know.

"Because we don't work for Alfred. We never did. He expects too much. We are not his minions. We bring the truth to the world. And as Alfred consolidates his base, soon he won't need us, and then he will try to destroy us. He thinks I don't know that. He always thought he was smarter than everyone.

"We follow only our God, and even our God, who cares not a whit, gets His justice in some way. Zeke has a fondness for the younger. You probably know. Some things every man should find distasteful – Kings, bandits, Christians, everyone. I'll leave him to you. Just remember, alive, or one of you will have to take my brother the message, and Alfred is likely to blame the messenger."

He nodded to Ripper, and the two walked out the door. I jumped up, pulling Addy to her feet. Zeke was struggling to his feet, too. I grabbed for anything I could use as a weapon, anything at all, and my hand closed around a piece of firewood.

"You still think you can escape, don't you?" Zeke said, clutching at his chest.

He pulled out a pistol, hidden in his coat, and pointed it at me.

I pushed Addy aside, the gun followed her, and I hurled the piece of firewood at his head.

I missed, the wood flying wide to hit the wall behind him. He flinched though, and his wild shot missed. I ran right at him. I kept low, jumping feet first into his shin. He was pointing the gun, pulling at the trigger as I hit him. I went down, the bullet going over my head. Zeke stumbled, but righted himself.

Addy skipped right by us and grabbed a proper weapon. The knife she grabbed was covered in blood and gore from Robbie. She jumped towards us swinging, and the knife went in Zeke's shoulder. He dropped the gun with a scream.

"No Addy!" I yelled, as she pulled out the knife and went to drive it back in. "Alive, leave him alive."

She moved back. Zeke was against a wall, trying to reach the wound in his shoulder. I managed to get up, the gun in my hand. We stood, across the room, gun pointed while Zeke tried to stem the bleeding.

I grabbed the firewood from where it had hit the wall and took it over. He tried to stop me, to hit me, but I ducked and smashed it down on an ankle. He screamed and fell. Then I hit the other ankle.

"That's for Jimmy," I told him.

Then I smashed his face. The nose I'd broken so long ago gushed blood anew.

"And that's for me."

He was sobbing and screaming..

We gathered what we could quickly. The bed rolls, and the food. I looked at Zeke, bleeding on the floor, and wondered if he'd live. Ted was still outside. I took Zeke's blanket, and while Addy pointed the gun, I ripped it and tied it tight around his shoulder to stop the bleeding.

We went outside. Ripper stopped us with a raised hand before he poked his head inside. A professional glance.

"He'll live," he told Ted.

"Thank you, Ladies," Ted said. "You're free to go. Bring my message to whoever you meet. The Kings offer mercy to those who will come to our God, the God of the end times. To all else, we offer only death."

"Why?" I asked.

He shrugged. "You've done so much to stop Alfred, you get a pass. For now.

With a tip of imaginary hats, they got in their truck and left.

Epilogue

The truck was just where Robbie had said it would be. He'd already topped up the gas. We drove on. We avoided New Bethlehem, taking side roads. After dawn, we saw wavy footprints in the snow and followed them to find Alain slumped under a tree. We took the gun off him and helped him into the back.

We drove on. South and east and south and east. Far enough that the snow stopped and cleared. To areas of scorched earth and desert. Past a city of foundations, everything above it gone in a blast. We drove fast, avoiding what radiation lingered there. On and on, south and east. Day and night, stopping only to change drivers and top up the gas from the barrel in the back.

Addy learned to drive. I couldn't last long with my shoulder killing me and Alain needed rest after two days in the snow. I watched Addy go, trying to peer over the wheel as she stretched to reach the gas. The landscape blurred and changed. We drove on.

The drum in the back was empty and gone and we'd been driving two days, moving on fumes when we crested a hill. And there, glimmering in the low winter sun, we saw it.

The ocean.

***

Spring was here, and we kept going. Walking and then cycling when we found bikes. We avoided communities, avoided all people, just moving as far and as fast as we could. We went east as far as we could. Not to Florida. Florida was gone. The glaciers had melted, yet to reform, and the seas were higher. Florida was a memory, an Atlantis for the future, a world beneath the waves. Somewhere in Texas or Louisiana, we were at the ocean.

We were sitting on a hill in a small town we thought might not be too radioactive. A bank still stood, and we stayed there. Food was already growing around. Plants were alive. Occasionally, we caught something, Fish, a bird, a deer once. A storm was coming in. We were safe, for now, a concrete vault and firewood aplenty. Miles and miles from the Patron and Ted and anyone who might come for us. A war was coming, we knew, but here we could rest a while.

I sat on the hill, watching it come in, the lightning flashing off purple clouds on the horizon, a waterspout forming off the ocean and fading before it made land, the waves building and building and as it started to rain. I took shelter in the doorway and watched.

Waves, ten feet, fifteen, twenty. Then wind came and huge waves, thirty feet, forty, breaking far out to sea and still the surge came up the hill further than I thought possible.

"Get inside," Addy was calling. "Close the damn door."

I'd have to stop her swearing; she picked that up from me.

I thought of Marley, out across the raging water, who swore like a fucking pro.

"I'm coming," I told her, through the waves and the storm.

I closed the damn door.

Acknowledgements

It takes a village to write a novel and a lot of people helped bring Haley and Addy to life. I'd like thank them all, but I know I will miss a few, so offer a generic many thanks to everyone who helped bring this novel out.

The Sherman Oaks Writers group gave me invaluable feedback and moral support as I worked through this. Special thanks to Scott, Janet, Chelsea, K, Dub C, Keven, Kevin, Kit, Megan, Doug, Shawn, Sara, Elaine, Sam, Alex

My editor, Charlie Knight, deserves a medal for patience as it took me year(s) between edits to process my trauma about Oxford commas.

My test readers, Imelda, Gio, Conor, Sinead, Damien, Suz, Colin, France, Bryan and especially Fritz Hudnut who explained about carburettors. That was a big mistake. Did you know how many carbs are in a car? I didn't, but Haley got it right thanks to Fritz.

Thanks to Ronan who took a quick description over coffee and captured the novel in the amazing art for the cover.

I've missed a lot of people in this list, and I admit that I didn't take everyone's advice. If I had listened to them, the book would have been better. If I didn't listen to any of their advice the book would have been much worse.

Thank you all for your moral support as I tried to do all of this. It means the world.

Gerry

About the author

Gerry Gainford is a nerd who spends the workday talking about computer security. Please change your password. Repeating that over and over is his 9 – 5.

The rest of the time he lives in Los Angeles, with a wife and kids. He likes to go camping, ride motorcycles, do woodwork badly, tell bad jokes, drink good beer and write.

He's originally from Ireland and hopes some day to know what he wants to be when he grows up.

To find out more, and to see when the next book is out, check out the website https://gerrygainford.com.

Cover art
Cover painting is by Ronan McCabe. You can see more of his work at www.deviantart.com/ronanmc.

www.ingramcontent.com/pod-product-compliance
Lightning Source LLC
Chambersburg PA
CBHW061423150726
47987CB00001B/75